African Beginn

Also by Olivia Vlahos

HUMAN BEGINNINGS

THE BATTLE-AX PEOPLE: Beginnings of Western Culture

African
Beginnings

BY OLIVIA VLAHOS

Illustrated by George Ford

The Viking Press   *New York*

For John

Copyright © 1967 by Olivia Vlahos
All rights reserved

Viking Compass Edition
Issued in 1969 by The Viking Press, Inc.
625 Madison Avenue, New York, N.Y. 10022

Distributed in Canada by
The Macmillan Company of Canada Limited

SBN 670-10768-9 (hardbound)
SBN 670-00257-7 (paperbound)

Library of Congress catalog card number: 67-24859

Printed in U.S.A.

Fourth printing January 1971

Author's Note

The reader must not expect to find here stories of the great European explorers who charted unknown Africa and opened it to travelers from the West. He will not find a history of colonial occupation and little more than a remark or two about Africa's new emergent nations.

The heroes of this book are simply Africa's people in all their rich and splendid variety, and the quest is for their cultural beginnings. In the absence of written records, the searcher turns to the archaeological record, which daily uncovers new surprises, and to the accounts of ethnographers who have lived with and studied living African peoples. These sources reveal a shadowy outline of Africa's past—and sometimes more than that.

The ethnographers on whose writings I have depended in preparing Parts II–V are listed in the bibliography. I have tried faithfully to reflect their views of the people in question. To the following specialists and their works I have a wider indebtedness: George Peter Murdock for orientation; Desmond Clark and A. J. Arkell, archaeology; Joseph H. Greenberg, African languages; Dudley Stamp, geography; Max Gluckman, interpretation.

To Dr. Irving Goldman, who read every word of the manuscript, I offer my deep thanks. His thoughts and suggestions have improved the book and enlightened its author.

The research on which this book is based was begun after many long talks with my friend Mr. Arthur B. Ojwang, of Kenya. I am grateful for his enthusiastic interest. Thanks, too, are due to Miss Ruth Adams of the Westport Library for patient help with research.

Contents

List of Maps

African Beginnings

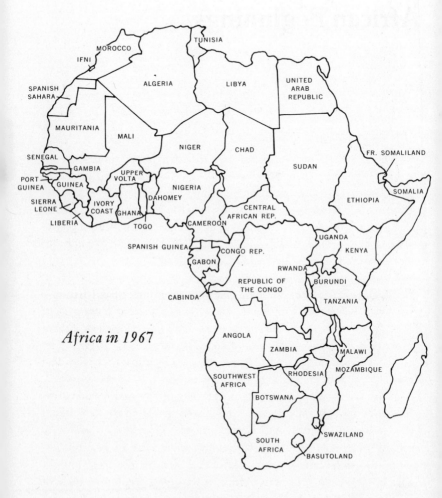

Africa in 1967

Foreword

What's in an Image?

"I didn't know there were ruins like that in Africa!" exclaimed the young lady. We were looking—she and I—at pictures of Great Zimbabwe, the still-magnificent remains of a vast palace or temple-complex built during medieval times in what is now Southern Rhodesia. "I always thought Africa was half jungle and half desert, with savages in one and nomads in the other. At least," she went on to amend the statement, "in the old days, anyway."

Right or wrong, whatever we may see or know to the contrary, that is the picture most of us imagine when we think of old Africa— of Africa before the white men came. It is a picture composed of bits and pieces from old Tarzan movies, from novels such as *Trader Horn* and *King Solomon's Mines* and *She*, from P. C. Wren's tales of the Foreign Legion, and from countless newspaper stories that cater to our appetite for the exotic and marvelous. All these have, in turn, been drawn from real-life adventures of the first Western explorers ever to see the interior: Caillié, who struggled over the desert to Timbuctoo; Burton and Speke and the Bakers, who painfully sought the sources of the Nile; Stanley, who went to find the lost Dr. Livingstone and sent out stories that gave us the most unsinkable image of all—"Darkest Africa." Before the explorers, tales of Africa were told in the West by slavers who—ever since the fifteenth century, when Europeans took to the high seas—had coasted Africa's shore lines in search of human cargo.

Men who exploit other men for their material possessions or their muscle tend to emphasize the animal in their victims rather than the human element. Such an attitude sits more easily on the conscience. The slaver must see himself as an ordinary businessman, even a benefactor bringing the advantages of civilization to a poor benighted heathen folk; else he might have to give up what he is doing and move on to something less troubling to the conscience but perhaps less profitable as well. No wonder slaving records of the eighteenth and nineteenth centuries read rather like commercial transactions, with little notice being taken of Africa's people as people, and none at all of those people's accomplishments.

Westerners of Victorian times were very pleased with themselves, with their progress, and their standing in the world. Self-consciously humanitarian, they were willing to see all men as MEN but liked to emphasize the achievement gap. Those who sincerely worked hard to bridge the gap tried to turn Africans into model Europeans. Privately they thought the task hopeless. What, they wondered, could be done with a people so persistently childish and backward?

Arabs knew better. They had come to Africa in the early years of the Christian Era and had there encountered great kingdoms whose merchants had gold to trade, whose women were adorned with jewels, whose courts dispensed justice of an exceedingly high order, whose kings ruled with pomp and splendor. Knowing a good thing when they saw it, the Arabs took pains to keep the rest of the world out. They did this with power when possible, with fear otherwise. Artful tales were spread, tales concerning Africa's savage animals and even more savage men, of its giants and cannibals and monstrous rites of evil in the jungle night. They embellished the dangers of inaccessible plateaus, of iron scrub, of waterless deserts, of fevers and rots which (supposedly) only the black man could withstand. All these horror stories meant for Western ears traveled first to the slavers, from them to the explorers, and from the explorers to the modern storytellers of the West. And each group has added its favorite bias and point of view to what in time became the common, the popular image of Africa.

Like the Arabs, Western social scientists—almost from the beginning of social science—knew better. So did some of the missionaries and civil servants who preceded them in actual field work. Nowhere have peoples been more fully and appreciatively studied than in Africa by these conscientious students of mankind. But their writings have been read mostly by other students, and the popular image has not been very much changed.

It has not been changed because, first of all, it is an exotic image and an easy one. Like all images, it has some basis in fact. A lot of Africa, for instance, *is* desert, though there is a good deal less jungle than you might think, judging strictly by its publicity. And what there is falls far short in size of the Amazon jungle in Brazil. The rest of the continent is grassland, hill land, scrub—a little of this and a little of that in about the same proportions as you'd find on any other continent. Africa *is* hot and disease-ridden, true, but not everywhere. A Westerner would find the various climates, on the whole, no more miserable than those of Southeast Asia, say, or South America.

There were once, it is true, plenty of dangerous animals in Africa (they are now vanishing so rapidly as to need protection). There were also dangerous men who shared with these predators a taste for human meat. But only look around and you'll soon discover that every continent has had its cannibals. Popping missionaries into pots seems to have been a favorite activity among any number of people here and there about the globe—though for some reason, cartoonists always make their cannibals African.

It is true that Africa shelters and has always sheltered people with very simple ways of life—people with few possessions and little awareness of life beyond that lived in the bosom of the family. But Africa can show us not just one way of life but every way of life man in his time has ever developed (except the technological one, and it won't be long before that's added). Besides hunters and gatherers there are (and have been for a long time) herders and farmers, villagers, and city dwellers whose ranks include (now as ever) doctors, merchants, craftsmen, and caravaneers. Some villagers and urbanites are (and have been) musicians whose rhythms and harmonies, changing over the long years and traveling by many a roundabout road, have given us Western jazz. Some are (and have been) sculptors whose works, though hidden away in museums of "primitive" art, have nevertheless influenced the development of artists and art in our own world and time.

Africans are political people. Maybe more so than the inhabitants of any other continent. As in a living textbook, there are examples of every form of government (or nongovernment, as the case may be). There are primitive democracies in which everybody has a say and says it loudly and at length until consensus is reached. There are republics whose representatives are chosen according to age groups or family membership. There are old kingdoms complete with secretariats and civil servants, census and taxation, trade agreements and foreign policy, with systems of appellate courts in which litigious people can continue (as in the family) to have their say loudly and at length. And now, enfolding all, there are the modern states struggling to forge even larger unities.

African history did not begin yesterday—though the current ferment of emerging nationhood often makes it seem so. African history did not begin with the arrival of the Europeans or of the Arabs or with any special people at any special time. It did not, because Africa is where people themselves began. It is the place in which man learned the things that made him human and from which he went forth. Other histories may be better documented, but none can claim greater seniority. African beginnings are human beginnings.

Now there's an image for you.

Part I

ANCIENT HISTORY

Climate and Vegetation

Desert and dry steppe (0–20 inches rain)

Grassland and trees (4–60 inches rain)

Rain forest (over 60 inches rain)

1. Stones and Bones and Pictures
Jigsaw Pieces from the Past

Africa is a big continent. It is old, too—old and unchanging. Over two hundred million years ago its basic structure took the shape it has kept ever since. Those mighty upheavals that wrinkled mountain chains into the skins of other continents hardly touched Africa. Like some mighty butcher's block, it rose slowly, majestically, from the sea. And now, dimpled by shallow basins and weathered nearly flat, it towers above its delta lands, its coastal fringes, tumbling its rivers down upon them in thunderous falls, in stair-step cataracts.

This old, flat block is, all the same, a cracked block. The stresses and strains of the long continental rise split a seam down its eastern flank. The seam widened into a double-branched chasm and then into valleys—the Great Rift Valleys—in whose almost bottomless depths there collected a series of ribbon lakes, very dark, very deep. The land between the rifts collapsed into a shallow basin which in time held Lake Victoria, that vast inland sea where monsoon rains, blowing inland from the faraway Indian Ocean, end their journey.

With the tearing and splitting of the Rifts—hundreds of thousands of years ago—came volcanoes bursting fire. All along the chasm's edge lava mountains began to form. Some are forming still and nightly pierce the East African darkness with flame. The oldest peaks are cold now, crowned with snow. Tall Kilimanjaro, sentinel over wide plains alive with game, wears a precious jewel as well—a diamond glacier in which a leopard lies frozen, his spots still bright as the day when, living, he stalked antelope and giraffe on the plains below. Bejeweled Kilimanjaro and her sister peaks are sacred to many of East Africa's people. There, it is said, the high god chose to make his home—as on another mountain, half a world away, the Greek Olympians loved to dwell.

From beneath the sacred peaks, from in and around the valleys of the Rift, have come fossil bones to document the past of living creatures for whom this land was home. The story of the bones is this: old Africa was the source, the center in which many mammals evolved and diversified, and from which they moved out over the earth. Certainly this was true for the Old World monkeys and apes, who are our closest primate relatives. And with every year fresh evidence makes us surer still that Africa was our first home, too.

Nowhere can a possible sequence of development be more clearly read than at Olduvai Gorge in Tanzania. Like a giant layer cake— weatherworn and water cut—it displays its ancient sediments, laid down one by one on the basalt foundation. For years the British anthropologist L. S. B. Leakey and his family have searched those layers for clues of man's past. And clues they have found. First came a sequence of tools (sophisticated ones on top, simple ones in the deeper layers) and then, at last, remains of the toolmakers themselves.

Most sensational of these ancient beings was *Zinjanthropus* (East African Man), who, in his combination of man and ape features (apelike brain case, protruding muzzle; manlike teeth and erect posture), much resembled numerous other finds from South Africa. These had been labeled, collectively, the Southern Apes, or australopithecines, and had been found in two varieties—big ones which appeared to have been vegetarians (*Zinjanthropus* belongs in this group) and little ones that could have been meat eaters. None of the australopithecines had been found in uncontestable association with tools—those simple stones chipped and flaked to a pattern, the pattern which reveals human manufacture. Zinj *was* found with tools at hand, or so it seemed at first. Furthermore, he appeared to be older by far than his relatives down south. Tests of the volcanic materials surrounding his skull suggested an age of nearly two million years. Certainly he had preceded the South African near-men, perhaps by a million years.

A later find then cast doubt on Zinj's status as first toolmaker. Somewhat below the spot at which Zinj was found and a little distance away the remains of another man were discovered. This one had been small and primitive, to be sure, but he had been a man—man unmistakably in brain and form—and, so Leakey believes, a man much closer to ourselves than Zinj or any of the other australopithecines. He, too, was found in conjunction with tools—those same chipped pebbles which had first turned up with Zinj, plus a beautiful scraper made of bone and bearing evidence of use. Dr. Leakey dubbed him *Homo habilis,* Able Man, and still another picture of man's past began to take shape.

Apparently two sorts of men had existed at Olduvai, side by side. Was it in harmony? Or were they hunter and hunted? Did the small man with tools stalk the large, dull near-man or was it the other way around? One thing at least we know for sure. For the small man an evolutionary future stretched ahead. Zinj, poor Zinj, was already moving down a dead-end street, on his way toward eventual extinction.

Even so, the two sorts of men coexisted for a long, long time, and in many places. The remains of large australopithecines together with those of an early true man have been found in the same lime deposit at Swartkrans in South Africa. And in Java, too, bones of what appear to be true men and bones of large australopithecines have been found on the same site. Near-men and true men, it would seem, had not only coexisted; they had also traveled together—if not in company, at least along the same byways and in the same direction, out from Africa.

But it was not to be so forever. Eventually the australopithecines died out, and—perhaps as much as a million years ago—early Able Man was succeeded by (or developed into) Erect Man, a larger, more advanced true man. His brain approached our own in size, and his tools were hand axes roughly flaked by hammerstone from flint cores. Such tools have been found all over Europe and it was a town in

France that gave them their type name—Chellean. Both Chellean tools and their makers have now been uncovered at Olduvai. Europe, it seems, was simply an outpost of an industry and a human type that had their beginnings in Africa.

The picture for later man in Africa is somewhat less clear. Stones and bones have not always been found together. The only certainty is that over the long years both tools and their makers changed and developed and improved. Axes, bolas, and cleavers were ever more skillfully worked and shaped to fit differing human needs. Eventually hafted tools appeared, spears and arrows fashioned with points that fit into wooden shafts, and punching tools and backed blades were devised. There was a special assortment for the forest environment; others for savannah zones. Africans who find these antique tools today believe them to be thunderbolts, lightning hardened and flung by storm spirits from the skies.

By fifty thousand years or so ago, men of our own species had appeared in Africa. Their beetling brows and sloping foreheads re-

mind us of Neanderthal men, who lived at about the same time in Palestine and Europe. But the Africans—called *Homo sapiens rhodesiensis* in honor of their place of first discovery—seem to have been a good bit taller than their northern contemporaries.

Sometime later, truly modern man, *Homo sapiens sapiens*, came into his own in Africa, though in what varieties we cannot now be sure. Many remains look like nothing so much as Bushmen grown tall. They were mighty hunters, these new men, with weapons and techniques equal to the most formidable of animals. So efficient were they in their work that they may have depleted the game. Of course, we can only guess about that. All we know for certain is that after the high hunting period, men began to fashion tiny blades and points of stone (microliths), used, it would seem, in arrows meant to bring down smaller animals and birds or perhaps to be daubed with poison. The knowledge of poison must be very ancient, for it is certainly widespread among living hunting tribes. In Southeast Asia and in South America, as well as in Africa, are to be found men who daub their tiny darts and arrows with poison. One of these, the

paralyzing curare, has given modern medicine a useful drug. Bushmen of the Kalahari Desert manufacture poisons so lethal that even a nick from a treated point is sufficient to kill big game.

By 1000 B.C., men below the jungle were first-rate collectors as well as mighty hunters. Groups began to settle in fairly permanent communities along the seashore or around lakes. In time the shells and fishbones from ancient dinners made considerable dump heaps there. Similar shell-mound villages were found in modern times by Dutch colonists moving upward from the Cape. They called the beachcombing Bushmen who inhabited them "strandloopers."

Toward Africa's north a general settling-in slowly impelled men toward farming. Above the great jungly Congo Basin, all along the Sudan, incipient farming appears to have had its beginnings by 3000 B.C. Some scientists, however, think it may have got under way even earlier in the west along the headwaters of the Niger River. Of this, more later.

When one considers the changes in African Man's life ways—his travels, his adjustments, his homes—one has to begin with the weather. It is not so much a story of hot versus cold as one of wet versus dry. And even today it remains so. For over parts of Africa the rains are scanty or absent altogether, over others torrential and destructive, and over all thoroughly unpredictable. No wonder men's concerns in Africa have always centered on water. No wonder the place of honor has always gone to leaders who believed they could command the clouds (or, in areas of constant downpour, hold them back).

During the last two million years or so—the time of man's appearance and development—while Europe, Asia, and North America were being subjected to four alternating periods of sunshine and snow, Africa was alternately wet and then dry. At roughly the times when great glaciers crept over northern continents, the rains came to Africa, woods and grasses spread out and grew, and men followed. When glaciers retreated up north, Africa's deserts advanced, lakes dried up, and life moved south again.

Nowhere is this cycle better illustrated than in the Sahara. It has long been thought of as the chief barrier between Africa's north and south, the reason why men and ideas spread slowly through the continent. The swampy Sudd, an almost impenetrable mass of vegetation which plugs the Nile about halfway between Khartoum and the lakes, is another. But these barriers are relatively recent ones in the long view. The Sahara in times past has been a meeting place, too, where men of many races, languages, and ideas came together. Like a monstrous sponge, it has sucked people in during wet times and during dry ones has squeezed them out again.

You can find in the Sahara, even today, living mementos of the last wet time, which vanished altogether probably no more than three or four thousand years ago. In the desert hills of Tibesti a few monkeys remain. Hidden under rock ledges there are shrunken pools where fish still live. And now and then if you are quiet and observant (or perhaps unwary!) you might even see a relict crocodile emerge to scavenge whatever refuse he can find.

Early men all the way back to man's beginnings have left their tools and bones along the Sahara's now dried-up waterways. Later men—hunters and fishers and farmers just learning the way of plants— left their garbage dumps for us to find. And in the mountains all through the desert, along cliff faces, under rock shelters, there are paintings and engravings made by immigrants who arrived to find not a sea of sand, but one of grass; not a land scrubbed bare of life, but one teeming with game, abundantly watered, welcoming and fair.

The first artists of the Sahara arrived perhaps ten thousand years ago. They were hunters who literally cut their records into the rock, records of themselves and of the animals they followed and hunted. Their favorite prey seem to have been the wild buffalo and the wild sheep. Both of these must also have been venerated, perhaps even worshiped. For between the horns of these animals there was often drawn a round mark of distinction, something akin to the halo which in our old religious pictures always identified the saint.

A little later other hunters arrived in the Sahara, perhaps moving upward from the south. They knew how to use ground-ochre paints, first in one color, later in polychrome. Styles changed, and the artists

*Rock painting
of hunters*

Horned grain goddess,
from a Sahara rock painting

took to drawing men who looked (as Henri Lhote, the French anthropologist and discoverer of many of the frescoes, has said) like science-fiction cartoons of Martians in space helmets. Rock shelters were often used as temples, not homes, and were covered with giant gods and suppliant women. Still later there were goddesses, too. One bears tribal scars and is crowned with horns. Over her head there appears to be a field of grasslike plants showering grain down upon her. Was she painted by men who had taken up a farming way of life? We can only guess.

Saharan rock painting of cattle herders

The finest of the Sahara's art works were painted by a herding people whose animals were first sheep and goats and later cattle. Where the herdsmen came from nobody knows. Perhaps from the upper Nile, perhaps from somewhere in Ethiopia; perhaps they had even been in the area all along. Theirs were all pictures of daily life: hunting scenes, records of cattle drives, furious battles with rustlers. They painted themselves eating and sleeping and caring for children and riding their oxen to and from pasture. Not very religious in nature, their painting seems to have been all for fun and for the glory of the painter. But what painting, and what people! Tall, red-brown, with straight backs and proud faces—an ancient aristocracy of the plains.

Sometime around 2000 B.C. the last drying-up began. Perhaps the great herds had hastened the process with overgrazing, uprooting the grasses and exposing the soil to sun and wind. Whatever the reasons for the disaster, all the good life, the easy life was over. Slowly, slowly the herds were driven away, perhaps into Egypt, perhaps into the oases which still dot the Sahara or up into the mountain peaks that rise above the sandy wastes. Or perhaps they went southward, ever southward following the grasses that followed the rain.

The Sahara in its palmy days was not Africa's only ancient rendezvous. Everywhere men of many shapes and sorts came into contact with one another. It was not so on other continents, each the home of a single race of men, monotonously similar in face and form. To Australia, for example, came the Australoids, who had their island continent all to themselves until the white man came. *His* racial type (Caucasoid, to give it a proper title) originally occupied Europe. Northern Asia has nearly always been a Mongoloid preserve. So, for that matter, was the New World. For it was men from Asia, journeying over the Bering Strait, who peopled North and South America and who became in time the American Indians. It was not until five hundred years or so ago (eight hundred if you give Leif Ericson priority over Columbus) that the Western hemisphere began to be the melting pot it is now.

In the matter of melting pots Africa has America beat by a country mile and goodness knows how many millennia. To begin with, not one but *two* races came into being there. The racial type represented by the Bushmen and Hottentots was one. Gold to golden-brown in color, the Bushman has an elfin, diamond-shaped face with wide cheekbones and puffy-lidded eyes that look almost Mongolian. His hair grows in tight little whorls something like peppercorns. He is small and graceful, with a sway-backed posture that gives him a natural bustle aft.

Negroid peoples are also thought to be native Africans, though the fossil evidence is not so clear as for the Bushman. One thing, however, is very, very clear. This type includes the world's most remarkable variations. Negroes are the tallest people and the shortest ones as well. A Pygmy of four and a half feet has to tip his head very far back to view a tall Watusi towering perhaps three feet above him. Negroes may be stocky or stringy, sturdy or frail. They may be hawk-nosed, flat-nosed; thick-lipped or thin-lipped. The skins of some are nearly black in hue; others are pale buff. Trying to settle on representative features is like looking into a kaleidoscope. Colors and patterns shift before your eyes, leaving you with an impression only. No wonder some anthropologists prefer to catalogue Negroes in several races instead of just one.

To the original combination of Bushmen and Negroes in Africa was added an influx of Caucasoids, who came (nobody knows how long ago it was) to settle all along the northern shore, in Ethiopia, and down the east coast as far as modern Kenya. The rock pictures of the Sahara document the meeting. There you can see Negro hunters and farmers (all with masks, markings, and costumes similar to those common to certain tribes in West Africa today). There, too, are people with a Caucasoid cast of features. Some—like the red-skinned herders—are in between. Living people in the desert today also bear witness to ancient migrations, and ancient marriages, too. For they come in all possible variations of color and size.

And then—sometime around the beginning of the Christian Era—still another racial ingredient was added to the African melting pot. Mongoloid travelers from Southeast Asia, sailing westward in their great outriggers, made landfall in East Africa. From there they sailed on, leaving some of their farm crops and perhaps descendants behind. They settled permanently in Madagascar, the large island off Africa's southeastern coast. There they mingled with local inhabitants and later migrants to produce a racial type often combining dark skin with slanted Mongolian eyes.

The effects of Africa's melting pot can be heard as well as seen.

Over seven hundred languages are spoken in Africa. Joseph H. Greenberg, an American anthropologist and specialist in African languages, groups them into four major divisions and several minor ones, distinct but with small distribution and few speakers. In most of these language groups you will find speakers both black-skinned and white. Take the Afro-Asiatic group, for example, which includes the Semitic languages (Hebrew, Arabic, Amharic) and the Hamitic languages (Berber, Cushite, and ancient Egyptian). Speakers of these languages were (and are) mainly Caucasoid in racial type. But wait. Also belonging to this family are the languages of the Lake Chad region (Hausa is the best known of these and the trade language of West Africa). Speakers of the Chad language are mostly Negroid.

The languages of the Sudan and the upper reaches of the Nile belong in yet another large division. It is called Nilo-Saharan so as to include related languages native to some of the desert nomads and to farming folk on the desert's fringe. Like those who speak Afro-Asiatic tongues, the Nilo-Saharan speakers have mixed racial backgrounds. In Madagascar, the large island off Africa's southeastern coast, you will hear the languages of the East, specifically, a form of Malayo-Polynesian.

The Khoisan languages used to be called simply Click languages, because that is exactly what they are—all a-bristle with consonants not so much voiced as expelled, rather like the sounds of reproof we

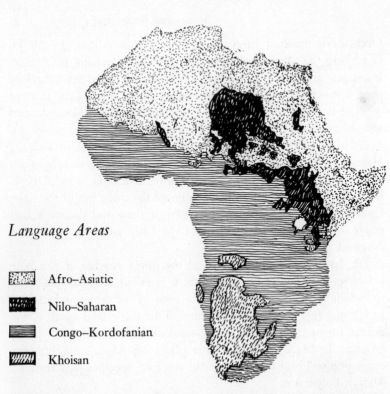

Language Areas

- Afro–Asiatic
- Nilo–Saharan
- Congo–Kordofanian
- Khoisan

make with our tongues and write as *tsk, tsk*. Khoisan languages are largely monopolized by Bushmen and Hottentots of Southwest Africa and by remnant bands of eastern relatives, whose presence demonstrates the extent of old homelands. There are, however, Negroid hunters in the Kalahari Desert who have borrowed the Bushman's language as well as his way of life. And neighboring peoples around and about have fancied up their own languages with imitated clicks.

The largest language division covers a vast geographical territory and includes a bewildering variety of forms. One can hear them spoken throughout the core, the heart-land of Africa, which stretches from the Niger and its tributaries to the Congo and its tributaries, all the way to Kordofan, the hill lands just west of the White Nile. And so the division's name: Congo-Kordofanian. Speakers of one of the Congo-Kordofanian languages spread out to occupy all of Africa in and below the jungle. These were the Bantu, of whom we shall have much to say in later chapters. One Bantu dialect of the east coast borrowed quantities of Arabic words and became Swahili, the trade language for its part of the continent as Hausa had become in the west.

The last additions to the language brew were, of course, the Indo-European languages of the West. Sound confusing? Think of this: many (if not most) of Africa's people are, because they must be, multilingual. A man might speak three languages without thinking very much about it—his native tongue, the trade language for his area, and the European tongue of those who once occupied his country and administered its affairs. If he is a practicing Moslem, he will add a generous dash of Arabic as well. How many of us can converse fluently in another language? We may study one in school, but without the opportunity to practice, what good are grammars and translations and vocabulary cards?

So much for melting pots.

The words and faces of living men hint of ancestral travels, of meetings and partings and ideas left behind. Pictures on rocks, broken bits of tools and pots and buildings sometimes tell us more. But none of these clues tell a complete story—not the kind of story that even a sketchy written record can provide.

Alas, only one of Africa's people knew writing in the old days. These were the Egyptians. Their records reveal something about Africa south and west of the Nile and suggest even more. But they do not answer one very big question. What, after all, were Egypt and the rest of Africa to each other? Was Egypt a splendid oddity, a bright thread in the midst of darkness? Or was she the splendid sum, the high point of all things African? Was Egyptian civilization the beginning of African high cultures or the fulfillment of African beginnings? Was Egypt *of* Africa or only *in* it?

We can never really know, but we can search for answers all the same.

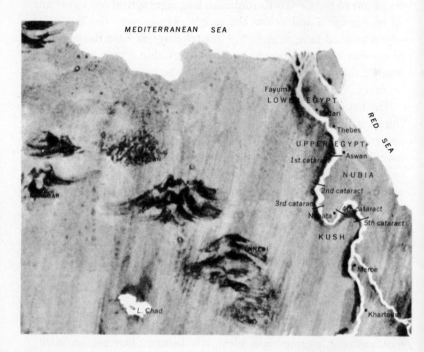

MEDITERRANEAN SEA

Fayum

LOWER EGYPT

Badari

Thebes

UPPER EGYPT

1st cataract — Aswan

RED SEA

NUBIA

2nd cataract

3rd cataract — 4th cataract

Napata — 5th cataract

KUSH

Meroe

L. Chad

Khartoum

Nile Valley and Points West

2. Egypt and Africa
In It or of It?

Egypt! Just say the name and visions appear—visions of lotus-columned temples, of pyramids silhouetted blackly against a dawn sky, their peaks touched with flame. Enduring Egypt, built to last. We see gorgeous Pharaoh, rigid as any statue, crook and golden flail crossed on his breast. We see almond-eyed princesses, elegantly slim, and lines of shaven priests intoning mysteries half as old as time. O wise Egypt, magical Egypt, bearer of secrets lost and forgotten. Egypt, first and oldest of civilizations, bringer and begetter of a light all the more brilliant for the darkness of its African backdrop.

This has been the image—an image very nearly as old as Egypt herself and as enduring. Untarnished and untarnishable, it outlasted time and change and invading armies whose generals, one by one, paid homage to Egypt's antiquity and marveled at her monuments. Scholars, even into the last century, fell admiringly into line. And then the stately hieroglyphs were fully translated, and modern men began to read the Egyptian past.

Very quickly it appeared that things had not been exactly as they seemed. Far from being otherworldly, the Egyptians were quite as this-worldly as you or me or anybody else. No speculative philosophers, they, no mystery men. Just hardheaded, practical people intent on getting along and living well. And all their elaborate funeral rites seem to have been as much an effort to hang on to the good things of this life as to prepare for the next. Indeed, in the days before there was writing to record the custom, men of importance liked to stuff their graves with wives and retainers as well as furniture. "You can't take it with you," our old saying goes. But the Egyptians certainly tried.

As Egypt's reputation for mysticism dimmed a little (at least in the eyes of scholars), so did her claims as first civilization. Archaeologists digging in the Tigris-Euphrates area unearthed cities clearly prior in time to Egyptian cities. Samples of writing found there were older than Egyptian samples and the line of script development was clearer. Even the humble mud brick appeared to have had its beginnings in Mesopotamia instead of along the Nile. After these discoveries, certain puzzling pictures drawn on the walls of very early Egyptian tombs could be read in a different light. Those pictures, it appeared, were meant to represent Mesopotamian ships with sailors wearing Mesopotamian costumes and striking Mesopotamian poses. Perhaps the *idea* of writing and sundry other inventions had traveled westward with them.

Soon it became plain that farming, too, had developed later in Egypt than in the Iranian highlands above Mesopotamia. Even Egyptian farm crops—wheat, barley, flax—had been gifts from the Middle East, and maybe the domestic animals as well. Quite suddenly, the hub of civilization shifted away from the Nile.

Egyptian scholars were quick to point out that for all the borrowings, Egypt had been no copycat but a powerful civilization in her own right. And a very *different* one at that. There was, for example, the matter of kingship. Other ancient rulers might well have been feared and absolute; they might have claimed divine kinship or the right to act as stewards for divinity. But they were, all the same, men. Not so Pharaoh. He neither claimed nor represented. He was a god, so his people believed. So he believed himself. Living or dead, he could expect to be worshiped. Even before Egyptian writing became explicit about that fact, the ancient pictures said it plainly enough. Always the figure of Pharaoh was made to tower over everyone else. Only fellow gods were drawn to his measure.

Pharaoh not only possessed Egyptian land, he *was* the land and everything that made the land fruitful. "The king is food and his mouth is increase," his people sang of him. He was drink as well. Yearly he caused the Nile to rise and reclaim its valley from the desert above. And though rain in Egypt was almost unheard of, foreign rulers considered Pharaoh the world's greatest rain maker and regularly applied to him for help when their own kingdoms suffered from drought.

Pharaoh's mother and sister were almost as powerful, as sacred, and as large as he. They were, that is, in statues. Wives were smaller

King Thutmose IV and his mother

both in importance and by artistic convention. Of course, since Pharaoh's chief wife was frequently his sister as well, she couldn't very well complain of being slighted. Some scholars believe that the divine right to rule descended mainly through the Egyptian royal women and that marrying his sister was Pharaoh's way of clinching the inheritance. However they came about, Egypt's royal marriage customs were certainly different from those of other Old World kingdoms.

Because Pharaoh was god as well as ruler, the royal routine was something special. Nothing ordinary for Pharaoh. No rise-eat-work-eat-sleep schedule for him. No rush, and no relaxation either. Not ever. His days and hours were frozen in a slow, stately round. His slightest gesture was fraught with magical significance, perhaps peril, for his people and had to be properly performed. This was doubly true for religious ceremonies.

These ceremonies often took place in the presence of god figures which were part animal, part man. Pharaoh himself—even into later times—wore costumes ornamented with lion or bull tails and celebrated a special festival which had the name "tail." People in other ancient lands had rather quickly lost interest in animal symbols. Not so Egypt—different Egypt.

Imagine the amazement of European explorers of the nineteenth century when they found, below the Sahara, kingdoms which oddly reminded them of old Egypt, the Egypt they knew from history books and ruins. Like papyrus paintings come to life were the black kings they saw there, divine beings, worshiped in life and in death. They saw fertility kings and rain-maker kings who might be deposed with the noose if their magic failed. They saw powerful queen mothers and queen sisters, and royal wives who were not powerful at all. They saw carved animal heads and tailed costumes and even, now and then, beards and hair-dos in the old Egyptian style. They noted the funeral rites of kings: how the royal bodies were preserved, wrapped mummy-like in cloths or hides, and entombed in groves made sacred by the royal presence. And everywhere, in every kingdom they found government as complex and organized as ever government can be without written records to keep things straight (or confuse matters, if you prefer). How very reminiscent of political life under the Pharaohs.

Such news made the Egyptian experts of those days smile and say, "We knew it all along." What a satisfaction it must have been to have proof of old Egypt's vitality, to know that the glory on the Nile had been reflected southward, across the desert and beyond. Clearly the distinctive elements of Egyptian civilization had left their mark on the hinterland. Clearly it was from Egypt that culture had spread to the rest of Africa.

But was it clear? Had things really happened in just that way? One odd question remained. If Egyptian influence on the rest of Africa had been so thorough, why was it that Egyptian farm crops had never penetrated further south than the Saharan oases? Why, even in Nubia—so long under Egyptian domination—had wheat and barley never replaced the native grains, pearl millet and sorghum? Was it, perhaps, because land and climate below the Sahara and in Nubia had proved inhospitable to the Egyptian crops? Perhaps so. In any case, there was certainly no disputing the fact that the *idea* of farming had spread outward from Egypt and had been put to use with hardy wild grasses, native to Africa. Somewhere between Nubia and the Ethiopian highland was settled on as a likely spot for this secondary source of domestication. From here, it was thought, domesticated millet and sorghum had traveled slowly over the rest of the continent. It was to be a long time before another, more interesting possibility was suggested. More about that in Chapter 3.

Meanwhile, the archaeologists had begun to dig. In many places along the Nile they found stone hand axes made in the style of the forest dwellers far to the south. Near Khartoum they uncovered the remains of a settled community. It was Neolithic (New Stone Age, early farming times), and in many ways it resembled another such farming site already discovered far down-river in the Fayum, a dried-up lake bed near the delta. British archaeologist A. J. Arkell thinks the two communities might have been contemporaries, or very nearly so, perhaps as far back in time as 4000 to 4500 B.C. In

both places the people had probably known how to domesticate animals, though only in the Fayum had they grown grain. Both sets of villagers had admired ornament—particularly beads made of blue-green amazon-stone—and they used the same sorts of tools. The amazon-stone could only have come from the Tibesti hills, far out in the desert—what is now the desert, that is. And tools found in those hills are almost identical in style to the ones used by villagers of the Fayum and of Khartoum. Even in those early times, apparently, a lot of traveling was going on. Certain marketable items, at least, were moving *into* the Nile Valley as well as in the other direction.

In neither Neolithic site are human bones to be found, not inside the settlement, not outside in cemeteries. Perhaps it was customary to give the dead to hyenas for disposal even as some people living along the White Nile still do. No disrespect is ever intended in this sort of "burial." Among the Nilotics it is considered the proper tribute to loved ones. Whatever the attitudes of the Khartoum and Fayum people, the interesting thing is the similarity of custom. Here were two societies, separated by the whole length of the Nile proper, and yet holding much the same ideas about death and burial (or nonburial).

In this they were quite different from people who lived later in time and in other settlements along the Nile; people who not only built cemeteries but sectioned them off as well—men alone on one side, family graves on the other. The Neolithic folk of Khartoum and the Fayum were different from earlier people, too, people who had liked to keep *their* loved ones close to home and dug graves right in the middle of camp.

One such early camp was found near Khartoum and may date back as far as 7000 B.C. No hearths, no remains of farm animals were uncovered here. For this had been only a simple fishing-hunting community—what is called Mesolithic, or Middle Stone Age. Simple or not, its people made pottery. For all we know, they may even have invented it. Very good pottery it was, combed with a catfish spine perhaps to give a basket effect and nicely fired. It was popular, too. Some samples have turned up as much as a thousand miles away from

Bird-headed "goddesses," from a Tassili rock painting

Khartoum, far out in the desert in the hills of Ennedi and Ahaggar.

The same wavy-line style, with certain added improvements, was used by people of the Khartoum Neolithic settlement, and again—far down the Nile—in Badari. The people of Badari lived much, much later in time than the fisherfolk of Khartoum and probably later than the villagers of Khartoum or of the Fayum. The Badarians were a sophisticated lot, perhaps dabbling in sailing and trade as well as farming. Besides their beautifully crafted pottery, they made the oldest ivory figurines yet found in Egypt. They may have been the first bread bakers, too. Beads and small objects of copper have been found in Badari, but whether these were made on the spot or imported from abroad nobody knows.

The bones of Badari's people—proper Egyptians in terms of locale —are thought to be Negroid in type. So are those of the Khartoum fisherfolk. The two sites are separated by several thousand years in time and at least a thousand river miles in space. All during that time and over those miles men of inner Africa were, without a doubt, moving north and taking their ideas with them.

Detail from wall painting in the tomb of Rameses IV at Thebes

In recent years scientists have begun to search the Sahara as diligently as they have searched along the Nile, always on the lookout for clues to the past. As everyone now knows, the Sahara was not always desert and never, even in dry times, entirely without inhabitants who left records behind. The real trouble has always been getting to the records and staying long enough to learn from them. Desert work requires the support of real expeditions, and as expeditions cost money in great quantity, there have been all too few of them. Those few, still and all, have brought back marvels. Henri Lhote and his artists have copied the desert rock art of the Tassili Mountains: the beautifully drawn herds and herders, the goddesses, the hunters dressed in animal heads and tails. Was it here, perhaps, among just such hunters, that Pharaoh's ceremonial costume had its beginnings? Could it have been that gods with animal heads traveled from the Sahara eastward into Egypt? Some scholars now think so. "Isn't it odd," they say, "that Egyptian art—once just stick figures like overgrown doodles—suddenly blossomed, about 3200 B.C., into that stately elegance we all admire? Perhaps the new-found art was learned from painters of the Sahara." But then, who can be sure? Rock paintings are notoriously difficult to date.

A dig often gives a clearer notion of time, especially when it uncovers materials which can be tested by radioisotope methods. Two very recent ones have turned up interesting (even spectacular) finds. In the rocky hills of the Fezzan there was found the body of a Negroid child, mummified, flexed, and buried beneath the dirt floor of the family shelter. Now, when I say "mummified," I do not mean simply wrapped up and put away. I mean that the body was carefully preserved (in this case by drying) before burial. The discoverer, Italian archaeologist F. Mori, claims a date of 3500 B.C. for his find, and the tests back him up. The spectacular thing about that date is that it makes the Fezzan mummy older than the oldest known Egyptian mummies, thought to have been prepared no earlier than first dynasty times, perhaps 3000 B.C. There is one thing more. On the wall of the rock shelter in which the child was buried someone had painted a mummy figure bound in many cloths and tied with red bands. This is the way the dead were represented in Egypt during later times. And yet Dr. Mori believes the painting may date even further back than the child's burial. Another blow to the Egyptian

image, to her reputation as premier undertaker. It seems likely that at least some Egyptian mortuary practices were learned from people living far to the west of the Nile.

A second carbon dating in the Fezzan and a good many as yet undated remains suggest to Dr. Mori that the Sahara was already home to one kind of cattle in 5500 B.C. If his opinion can be confirmed, then the great herds of the rock paintings may have traveled *from* the Sahara to points east. Indeed, the Sahara may have been their original home, the center of their domestication. Although specialists have often noted the presence of certain wild cattle, potentially tameable, among Saharan fossil finds, few have seriously considered Africa west of the Nile as a possible source of domestication.

But all along the pictures have hinted at it—those old Saharan pictures dating back, some think, at least 5000 years and probably more than that. In those pictures one can see cattle whose horns have been twisted—doubtless by their human masters—into fanciful shapes. Temple and tomb paintings from later times along the Nile show that Egyptians liked to do the same thing to their cattle. And cattlemen living today along the White Nile still follow the ancient custom. Who started it all? Nobody can yet be sure.

Cattle with twisted horns. Left to right: from a Tassili rock painting; from an ancient Egyptian temple carving

At least one thing seems plain enough. There *were* connections. Egypt was not a splendid oddity stuck all alone and lonely on the Nile. A tree does not grow without roots and without a beginning. And the Egyptian tree, for all its fine Eastern graftings, had its roots in Africa and its beginnings, too.

Far into Neolithic times, it seems likely, most Africans—at least those above the Congo Basin—shared a community of ideas and outlook. Perhaps it was increasing dryness that sent refugees straggling into the Nile oasis and drew immigrants from up-river. Perhaps not. In any case, the population grew. There was a great congregating along the Nile, a congregating of men and minds. Into this supercharged population came merchants from Mesopotamia, bringing goods and influences. Old African ideas were intensified and transformed. And Egyptian civilization was born. In later times, men would take the familiar patterns, tricked up in newer dress, back again into the lands from whence they had come—westward and southward into Africa.

Right from the beginning it was always the southerners who were Egypt's strong men. They were less in touch with foreign ideas, less exposed to luxuries and niceties than the men of the delta up north. But they knew how to fight, and they knew how to rule. Three times leaders from the south rose up to unify Egypt, to restore her glory, and to establish those long historical periods we know as "kingdoms" —old, middle, and new.

It was in a contest between north and south (about 3100 B.C.) that Egypt as a nation really began. The conqueror and first king of unified Egypt was probably Nar-Mer, a southerner, whose stone palette shows him in the act of slaying his rival, a king of the delta.

Soon after this event the southerners turned their attention upstream toward Nubia, Ta-Nehesi, Land of the Blacks. Just below the Nile's first cataract (site of the modern high dam), a trading post began to grow, a place where the exotic goods from Africa could be exchanged for Egyptian wares. It was called Suan (now modern Aswan), which means simply "market," and the goods displayed there must have been tempting indeed, because Pharaoh Snefru of the third dynasty (2650 B.C.) sent his southern armies raiding into Nubia. He had this to say about the expedition and its success: "I brought back seven thousand prisoners and two hundred thousand cattle, large and small."

Some years later the country around the first cataract was enough at peace to permit another Pharaoh to make the voyage south and himself receive the homage of Nubia's chieftains. A southern nobleman of yet another Pharaoh explored far into the interior and brought back many marvels. Most wonderful of all to Pepi II, the little boy who then sat on the throne, was news of a small, dark, dancing man who must have been a Pygmy kidnaped from his forest. "My majesty desires to see this dwarf," Pepi wrote the expedition leader, "more than the gifts of Sinai and of Punt. If thou arrivest at court this dwarf being with thee alive, prosperous, and healthy, my majesty will do for thee . . . according to the heart's desire of my majesty to see this dwarf." He may have been a living god, Pepi II, but what he wanted most of all was a playmate.

It is probably fair to say that without Nubia, Egypt might not have been so splendid by half. For Nubia was treasure land. It filled Egyptian coffers with gold, put slaves in Pharaoh's fields and soldiers in Pharaoh's armies. They were famous archers, these Nubian soldiers. Because of their prowess, Nubia herself was called "Bow Land." More and more of that land came under Egyptian rule. From the second cataract to the third the soldiers went, leaving fortresses of stone in their wake. And the frontier stretched ever farther south.

By Middle Kingdom times, the center of Nubia was very far distant from the Egyptian political center. The dynastic struggles and religious controversies that shook the north scarcely caused a ripple in Nubia. Egyptian viceroys were becoming powerful lords in their own right, small-scale models of Pharaoh himself. They married Nubian princesses, acquired wealth, and occasionally followed the very old-fashioned customs of group burial, taking with them into the tomb still-living companions instead of clay replicas. Some viceroys took on such airs that royal discipline had to be exercised and certain records of viceregal exploits erased from monuments and

tombs. This was the unkindest cut of all, at once removing a man from office and from favor in the hereafter. More and more, Nubians began to think of themselves as truly Egyptian. During the unrest of late Middle Kingdom times some even began to claim rights to the throne. Proud of his origins, one such pretender added to his inscriptions everywhere the word *Nehesi*, which means "the black one."

In 1750 B.C. or thereabouts invaders from the desert—Hyksos, the "Shepherd Kings"—overran Egypt and settled down for a long stay. But, except for the increasing demand for gold, more gold, Nubians scarcely knew what was going on in the north and cared less. Eventually the invaders, encamped in the delta, tried to negotiate an alliance with Nubia and were soundly trounced for their pains by the Prince of Thebes, who then drove them out of Egypt.

His descendants, the Pharaohs of the New Kingdom, pushed an empire into Southwest Asia all the way to the Euphrates. There Egyptian soldiers marveled at the odd river that flowed from north

to south instead of south to north as normal rivers should. Was that not the way of blessed River Nile? (We today are still stuck with that ancient confusion. Upper Egypt and upper Nile are "down" on our maps; Lower Egypt is "up." Any mention of either requires us to make a mental switch in directions.)

New Kingdom Pharaohs also moved still further south, past the third cataract and the fourth, into the land of Kush. In 1486 B.C. Hatshepsut the queen—or, more accurately, the woman-king—occupied the Egyptian throne. She did not make war, but she did build, and she renewed the lapsed trade with Punt, a semilegendary land probably near what is now Somalia. Like her forebears, she was a collector of treasures and perfumes, not entirely for herself but also for Amon, a ram-headed sun god, once chief god of Thebes, later chief of the Egyptian pantheon. This is what she caused to be written of Punt: "For so, says the god, it is a glorious region of God's land. It is indeed my place of delight; I have made it for myself in order to divert my heart."

One of her descendants, a religious reformer named Akhnaton, wanted to expel all the gods but one—Aton, the sun's disc, sign and embodiment of a universal as well as Egyptian deity. He did have some success and nearly turned Egypt upside down achieving it. Not so in Nubia, conservative Nubia, which gave its loyalty to sun-god Amon, chief of gods and patron of Thebes. In his honor ever more regal viceroys built ever costlier monuments, expecting his divine intervention to stretch over a land now thoroughly Egyptianized all the way past Napata, its chief city.

In time Napata itself produced a Pharaoh, the valorous Piankhi, lover of fast horses, who took all of Egypt for Nubia and became ruler of the two lands. About 720 B.C. that was. His dynasty did not last long. Assyrian invaders pursued his descendants all the way to Thebes. For safety's sake the king moved his capital from Napata to Meroe, above the fifth cataract. And his great empire shrank to the Kingdom of Kush.

The Kushite kings continued to build tombs and monuments in the Egyptian style, to worship Egyptian gods, and to give themselves the royal titles of Egypt. But they began to write in what was presumably the local language, and these writings have not yet been deciphered. And something new was added. It was the use of iron. Egyptians had long known iron, but they had somehow never learned to smelt it—or perhaps they had simply never found enough ore in their land to make the smelting worthwhile. But there was such ore in the soil of Kush, and invading Assyrians unwittingly gave Kushites the smelting process. From Meroe iron went out to inner Africa, allowing her people to graduate overnight from stone tools to iron ones with never a period of copper using in between.

Though small, Kush was brave enough to threaten first Ptolemaic and then Romanized Egypt. In 23 B.C. the relentless Roman legions sailed all the way to Napata and sacked it in retaliation. Another withdrawal for Kush, another defeat. Christian times were at hand. The lands around Kush raised up their own kingdoms and offered battle. Between Meroe and the Red Sea was Semitic Axum, soon to turn Christian. To the north, tribes of desert men, invited by the Romans to occupy Nubia, cut off the way to Egypt. About 350 A.D. the city of Meroe, last remnant of Pharaohic glory, collapsed and its people fled—who knows where? Perhaps westward along the desert's fringe. Perhaps eastward into the hill country. Perhaps southward, ever southward along the Nile and into the heart of Africa. Perhaps to found—or to find—other kingdoms, kingdoms which would echo Egypt but also rephrase what had been a common, an African beginning.

Part II

KINGDOMS
BELOW THE DESERT

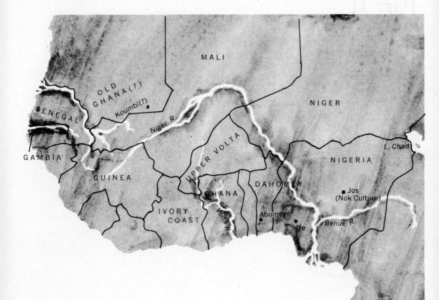

West Africa

3. The West African Kings
Metals, Mothers, and Amazons

Once upon a time there was a great West African kingdom called Ghana. The name was already well known in 680 A.D., when Arab armies arrived in the north. Nobody knew then just how old Ghana already was. Tradition held that the kingdom had been founded in the fourth century, but it may have been earlier. Nobody living along Africa's northern coast could say exactly where it was, either. All that was known for certain was that now and again, caravans appeared from out of the desert, and those caravans were laden with gold—gold from Ghana.

I should say immediately that there is no connection whatever between ancient and modern Ghana, though both had a reputation for treasure (modern Ghana was once called The Gold Coast). They are not even close on the map. The ancient kingdom, it is thought, lay somewhere between the headwaters of the Niger River and the Sahara. Its capital city (long lost under the sand), was said to touch the very fringe of the desert, perhaps somewhere near modern Oualata in Mauritania.

To this city in the tenth century came Moslem writers and explorers, traveling by overland caravans. Ibn Haukel and after him El Bekri were both astonished by the wealth of Ghana's ruler, from whose royal title the country took its name. Both writers recorded their impressions for the folks back home. And well they might. Gold was everywhere and silver, too—on the king, on his councilors, on the royal drums, the royal horses, even the royal dogs. The king apparently exercised a monopoly on all gold nuggets found in his domain. He also collected the taxes and tributes customarily due rulers everywhere. No novice in the world of commerce, he encouraged a thriving caravan trade and permitted foreign merchants and caravaneers to set up their own township near the capital. It was called Koumbi.

Besides being wealthy, Ghana's ruler was also considered at least semidivine. According to El Bekri, he lived in a palace of stone, and the pageantry of his public appearances was something to behold. Drums thundered news of the impending event, and subjects fell to their knees, throwing dust about their heads and shoulders by way of doing homage.

The royal cathedral was a grove of trees so large as nearly to surround the city. Here were buried all the former kings of Ghana. Here each reigning monarch could himself expect to be laid to rest. Here, too, would go his mother and sister, in death as in life of nearly as much importance as he. Heir to Ghana's gold and glory was always a royal nephew, never a royal son. The old reports are clear on this point.

The first known kingdom south of the Sahara is interesting not just because of its history but because of its location as well. It lay in an area where true African farming may have had its beginnings. Perhaps here in this land between river and desert may be found the answer to that old question: Why were there no Egyptian crops below the desert and why so few in Nubia? Was it indeed because of inhospitable climate? And were the native domesticates simply substitutes? Not so, says the American anthropologist George Peter Murdock. African crops were not substitutes; they were not domesticated in Ethiopia; and if they enjoyed (and enjoy) priority in Africa below the desert and in Nubia, it was because they had arrived there first, before the Egyptian agricultural gifts could work their way up the Nile.

Wheat, barley, and flax were first brought to Egypt's delta region around 5000 B.C. They came from older centers in the Middle East.

It was also around 5000 B.C. that pearl millet, sorghum, and cotton were domesticated in the western Sudan, almost certainly as a result of independent invention. From there they moved slowly eastward to arrive at last in Nubia and Ethiopia. Why does Professor Murdock believe this to be so? Certainly there is no archaeological evidence that gives us cause to say emphatically, "There was farming here in Nubia, African-type farming, and by 4000 B.C. at that!" Nevertheless, farm crops, when they first appeared, *must* have been of the African sort, because even now the basic crops in Nubia, though supplemented by some Egyptian ones, are African. And elsewhere in the Sudan, Egyptian crops are almost never to be seen.

And there is one thing more. You will recall that in the area near Khartoum there is one Neolithic site, tentatively dated at 4000–4500 B.C. No evidence of grain has yet been unearthed there. But wait. In one of the fireholes there was found the charred fragment of an oil-palm fruit. Now, the oil palm is native to West Africa and is extensively cultivated there. If one plant had been carried across the continent, perhaps others were on the way.

How Professor Murdock arrived at his belief in a West African center of farming is almost as intriguing as the theory itself. First of all he made lists, sorting out Africa's cultivated plants by country of origin—the ones that had been at some time introduced from India, from Southwest Asia, from Southeast Asia, from the New World. What remained were the true natives, the plants that had been domesticated from African wild forms. He then tried to find the place in Africa where most of these natives were cultivated—not just the popular, important ones, but the lesser known plants as well. The area which fitted this requirement turned out to be savannah land centering around the upper Niger River, an area which covers parts of modern Mali, Guinea, Senegal, and Gambia. Its people today speak Mande, one of the Congo-Kordofanian languages. Perhaps it was their ancestors who did the original job of plant domestication. Certainly they have long had the reputation of being energetic, expansive, and go-getting.

No wonder Ghana, the first African kingdom, appeared just here

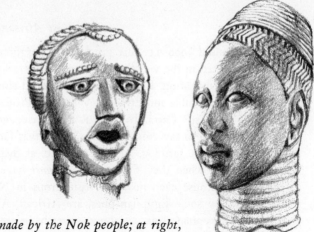

A clay head made by the Nok people; at right,
portrait in fired clay of a king of Ife, Southern Nigeria

among such people and in such a setting. Many great kingdoms were to follow. Perhaps there were others that came before. Nobody knows. Indeed, there is no real archaeological proof for the beginning of African farming in this area. This may be so not because the evidence does not exist, but because the digging has not yet been done. No one has subjected the banks of the Niger to the same fine-tooth combing applied along the Nile. The immediate incentives, it must be said, are not quite the same. Flooding behind the high dam at Aswan has made archaeological investigation in Nubia a scientific must. What is more, a man could dig there with some definite expectation of success. After all, everybody knows what happened along the Nile. The Niger is something else again. There one has only the possibility of great discovery, however exciting that possibility may be.

Whatever remnants we have from West Africa's distant past are ours mostly by accident. Strange stone figures are often found all the way to Lake Chad and down to the Guinea Coast. West Africans say they are unlike anything made today. Badly surface-weathered, they look to be very old. Who can be sure?

The luckiest of the archaeological accidents happened near Jos, Nigeria. Modern tin miners in search of ore uncovered the remains

At left, portrait in bronze of a king of Ife, Southern Nigeria; bronze head at right is from the altar of a Benin queen mother in southwest Nigeria

of an old and particularly long-lived settlement—now called the Nok Culture. It began around 1000 B.C. and flourished until 200 A.D. or thereabouts. In the early days of the settlement, stone tools were used. Toward the end, the same tool types were made of iron. The Nok people were farmers. Grains of their millet have been found (and age tested). They were artists, too. Beautiful little heads of fired clay found all through the site prove this beyond a doubt. They suggest even more. They suggest a long artistic tradition among the Nok people and a society with enough means, enough leisure time to allow such a tradition to develop.

That tradition outlived the Nok Culture itself. It followed migrating groups and tribes as they moved south, away from savannah lands and down toward the great forest fringe along the Guinea Coast. A thousand years after the last Nok head had been modeled, city artists in southern Nigeria captured in clay the likenesses of their kings. Their work is glorious by any standard, rivaling the best sculptures of Egypt or Greece.

Later on the same artistic tradition was expressed in bronze and brass, still with the same elegance and grace. How the knowledge of bronze developed we do not know. Did it come as a gift from other people, or was it home-grown? Certainly the use of bronze was a relative rarity in Africa, where iron was everywhere the metal of preference.

From southern Nigerian cities the art of casting metals spread along the coast. Eastward it went, to the Niger delta, where heads of bronze were placed on royal altars, there to house the souls of kings. Westward it went, to the area that is now modern Ghana, where kings leaned on golden stools and had their faces masked in gold.

On the coast between modern Ghana and Nigeria there is a break in the rain forest. In that wedge of clear land lies Dahomey, which was, until French conquest in 1892, a powerful kingdom, perhaps the most powerful in its part of the world. To Dahomey also came the knowledge of casting in silver and gold and brass. It became the closely guarded secret of a family guild. Metal workers were courtiers who produced king's treasure, art objects suitable for royal gifts and royal rewards. Almost nobody owned the brasses of Dahomey except as a mark of the king's generosity.

News of Dahomey and its treasures had reached Europe by the seventeenth century. A hundred years later the kingdom was to be famous among sea traders. Many perceptive travelers and fine writers have, at one time or another, visited Dahomey, among them the British explorer Sir Richard Burton, who in 1864 undertook a diplomatic mission to King Gelele. In 1931 the American anthropologist Melville Herskovits and his wife went to study and to stay. And though the monarchy was, even then, forty years in the past, they found Dahomey much as Burton had described it.

Just when and where the first king of Dahomey got his start is not certain. From the north toward the Niger, perhaps. By 1625 A.D. his war bands had taken Abomey, which became their capital city. From there they pushed on until they reached the sea. Village after village capitulated. Each local chief or "king" did homage to the invading monarch, bent his knee and cast dust on his head—or found himself replaced by someone who would. Home rule was lost forever. After the conquest village chiefs were appointed to office and stayed in office only at the king's pleasure. Local courts could hear only minor disputes and could decree only minor punishments—no more than four days in jail, a sound slapping (by hand, not strap), or a small fine. Offenses requiring major punishment (or larger fines) had to be heard at the provincial cities. The prospect of high court costs there was usually enough to scare quarreling villagers into quick settlement on home grounds.

Final appeals went to the king, as did all cases for which capital punishment or enslavement might be the result. "Death is mine," said the Dahomean monarch in effect. "Everybody else, hands off." The rule applied to all—noble or commoner, slave or freeman. To enforce the rule, coroner's juries were ordered to check every death in the kingdom, making sure there was no suspicion of foul play.

The king's long arm extended into the family itself. Whatever a deceased father's wishes; whatever the sworn statement of his "best friend" (a sort of living last will and testament)—the king had his own say about who would inherit and who would not. Chosen heirs could not succeed their fathers—particularly if they headed large and influential family groups—unless and until they had sworn loyalty and paid their inheritance taxes.

The king had a bit more trouble controlling local leaders of work gangs—groups of young men who helped build houses, clear fields, maintain roads, all to the accompaniment of feasting and song. For as long as anyone could remember these leaders and their fathers before them had been on the land. They were, in a way, the original owners of it. Before the king came, even before the village chiefs had come, the work leaders had been there. It was really something more than land and work that these leaders symbolized. It was the whole spirit of cooperation. Cooperatively Dahomeans had always formed clubs for self-help. Not only was help at hand for house and field, but one could, in groups, beat the high cost of buying, of marrying, and of dying. Smiths and weavers, for example, regularly pooled funds for raw materials, and the potters did their firing together. For weddings and funerals—always occasions for ostentatious display—only mutual "insurance" staved off family bankruptcy.

As symbols of this cooperative spirit, the work leaders were potential rivals to the king's power. Worse yet (in the king's view), they were untouchable. Their ancient connections with the land and the spirits of the land kept them out of royal reach. The Dahomean king was a practical politician, however. What he could not beat, he joined. Village chiefs were ignored, but village work leaders were praised and pampered and loaded with honors. As each new leader succeeded his father he was given his day in court, with big doings, great ceremony, many gifts, and everybody who was anybody on hand to watch. What young leader, fresh from his fields and furrows, wouldn't have been awe-struck? It must have been rather like achieving knighthood in England. Especially when, just before the "dubbing," these words were intoned:

> ". . . the King orders you to allow even the poorest man to come to him, and the strangers who have no protectors in the capital, so that he may help them. And here is the rule of Dahomey: put dust on your head and rise to vow to the King your devotion. . . ."

And the work leader always did.

What the king gave with one hand, however, he took with another. Everyone paid taxes. Every man did his military duty. Or else. The king knew all. And he knew all because he took a census.

Dahomeans may not have been able to write, but they could certainly count. Every eight days the king received news of births and deaths in the area around Abomey and every three months from the provincial capitals. He was told whether the deceased were children or adults. If children, what ages and sexes; if adults, whether slave or free, and the manner of death. Pebbles in sacks gave the numbers, pictures on the sacks told the village, and color of sack and

various emblems supplied the other information. The count of children was kept in two sets of ingenious boxes—one for boys, one for girls—thirteen boxes to a set. Pebbles were put into the first boxes as births were reported and removed as deaths occurred or yearly as all graduated to the next higher box. After thirteen, girls became marriageable and boys subject to the "draft," and their pebbles were sent along to fill adult bags elsewhere.

The population boxes and sacks were kept in a long, low building with many doors and many rooms, each representing a king's reign. After an old king's death, always his favorite son and successor was brought first to the house of the census. Priests guided him from room to room, showing him Dahomeans in their numbers, reign by reign. "Make the people grow," he was told. "Protect them, nourish them, make them great."

After that first visit, the matter of population became both secret and sacred information. Only two persons shared this knowledge with the king: the chief census taker and one of the female advisers who were called "mothers." These special "mothers" of Dahomey were in reality wives of the king, and there were hundreds and hundreds of them. But instead of shutting them up in harems, the king put them to work. They were the country's recorders, its living file cabinets, its supervisors. And, as eyes and ears of the king, they were also the country's "F.B.I."

Each official in the government had his assigned "mother"—a watchful lady who accompanied him to every meeting, every conference, every commercial transaction. Whatever he told the king she was required to verify. And if she didn't, woe betide the official. From distant towns—Whydah or Allada or Savé—a constant stream of reports arrived at the palace, and always in two versions. As the information was memorized and carried by messenger, that meant two men per report. Royal messengers were former war heroes whose half-shaven heads and royal staffs proclaimed their office. Up and down the roads they pounded, night and day. Running in relays, they could cover the ninety miles between Abomey and the sea in three days.

Even the army had its *meno*—"our mothers." Each male soldier, be he private or general, had his female counterpart. Because the king much preferred his women warriors, he tended to pet and spoil them with praise, to the immense chagrin of the male warriors. Even so, Amazons were no stay-at-homes. They fought as hard as the men and, it is said, were even fiercer and more ruthless in battle. Like all the other "mothers" in the country, Amazons were also wives of the king, though usually in name only. As there were quite a lot of these celibate soldiers, the end result was a kingdom full of old maids and a declining population.

Royal "mothers" were not usually a fixture in religious life, but this does not mean that church and state were separate in Dahomey. The king usually maneuvered the appointments of chief priests and had some say (though discreetly) in a temple's financial operations. There were lots of temples in Dahomey and a respectable number of competing "denominations." Prominent were those serving the great gods of Earth, Sky, and Thunder. There were also smaller groups which honored less impressive but more personal gods. A universal favorite was the messenger of the gods, a cosmic cutup who might be induced to change the orders from on high, bringing down to earth a fate other than that which had been originally ordained.

In between and over all were the rites and shrines devoted to ancestor honoring. Most important, of course, were the royal ancestors. Their honoring was a national duty and a national rite, rather like our own pledging allegiance to the flag. In the old days of Dahomey, royal memorial services included much human sacrifice—the theory being that if lesser persons could afford to sacrifice grain or animals in worship, the king should go them one better and make the most expensive sacrifice of all. As Burton tells us, people in general felt quite strongly about this tradition, and even though the king might have had humanitarian scruples about the waste of life, public sentiment prevented him from discontinuing the practice.

The great temples were served by devotees with varying degrees of sanctity. There were what our religious people might call "lay brothers." There were "preaching brothers," and, of course, priests —garden variety and high. Even becoming a "lay brother" meant undertaking a novitiate lasting nearly a year. The training was rugged. Novices were never entirely sure they would last or even come out alive at the end. Strict though the priests were, however, they were certainly no snobs. Slaves were welcome to undertake the novitiate and, in time, could even rank high in the denomination. So could women. There were, in fact, always more women novices than men. Husbands grumbled about this and said their wives had joined only for the fancy costumes and the chance to take on airs at home.

Dahomean men had quite a lot to grumble about, actually, because women did take on airs and in many places other than home and temple. Of course, they could not hold office, but they could make and inherit money. And what they got, they kept. (Women of the West did not acquire this right legally until seventy years or so ago.)

Dahomey had a money economy long before the Europeans came. Cowry shells, copper, or iron bars served as currency, and very often women had more money than men. They could provide for their sons' weddings and (if broad-minded) help their husbands acquire an extra wife or two. They had money because they worked for it. Not primarily in the fields (though they did that, too), nor in the crafts (only pottery making was open to them), but in the market place. Women were the merchants of Dahomey. They bought and they sold. They managed whatever there was of high finance, remitting to the king his share of the take. So firmly fixed was commerce as a female way of life that little girls played at selling almost before they could walk, and a new baby was not fully named or recognized until his mother had introduced him to the market.

Economic rights were echoed in marriage. It was not thought gallant (or magically safe) for men to seek divorces in Dahomey. That was a woman's prerogative. And as to marriage, there was plenty of room for choice. In our world a couple has only two options in terms of vows. The bride can promise to "love, honor, and obey" or "love, honor, and cherish." That's all. But in Dahomey there were thirteen sets of vows, covering all sorts of marital circumstances.

There was even a provision for "woman-marriage," in which a wealthy lady, usually of noble birth, could create and head her own family. She did this by "marrying" slave girls or commoners and then lending them to her own brothers or cousins or male friends. Whatever children resulted then called the wealthy woman "Father," took her name, and inherited her wealth. Such a family never broke up. The children were lumped together for good and aye. Since most were not really related by blood, they were free to marry one another and indeed had to do so. In time the oldest granddaughter of the "founding father" took her predecessor's name, and the whole process was begun anew.

If Dahomean women could defy their husbands, Dahomean sculptors could defy the king. Work in brass and the precious metals and even the making of appliqué cloth were, it is true, confined to the members of tight family guilds, forever under the king's thumb. But wood working was an art open to anyone with free spirit and talent. Amateurs of wealth and importance usually preferred to work in secret, because for them this activity was considered not quite "nice." The rest of the lot, however, simply went their way with a fine disregard for convention. The wood carvers of Dahomey had a reputation for temperament. Women thought them dubious marriage prospects. Dreamy and unreliable, they were forever wandering around the forests looking for wood when they should be bringing home the bacon. They never finished commissions on time, and what is worse, they never seemed to care. The king himself was known to plead with artists and even, on occasion, to have them arrested and put under lock and key until their work was done. Never, never did he push an artist too hard, however, or threaten too seriously. "After all," he would say with a sigh and a shrug, "good artists don't grow on trees" (or the Dahomean equivalent of that old cliché).

It was from this land of Dahomey, a hundred years and more ago, that many slaves were taken for the New World. The kings and all the other native rulers up and down the coast (The Slave Coast, it was then called) earned a good part of their wealth by supplying the demand. They supplied it, in the main, with captives taken from tribes and kingdoms with whom they were at war. Convicted criminals, too, were often punished by enslavement. And the big "black birds"—slave ships, America-bound—offered native rulers a dandy way to dispose of princely political rivals.

Enslavement was a harsh and terrible fate. Many Dahomeans consigned to slavery did not survive the passage overseas. Many who did survive must often have wished for death. And yet, in spite of their misery, they brought something of Dahomey with them, something that worked its way into the fabric of life on these shores. They brought their gods, for one thing, and the spirit of god in all—the *vodu*, which in Haiti became the familiar voodoo. They brought their mysticism—their belief in possession by gods and by evil men— a concept symbolized by the zombi. They brought their ways of worship, too—the use of song and dance and hand clapping and antiphonal response. They brought their talent for organization and used it again and again (especially in the Caribbean) in bloody revolts. They brought their elaborate etiquette, their formalized good manners and ceremonial address. They brought the tradition of strong-minded, resourceful women. They brought the spirit of both cooperation and competition and the capacity for optimism and good cheer that marked them in their homelands and marks their descendants to this very day.

4. East African Kings
Caste, Class, and Cattle

Though all African kingdoms were alike in their casts of royal characters, they certainly followed different scripts. In Dahomey, life was a hurly-burly of activity. People cooperated when they had to, but they competed with even greater enthusiasm. They competed for wealth, for honors, for importance, and their hearts were in the market place. (Even the king was something of a businessman.) There it was possible for a man with talent and energy to move up the social ladder no matter what his forebears had been.

Across the continent in East Africa, however, what a different story! There, clustered between Lake Victoria and the lake chain of the Rift, were six large kingdoms and several little ones. You would not have found much social climbing in these kingdoms. You would not have found pampered, temperamental artists or market women selling their wares. Women were, by and large, confined to their own back yards, and there was precious little interest in markets anyway. Wealth was a matter of concern, of course (as where is it not?), but in most of the lake kingdoms, wealth was not reckoned in cowry money or even in copper ingots. It was reckoned in cattle. And yet, cattle could not be called currency. They were much, much more than that. Cattle represented honor, respect, prestige, all that made life worth living—for a chosen few. Cattle were, after all, a restricted commodity. Only members of the upper class—the ruling class—could own herds. Subject peoples—the farmers and the hunters

—were obliged to remember their "place" and not meddle in the affairs of their betters.

The whole of society in many lake states presented a sort of layer-cake arrangement, with the hunters (the Twa) on the bottom, the farmers (in some states called Hutu, in others Iru) in the middle, and the herders on top. These were called Tutsi or, in some states, Hima. Occasionally both names were used so as to distinguish the social elite from common, ordinary herders.

In any case, it was in the old days (and often still is) very easy to tell the rulers from the ruled. Tall Tutsi towered by at least a foot over the smaller Hutu and sometimes two feet over the Pygmoid Twa. And they tried very hard to maintain their mark of distinction. Marriage between classes was forbidden, for purity of blood and social pedigree were terribly important, to the Tutsi, at any rate. In the process of maintaining the differences in looks, differences in occupation tended to freeze as well. A boy was fated to do and be exactly what his father had done and been before him. What resulted was a caste as well as class system. And it has continued well into modern times in independent Rwanda, Burundi, and parts of Uganda.

All the well-born Tutsi male could, in honor, do with his time was fight, play politics, and herd cattle. His wife did a little light housekeeping, a little fancy basketwork, and carried on some political intriguing behind the scenes. She might even be relieved of child care by governesses—women of good family in somewhat reduced circumstances. Both men and women had ample leisure in which to cultivate the social graces and an air of hauteur. The aristocratic Tutsi gentleman valued above all else the achievement of political power, his wealth in cattle, his reputation, and his impeccable manners. The Tutsi lady also valued power and wealth and, in order to acquire them, spent a great deal of time making herself elegant and appealing. And though she lived in what was strictly a man's world —a world in which women were meant to be often seen, seldom heard, and *never* consulted—she managed to get her own way nonetheless.

Farming, of course, was beneath contempt. That was the business of the Hutu, who were forbidden to own cows other than malformed or barren ones. Even farm foods were publicly scorned. Self-respecting Tutsi professed to live entirely on a liquid diet—the milk and butter (and perhaps in older days the blood) of their herds. Of course, they were not above a social pot of beer made from Hutu millet or Hutu bananas. And one may suppose that a good deal of porridge was consumed in private.

The farming Hutu, though technically free to come and go as they chose, became in time something very like the serfs of medieval Europe. Whatever hard labor had to be done, they did. Whatever was wanted, they gave. They had to. Any Tutsi might at any time cart off their goats or barren cows, and unless they were in service to a greater lord, there was nothing that could be done about it. Protests were often punished with the spear. Of course it goes without saying that a Hutu did not seek revenge. It was not his right, and it would be stupid, besides. For the Hutu who did harm a Tutsi would certainly see two of his own family killed by way of reprisal. The farmers endured and, while enduring, served. They fed their masters, clothed them in bark cloth, supplied them with beer. They were also the doctors who cured great lords, the blacksmiths who made their weapons, the sorcerers who cast spells on order, the drummers who manned percussion orchestras.

It was up to the Pygmoid Twa to keep the upper class amused. They sang, they danced, they mimicked. They also hunted in the forests, and their women sometimes made pottery to sell. Neither Hutu nor Twa worried much about maintaining an image. Both were far too busy attaching themselves to great lords who would provide some measure of protection to lose their tempers and make fools of themselves. Beyond security in his home and for his small possessions, the farming Hutu's aims were to work hard and become as well to do as possible. The Twa hunter was interested in nothing beyond stuffing himself on a good dinner. This, at least, is how the Tutsi *imagined* their underlings to be. How proudly they bore the tall man's burden in allowing these small, ill-mannered underlings to serve them!

The way the caste states came into being is unknown. It is probably safe to say that the herders were originally migrants in the area, having appeared some time after the farmers' arrival and long, long after the Pygmies were established there. Their love of cattle and their tall stature seem to relate them to peoples living further north along the Nile, wandering warrior-herdsmen whose simple way of life includes almost nothing of the sort of organization we call "government." Because ancestors of the Tutsi were probably just such a people—fierce, proud, and strong—some scholars have imagined a sort of Norman Conquest taking place in the lake region. The tall warriors, they say, subjugated the small farmers, erecting on the wreckage of their villages the superstructure of great kingdoms. Others have seen the answer in persistent snobbery, with the aristocratic Tutsi simply awing their farming neighbors into submission. However caste and class developed, it is certainly true that the great kingdoms resulted from the mixture of peoples—herders with their simple ways and snobbish sense of superiority, plus farmers with a background, it would seem, of more organization in community life.

The mixing produced yet another result. Though the herders very

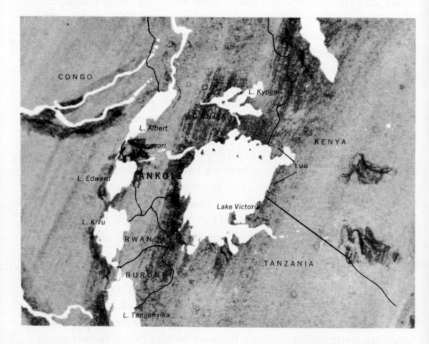

The Lake Region

likely entered the lake region speaking a Nilo-Saharan language (perhaps something like that of the present-day Nilotic Luo across Lake Victoria), they soon switched to the farmers' language. There were, after all, many more farmers than herders, and people in the majority do not give up their language no matter what an invader threatens to do about it. Unless he threatens in the proper language, nobody will know what he is saying, much less take fright. He who would rule must first become a linguist. And that is what the Tutsi did.

One of the most important of the lake kingdoms in prestige and population was Ankole. Nobody knows when the kingdom began. Fourteenth or fifteenth century, perhaps. But that is only a guess. Somehow English explorers of the 1860s missed calling there during their search for the source of the Nile. It was not until the 1920s and 30s that the kingdom and its people's ways were fully studied, most notably by anthropologist K. Oberg. Thirty years later, historian H. F. Morris collected and translated Ankole's epic poetry. The accounts of both men suggest that though much of Ankole's former glory has flown, the old ways can still be traced, even today.

The tall herders of Ankole, called there the Hima, say they came to their present home from somewhere in the north, driving their cattle before them. They had neither kings nor chiefs and lived peaceably with the farming people they found in residence. Then, they say, a strange people called Chwezi arrived, a fair, bright people with faces like the sun, people who lived in grass houses, people whose women covered their faces in modesty, people who were mighty hunters and mightier magicians; most of all, people who knew how to rule. Mysteriously they came and just as mysteriously they went away again, embittered by the ingratitude of their subjects.

Stories about the Chwezi turn up in many of the lake kingdoms. Always they are pictured as bringers of chieftainship and many other things besides. Professor Murdock believes this myth to be rooted in actual fact. The first inhabitants in the area (apart from the Pygmoid hunters) were, he thinks, a Caucasoid people speaking an Afro-Asiatic language related to those of the North African Berbers and the Egyptians. It was they who first met the incoming Bantu; they who retaught the knowledge of African grains—a knowledge lost during the long forest years of yam cultivation. Theirs were the great stone and earth works still to be found in parts of East Africa.

In the Hima version of the myth, times of arrivals and departures may be fictional, but the essential core of fact remains. So says Professor Murdock.

No fact at all, other scholars insist, but fiction through and through. A myth meant to glorify the past, to capture a group ideal, to hold up to view the very model of a model Hima gentleman.

Whether myth or reality, the Chwezi are long gone. But, say the Ankole, in their going, one of them was left behind—a young man named Ruhinda who lingered on to marry a slave girl and found the Hima royal clan. Interestingly enough, he was persuaded to remain by a small farmer (Iru in Ankole)—a clever fellow who also recovered the chief Chwezi symbols of royal authority: the beaded veil called *Rutare*, and the drum, *Bagyendanwa*, without possession of which no man may rule in Ankole. The cult of the vanished Chwezi and the cult of the royal drum were, in the old days, the main forms of religious expression in Ankole, along with the inevitable celebration of the royal ancestors. A creator god, Ruhanga, had been responsible for the beginning of things, say the Ankole, but he then went too far away to hear his people's prayers and be troubled by them.

The royal drum, however, was always there, a very present help

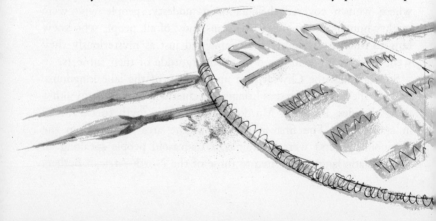

in time of need. Addressed as "He," housed and warmed and provided with a consort drum, tended by a clan whose members were devoted to "His" care, the drum was thought to be as royal as the living king and a good deal more compassionate. While the man might be capricious and partial to some of his subjects, the drum played no favorites. To "His" shrine came both herding Hima and farming Iru, singing "His" praises and bringing offerings. Both came when in need, and the drum (through "His" attendants) heard the sorrows of both and lent assistance to both from "His" collected wealth. The drum was truly the ideal king, all-loving, all-giving, and as an ideal, "He" mended the hurts of caste-bound men and held the kingdom together.

Like European monarchs of feudal times who moved in ceaseless progress from castle to castle leaving only when the larder was bare, the king of Ankole toured his domains. With him went his brewers and his bakers, his dancers and drummers, his soldiers, bodyguards, and young squires in military training, his wives and their guardians, great chiefs and herd boys, and, of course, his cattle. When these herds left a grazing ground, it was indeed bare. Technically, all Ankole's cattle belonged to the king, and a man's cows were his only in trust and by loan. To keep them, a subject had to make frequent gifts of cattle to the king. This was not so tyrannical as it sounds, for the huge royal herd was, in reality, the nation's insurance policy. If a man's herds were wiped out by sickness or in an enemy raid, he could reasonably expect the king to give him more from the royal reserves. And so to the king's huge grass compound—houses, courts, and cattle yard—came the lordly Hima from all over the realm. They knelt to the king and swore him fealty. Once home again, they could expect lesser Hima to kneel to them, so that nearly everyone was both client to somebody above and lord to somebody below. Except, of course, for the king on top and the Twa on the bottom.

The great lords held lands and herds at the king's pleasure and for so long as they rendered loyal military service in the frontier camps. Here they defended Ankole's borders. From here they sallied forth— led sometimes by the king himself—to raid neighboring kingdoms and neighboring herds. Epic poetry was composed to celebrate these adventures, songs to praise the warrior's valor and the invincibility of his weapons. Even cattle had their praise songs, for were they not a warrior's boon companions, things of beauty and a joy forever?

Cattle and weapons, like men, also had praise names. (Remember King Arthur's Excalibur?) In reading Hima epic poetry it is sometimes hard to tell whether the hero is a "he" or an "it." Here is a sample. Translated by Dr. Morris, it was composed in the nineteenth century to celebrate a cattle raid.

> I-Who-Take-No-Rest went for the cattle!
> With Rwakakuuto, I went for them as they stood without the kraal;
> Hearing the cries of their master they scattered. . .
> At Kajwamushana, they captured the foe whilst the frogs were croaking;
> They fought on without ceasing until they had vanquished them.
> He-Who-Is-Truculent fulfilled his word and The-Slayer-of-the-Enemy was with him;
> He-Who-Grasps-His-Weapons-Firmly slew the foe.

Each warrior was his own poet, and each poem was a personal thing to be made and sung on the spot. The poet might remember it later and sing it again; he might not. There was no writing in Ankole, after all. Many songs of the past owe their survival entirely to the devotion of Iru servants who learned their masters' songs and passed them on to their own descendants. In just this way the *Iliad* and *Odyssey* were preserved. And what were they, after all, but the collected praise songs of raiders in other places, other times?

As a leader of raids, the king was "The Lion." As the bringer of spoil, he was "The Leading Bull." And as "The Drum," he was the symbol of unity, the giver of law, and the final court of appeal. Even the Iru could repair to him when predatory Hima had robbed them once too often or when the royal tax gatherers had been feathering their own nests on too grand a scale. If enough goats and beer were offered to win his attention, the king just might do something to mend matters. He might scold the offenders. Or if he thought he himself had been wronged, he might punish, "eating up" all the culprit noble's estates and driving him out of the country. He could order executions if so minded, but in cases of murder involving Hima he sometimes allowed individual families to take personal revenge on the murderers' families. (Feuding in Ankole took place on the king's terms or not at all!) Of course, if an Iru were the victim, that was a matter of mild regret, nothing more.

The king owned all Ankole's cattle, and theoretically, he owned all its women, too. Hima fathers were anxious to call attention to their daughters, because the king gave generous wedding gifts. Besides, the lucky girl then had the chance of becoming mother to a future king, and that meant her whole family would share the glory. So of course the king's royal compound was crammed with women of all ages and descriptions. They did not eat with him, for royal meals were taken alone, but they did sing and dance and entertain him. Those who especially caught his fancy were force-fed with milk until they became roly-poly butterballs, barely able to walk. For heft as well as height was much admired among the Ankole. Girls who remained persistently slim in spite of the dairy diet were considered unfit for royal consideration and were bestowed on visiting chiefs.

To help him in his duties, the king depended on a council of ministers—especially one, called *enganzi*—the favorite. There were no hereditary positions in the Ankole court. And since the high offices were usually given to the king's uncles and cousins on his mother's side, an entirely different set of leaders came into prominence with each new reign. Always the king's mother and chosen sister were of supreme importance—always so long as one remained a widow and the other unmarried. Many administrative matters passed through these ladies' hands and some court cases as well. They even had the right to overrule the king's life or death decisions, and their own compounds were places of refuge. Daily the queen mother performed ceremonies meant to protect her son from the ghosts of his enemies. She also protected him from tiresome living subjects. Anyone who wanted an audience with the king had to apply first to the queen mother. This rule was especially strict when it came to foreigners.

The king was not only "Lion," "Leading Bull," and "Drum"; he was also "The Territory of Ankole," through whose vigor and by whose daily life the kingdom's good fortune was preserved. He could not bend a knee lest the territory shrink. He could not suffer illness or show age. Whatever a mother's feelings, whatever a sister's pride, the nation came first, and it could not be allowed to weaken with its monarch's advancing years. At the first sign of a wrinkle or gray hair his reign came to an end. Some say he died by poison, self-administered. Some say he was strangled by those who loved him best.

On that day the royal drum, *Bagyendanwa*, announced the awful message. Solemnly the funeral ceremonies went forward. Human sacrifices were made, and the king's body was taken to a sacred forest where it was left for the vultures and hyenas in the way of some Nilotic peoples farther north. Someday, the people thought, the king would emerge from the forest as a living lion. And in that hope, the new queen mother periodically sent a white heifer trotting into the forest, there to await the lion-king's hunger.

Because African kings had many wives, there were always many princes contending for every throne. Succession, even in commoner families, was rarely a predetermined matter. The eldest son was not automatically the chosen heir. Always there was plenty of leeway for favoritism and considerations of fitness. The uncertainty of succession in royal houses resulted, more often than not, in civil war. Many peoples tried to avoid it or head it off. In some of the lake kingdoms a likely candidate might scheme to eliminate his brothers before they could contest his selection. (His mother very often managed the process better than he with a judicious use of poison.) In Ankole, however, civil war was neither averted nor avoided. It was a ritual, foreordained and inescapable.

After the royal funeral, the contending princes of Ankole were invited to the former king's compound, where they witnessed a prologue to the pageant of death that lay ahead. A battle was fought between common herdsmen, spear against spear, until blood was shed. The winner was crowned king—a mock king he was to be—for the land could not be left leaderless while civil war went on.

Grimly, then, the royal claimants took their departure and sped away, each to his own stronghold, where his mother and her brothers and cousins waited to help him with weapons and with men. Each royal brother stalked the others in a mighty man hunt. Traps were set and ambushes laid. Assassins with their poisons and their silent knives were sent secretly into enemy camps. Sorcerers whispered magic litanies, summoning death from the skies. Often the brothers met in pitched battles, army against army, struggling for possession of the royal drum. And all the while, the great lords held the borders secure against the enemies of Ankole, lest there be war without during this dreadful time as well as war within. The weaker brothers fled the country. The stronger ones fell one by one. At last only the strongest, the fittest, the cleverest, the best served if not the best, survived.

Quickly he sought the royal drum, and finding it, beat on its skin a triumphant tattoo. Never in his life would he touch it again. One final obstacle barred him from the beaded veil, crown and sign of Ankole royalty. One final drama remained to be played. The mock king—the foolish one, the toothless baby, as his name implied—had to die, and by the new king's hand. Did he resist the young champion, already bloodied in a hundred brother-battles? Did he accept his fate and stand mutely, waiting for the spear? No one knew, and no one cared very much. For with the mock king's death there returned to Ankole once again a time of order and honor and calm. Once again the nation was whole and complete with new ministers, new royal women, new war commanders. Then came the noble Hima to renew their clientage and swear fealty. The king was dead. All his sons save one were dead.

Long live the king!

5. Kings of Central Africa
Mother's Brother and Sister's Son

Old Ghana we know through Moslem hearsay and Moslem writings. For news of early kingdoms below the jungle we can thank the Portuguese. Late in the 1400s they caught exploring fever and set out to coast around Africa. Past the Niger delta they sailed, down the jungly coast until at last they reached the mouth of a wide river and dropped anchor.

To their surprise they found themselves in the midst of a thriving kingdom—the Kingdom of Kongo. Actually, it was more a small empire than a large kingdom, encompassing as it did a number of minor states, themselves headed by kings. (From the title of one of these small kings, *Ngola*, comes the name of present-day Angola.) The year of the Portuguese arrival was 1482. Even then Kongo may have been nearly three hundred years in existence.

Inland the voyagers found Manikongo, the emperor, waiting in his capital. Later he would change its name to São Salvador in honor of his visitors. To the capital came provincial governors, district chiefs, and the headmen of villages. They came to hear the king give judgments at law, and they came bearing gifts, taxes, trade tolls, and items such as cowry shells, which belonged to the king alone. (As in Dahomey, cowries were used for currency.) In the capital lived the royal courtiers, the queen mother, and several royal nephews. From among the latter the queen mother and the council would later, after the emperor's death, choose his successor. It would then be the new emperor's responsibility to see his uncle properly mummified by thorough smoking, wrapped in many cloths, and buried with all pomp. Then might the sacred fire—extinguished at the death of kings—be relighted to burn undying throughout the new reign.

A fairly close relationship soon developed between Kongo and Portugal and lasted a long while. Royal princes were sent abroad to travel in Europe. Portugal was granted many trading concessions, especially in the matter of slaves. And then, less than a hundred years after the Portuguese came, Kongo was overthrown, conquered by war bands from the interior. The old aristocracy was wiped out or dispersed. All that was left of old days and ways were the records in dusty ship's logs and the scattered descriptions of Portuguese trade officials. Fragmentary tales, these were, often full of gaps.

Further inland, fortunately, there were other kingdoms much like Kongo in form and ways of life. Many of these lasted well into the twentieth century, long enough for us to learn what old Kongo must have been. All the way across the continent in that great swath of central savannah lying below the jungle these kingdoms could be found. They were, every one, kingdoms with much governmental machinery and a high regard for art. No cattle aristocrats here and no cattle, either, for this was the domain of the tsetse fly, transmitter of sleeping sickness to cattle and to men. Kings of the central savannah were solid farmers who might dabble a bit in trade. And like king, like people.

The farmers of the central savannah—indeed, nearly all peoples in the Congo Basin, in the lake region, and south to the Cape of Good Hope—spoke a language belonging to the Congo-Kordofanian group. It was called Bantu, and the people called themselves Bantu, a word which means, quite simply, "the men." Many people of early times have taken title to that name—as if they were the only human beings on earth and everybody else properly belonged with the lower beasts.

Even today most Bantu peoples claim to have traveled to their present locations from some place else. Always it's from neighboring country just over the hill. The people *there* will say they came from around the lake beyond or from across the river or through the

CAMEROONS HIGHLANDS
(Bantu homeland?)

Central and Southeast Africa

 Swazi

 Lozi

 Bemba

 Zulu—relatives and offshoots

Jungle

Savannah and dry forest

KONGO

L. Tanganyika

L. Nyasa

Zambesi

Limpopo R.

distant grove of trees. And so on and so on in fits and spurts, short hops or long ones.

By means of language studies and one or two other useful scientific guides, we can now trace those little travels all the way back to their ultimate beginning—to the ancient Bantu homeland. This seems to have been somewhere in the Cameroons Highlands, an open, dry parcel of real estate, jam-packed with humanity. If it is so even today, how much more crowded it must have been for those early Bantu—wedged as they were between powerful tribes on one hand and the inaccessible jungle on the other. Not a chance for them to move. Not a chance of breaking free.

And then sometime near the beginning of the Christian Era, new plants came to them—yams and taros and bananas—plants which could be grown in jungle soil as their own sorghum and millet could not. All the way from Southeast Asia these plants had come, carried in great outrigger canoes to the coast of East Africa. From there they had been passed from one farmer to another across the wide Sudan until they reached the Cameroons Highlanders, stuck in their own small preserve.

At about this time, too, the knowledge of iron came to the Bantu—iron for tools sharp enough, strong enough, to hew down the giant trees that hemmed them in. Armed with iron and with new farm crops, they moved out into the new land before them. Mile by mile, generation by generation, slowly they moved through the jungle, cutting out new plantations as the old fields ceased to bear.

After five hundred years of this slow progress, some of the Bantu groups had reached the jungle's end. At its eastern edge they emerged into the lake region where, in time, they met infiltrating Tutsi moving down from the Nile. Along the south they found a land untenanted except for bands of Bushmen here and there. Everywhere they relearned or were retaught their long-forgotten knowledge of grain.

The Bantu language is only a twig on a branch on a limb on one large bole of the Congo-Kordofanian family tree. And Professor Joseph Greenberg was able to trace the Bantu homeland by locating the other language twigs which, along with Bantu, belong on a common branch. When he found a whole cluster of them around the Cameroons Highlands—the border line for spoken Bantu—he knew he had hit the right spot.

Congo-Kordofanian languages in general and Bantu in particular are marked by a fondness for labeling. This is accomplished with prefixes which tell, before you ever get to the noun proper, something about what you'll be dealing with—whether people, objects, or abstractions, and often in what number, gender, color, size, and shape. For example, *Ankole* (the name of our lake kingdom of Chapter 4) by itself conveys a sense of special identity. Preceded by *ba-* (*Banyankole*), it means the people of Ankole; by *bu-* (*Bunyankole*), the country of Ankole; by *mu-* or *mw-* (*Munyankole*), one man of Ankole. The prefix *ru-* is especially interesting because it conveys the idea of height. Understandably in this land where height is a mark of distinction, many praise names begin with *ru-*. There is Ruhanga, the god of Ankole, and Ruhinda, the Chwezi who founded the ruling clan. In addition to height and honor, *ru-* also signifies language, as in *Runyankole*—spoken, of course, by Banyankole. The "tall language," one might almost say, of tall men.

It must be remembered that this "tall language" was also spoken by short men and spoken by them first. For it was the farming Iru who, in Ankole, were proper Bantu. The herding Hima, presumably, came from further north and originally spoke a Nilo-Saharan language which they exchanged for Bantu at some time in the dim past.

The people of the lake region, and of the jungle too, organized their families along patriarchal lines. Children took their fathers' names and considered themselves primarily members of their fathers' clans. The people of the savannah—though just as Bantu in speech and background as those of lake and forest—took a very different view of family life. Among them a man inherited titles and property, not from his father, but from his mother's brother, and he spent his life, not with Father, but with Uncle instead. It was all very reminiscent of Kongo's royal inheritance. Savannah people—small tribesmen and great kings alike—believed that a man's whole biological make-up came to him through his mother. We have an old saying: "Blood is thicker than water"—by which we mean relatives are closer than friends. The savannah folk thought so, too, but according to them all the blood ties were on the maternal side of the family, and the father's ties were the watery ones. Naturally, then, it was thought that a man must be biologically closer to his sister's son than to his own and that his nephew must be his proper heir.

Suppose you were a child living under such a family arrangement. You would look to your uncle, your mother's eldest brother, as head of the family. You would take his name (the same, of course, as your mother's) and try to bear it honorably. (You would hear from Uncle if you didn't!) He would make all the decisions as to what school you should attend and administer punishment if your grades weren't up to snuff.

If the society happened to be very strict (not at all like our present permissive one) and you were a girl, your uncle would choose your husband and provide your most expensive wedding gift (or receive it from the groom if that custom prevailed). Were you a boy, your uncle would help you decide on your future or decide it for you. Doubtless he'd insist that you come into business with him so that he could keep an eye on your progress. You'd take good care to toe the line lest he turn the firm over to some other nephew. Naturally, he would have a say in your choice of wife. (In our world, of course, she could not be the boss's daughter—your cousin—but in the central African savannah she most certainly would be. And what is more, you'd both wind up living with Uncle in his home instead of your own.)

Where would Father be in this arrangement? He would be your pal. He'd love you and joke with you and try to smooth things over when Uncle got huffy. He'd assist at all religious ceremonies that involved you and your uncle—at your *bar mitzvah*, for example, or your confirmation.

You, in turn, would help him—not because you had to, but because you genuinely wanted to. Father's whole family, in fact—his sisters and brothers—would be the really loving relatives in your young life, the ones you most enjoyed visiting. Perhaps this was so for the very reason that no inheritance was involved, that affection was not compelled, that neither of you was in any way duty-bound. How very easy, then, just to do what came naturally.

Of course your father would *want* to do for and give to you. He'd try to keep you in his home as long as he could, and if he happened to be socially prominent and wealthy, he might manage to keep you permanently. But all the while there would be his own nephew obligations to attend to and the family inheritance to pass on. Much as he loved you, he would have to give some thought to his heir. Perhaps one day you might hear your father bitterly echo the words of a Bemba high chief, councilor to a king in the central African savannah:

> "Why may my nephew not see my sacred relics? Because he will succeed me. He is the same as me. It would be a slight to the spirits while I am still alive. Besides, why should I show things to him who will one day get everything of mine? I am not going to teach him. I shall teach only my sons. My nephew can learn from other people when I am dead. How do you suppose I learnt myself?"

The Bemba of Central Africa lived (and live still) in hilly land between lakes Nyasa and Tanganyika, in what is now Zambia. They may have come there originally as a conquering army sent out by a neighboring king. They may have been pioneers seeking new lands and open spaces. We don't know. Their legends say the colonizing party consisted of three people only—two brothers and their sister, in whose hair was cached seeds of every plant grown in the mother country. A pretty, agricultural beginning, to be sure, for a people who were neither peaceful nor terribly interested in agriculture— who were, instead, the most feared, the most ruthless warriors in their part of Africa.

The Bemba were not empire builders. They had no interest whatever in incorporating other tribes into their kingdom. They kept themselves to themselves. "*Fwe Babemba,*" they still say proudly— We, the Bemba—all other people around and about being generally referred to as slaves. For that was exactly what the Bemba hoped to make of their neighbors, and that was what the incessant raiding and battling was all about. At first used as laborers on Bemba farms, captives were later sold as slaves to the Arabs, who paid for them in guns—guns which made the Bemba even more dreaded.

It is only fair to say that Bemba land is poor land, the soil thin and unproductive. Even today villages have to pull up stakes and move every few years. Perhaps because of that, perhaps because of the long dependence on slave labor, the Bemba are indifferent farmers, unskilled, more interested in the beer their grain might yield than in saving some for hard times ahead. They were so, at any rate, in the 1930s, when the British anthropologist Audry I. Richards went to stay with them and learn their way of life.

They were then poor, and during certain seasons of the year, regularly hungry. Conversation centered on food—its quantity, its acquisition, its preparation. A man ordinarily greeted his friend, not with something like our "How are you?" but with the query, "Have you eaten well?" To which the standard reply was, "Provided you have eaten well yourself." In the old days the king staved off outright famine by passing around his tribute grain. But when trade with the Arabs ceased, when taxes and tribute went to officials other than the native kings, then the pinch was all the more keenly felt. All day long people sat quietly in their houses, smoking and drinking water, trying vainly to dull the edge of hunger.

There has never been much market activity in Bembaland. Trade with Arab merchants was always in the hands of the king and his chieftains to the utter exclusion of ordinary folk. The Bemba were not distinguished as artists or craftsmen. Even in the old days metal work was imported from more industrious neighbors. Never was a powerful kingdom built on a narrower base.

And yet, though interests were few, they ran very deep. War, and next to war, hunting were passions among the Bemba. After them came a preoccupation with the ins and outs of politics. Not that the general run of Bemba folk had much to say about it. The base of Bemba government was no wider than the range of Bemba interests.

With the exception of certain hereditary priests, the royal clan—the Crocodile Clan, they were called—ran everything. They were the provincial governors, the district leaders. Even women could occupy these posts, provided they were Crocodiles. Commoners seldom had a finger in the pie. Very different it all was from the Ankole system, which, for all its violence, at least introduced a whole new set of leaders at the beginning of each new reign. In Ankole the king's advisers were invariably his mother's people, who might previously have been commoners, outsiders—no one cared. When change occurred in Bembaland, it was not a fresh, new leader who came to power, but only a distant relative in the same old Crocodile Clan.

The way this clan was organized for rule—the way its members achieved job promotion and the way an heir was chosen—surely was one of the most complicated in Africa. All Bemba offices were ranked and graded. The kingship and high-ranking chieftaincies went to the sons of Royal Mother number one. The next most important posts went to the sons of Royal Mother number two, sister to number one. Third in line were the grandsons of Royal Mother number one. As death created vacancies in the hierarchy, the whole of Crocodile officialdom enjoyed promotion, but in strict order of succession.

In theory, that succession was supposed to travel neatly from brothers to cousins to nephews. In fact, it simply did not work. A first-rate genealogist with stacks of charts and family trees at his disposal could not have kept things straight. And what happened was that periodically the whole intricate system blew up in civil war.

At the root of the problem were the queens. There were two—usually eldest sisters of the king. Each was established in her own village, surrounded by her own officials and courtiers, and exhorted to produce as many sons as possible. The fathers, of course, were of negligible importance. They might be slaves, no matter. Blood would tell—the mother's blood, the blood royal. The sister queens took their duties seriously, turning out squads of nephews for the king. There may have been a good deal of rivalry between the sisters, contention as to which was number one. Certainly there was rivalry among off-

spring on their mother's behalf. And the element of uncertainty as to whose son was really entitled to which post, and when, kept the succession in constant suspense.

Another thing bred frequent revolt. The Crocodiles, as the Bemba said, liked to bite. They dealt roughly with commoners, and the king was harshest of all—maiming, killing, impoverishing his subjects without a qualm. It was despotism, out and out. For as long as it lasted. When the king's behavior became too much for even the Crocodile-hardened Bemba to stand, some lower-echelon prince was encouraged to aim at the throne. War ensued, and if the pretender was successful, the old ruling brotherhood was booted out and a new slate of Crocodiles installed up and down the line. Different players, same play.

More benevolent rulers were the Lozi kings of Barotseland, studied in recent years by the British anthropologist Max Gluckman. Barotseland lies mainly along the Zambesi River where it curves into modern Zambia. Part of the territory is a great flood plain which is for several months of the year covered with river water. People can remain at home during these times, high in their mound villages above the flood—and some hardy souls do—but the influx of refugee animal life usually makes home so uncomfortable that nearly everyone moves to dry land around the plain. The annual migration is still led by the king in his royal barge. In the old days he was gorgeously attired in plumes and lion manes and leopard skins and armed with a

ceremonial fly whisk which he flicked idly, keeping time with the oars. Nowadays for this momentous occasion he wears the uniform of a British admiral of Victoria's reign.

In attendance is the whole royal cabinet. They are followed by another barge full of royal musicians and drummers thumping madly on the sacred drums as they do every night of the king's life to proclaim his continued good health. Then come the people in order of precedence, all in their holiday best.

There is no ceremony on the way back, for everyone is homesick for his gardens (by now fortified with silt), his fishing holes, and most of all, his mound village. All scramble home the moment the waters recede. The king comes along at his own convenience, sailing down one of the canals his ancestors cut long ago.

Lozi ways may once have been similar to those of other savannah Bantu. Perhaps they, too, once inherited goods from their uncles and took the name of their mothers' clans. But nowadays, says Professor Gluckman, the kinfolk who count among the Lozi are those who are close and those who are near. Never mind whether they are Father's or Mother's or even a wife's people. Each child has a choice of eight names—one for each of his great-grandparents—and the village in which he chooses to live, the one which has room for him, is the one in which he will inherit property.

Unlike Bemba children, who tend to view their uncle with alarm, Lozi boys and girls are especially attached to their mother's brother. Perhaps this is because he is not required to be the stern taskmaster he is among the Bemba. He neither bequeathes nor punishes but is, by custom, a playmate of warm heart and open purse. His nieces and nephews call him *me* (mother) or sometimes *malume* (male mother), a habit which (as Dr. Gluckman has said) caused no little confusion among colonial administrators in the area. After all, when a worker wants time off to visit his sick mother, and the "mother" turns out to be a man, what is an employer to think?

Changes from the usual system of family ties may have come about through contact with patriarchal, cattle-keeping people who moved into the land just south and east of the Lozi. They may have happened through necessity—the restricted size of the mound village, the constant need to move back and forth between hill and plain, between gardens, between relatives. The Lozi double life in time found a reflection in family arrangements, with both bloodlines (father's and mother's), both names, and both sets of relatives counting equally. (Except for our habit of taking our father's name, this is the very family system we in the West live by. Perhaps—as among the Lozi—our penchant for moving about has something to do with it.)

Other sorts of balances resulted as well. Loziland itself is divided into upper and lower kingdoms, the subordinate one being headed by the king's sister, who is called "The Earth of the South." Like the king, she wears an aura of divinity and represents in her person the land and its fruitfulness.

One is struck immediately by the resemblance between the Lozi kingdom and Egypt, and in more ways than one. Besides the two kingdoms, there are two palaces and two treasuries. Like Egypt's Pharaohs, the kings of Loziland (and its queen mothers and sisters too) have long been concerned with royal burial and royal tombs. These are not, like the Egyptians', of stone. They are simply the mound islands in which royalty is laid to rest. Planted thickly with trees brought from afar, these royal mounds stand out tall and black against the horizon. Each is staffed (or used to be in the old days) with priests who, in the Egyptian manner, conduct perpetual devotions to the dead king's soul. For, living or dead, Lozi kings have always been thought to keep the land in their care.

Like the Pharaoh, the Lozi king is believed to have the love of truth in his heart and the care of his people uppermost in his mind. It is said that he never snubs his subjects and that whatever is given him, he generously gives away. "The king is also a beggar" is a favorite adage. More than most African kings he was (and is) loved as well as honored. For almost as far back as the Lozi can trace their royal house, they remember specific acts of kindness, care, and thoughtful planning. They remember how one king provided for the families of men killed in war, how another saw to it that taxes were collected

fairly, how still another personally rescued this man and that from debt. Unlike the rulers of many African states, Lozi kings adamantly refused to deal with slave traders. "I do not sell my people like cattle," said one, contemptuously dismissing an eager flesh merchant.

Perhaps the king was also honored because his government—more than most—took care to be representative. (And that in the old days, when its power counted for something.) The office of prime minister has never been hereditary and by custom must be occupied by a commoner. The chiefs and subchiefs of districts are commoners, too. When the grand councils of both kingdoms met as they used to at stated intervals, these commoner chiefs sat on one large mat, the representatives of the aristocracy on another, and the king's personal stewards on a third. It must have been, all in all, rather like the British houses of Parliament met in joint session to hear an address from the throne.

The government also took care to be just and fair. Loziland was not a clear-cut tribal unity as was Bembaland. It included many different peoples—some refugees from times of trouble in the south during the 1820s and 1830s, some allied by treaty, some conquered.

The true Lozi—rather like our Mayflower descendants—were not allowed to exhibit pride of origin, and the word "foreigner" was considered insulting in the extreme. If, in a case at law, a plaintiff were to fling this word at the defendant, he might find himself sternly reprimanded by the judge. As one said:

> "All the different tribes—they are all people under our great king. . . . There is no such thing as a foreigner. We are one thing, with two eyes and two ears, and our children marry them. They feel hunger like us and ask us for land which we give to them."

Lozi judges and councilors had to live their roles. Reasonableness and impartiality were not to be put on like robes for public performances and doffed in private. Officials could never lose their tempers, could never engage in slanging matches or strike an adversary. They had to be grave and courteous at all times, soft-spoken, kind, and above all, fair. This was a tradition as powerful as law. And it applied in some degree to all the men of Barotseland—from the smallest village headman up to the king himself. No wonder the Lozi still say proudly, "Other people have magic. We need none. We have the medicines of government."

6. South African Kings
Cadres, Clans, and Cattle

Below Barotseland was cow country. How it came to be so is something of a wonder, for between the cattle people of East Africa and those of the south was the tsetse fly. And yet wave after wave of Bantu peoples, having acquired cattle from Nilotic tribes around the lakes, somehow crossed no-cow's-land driving their herds before them. Once they were in safe territory, range wars broke out; cattle raids were launched as late arrivers pushed earlier ones aside. All newcomers attacked the hunting Bushmen, the only inhabitants with really valid claim to the land. But who cared about that?

Nobody is sure just when the first cattlemen appeared in the south. It may have been as early as the tenth century. Certainly they were still expanding toward the Cape when Boer colonists from Holland moved in and began an expansion of their own.

The farming Lozi acquired from their neighbors some interest in cattle but declined to make them a way of life. Everywhere else the story was purely East African in style. As in the east, cattle were wealth and honor and religion, a constant preoccupation that left little time for any other interests. As in the east, dairy food dominated the diet. Beer might be served to outsiders, guests graciously invited to dine. But milk was sacred to the family, the food of real togetherness. Since cows were wealth, beef appeared on the menu only for feasts and ceremonies. Carving was very nearly a ceremony in itself. If you think portioning a Thanksgiving turkey is a headache, imagine the woes of the roast-carver in Southeast Africa. Diners had to be served, not according to their preferences, but according to protocol. Every rank and role in the family had its corresponding section of the cow's anatomy. And the carver had better know who got what!

As in the east, homes were built around the corral—or as the incoming Dutch called it, the kraal. Its main gate was angled to catch the first rays of the rising sun. Next to the gate lived boys and young single men, their hut a kind of barracks and they the sentries for the kraal. The kraal master would be buried under the gate so that the beloved herd could pass daily over his grave. Around the central cattle pen were grouped the huts and fenced yards of the women— the master's wives, his brothers' wives, and possibly his sons' wives, too. He himself lived at the kraal's western end, in a great hut that was also a family shrine. Here he invoked the ancestral spirits and offered to them libations of meat and milk.

As in the east, it was a man's world. Women stuck to their farming and kept strictly away from the herds. They did not milk cows or even enter the cattle pen lest their very presence bring contamination to the herd. And it was here, in the pen, that the canny kraalmaster sank his storage pits, knowing well that there the grain would be safe from profligate wives.

Among these southern herders, a man and his sons and their sons after them were of one blood and one name. It was through them that the precious cattle were passed on. A woman was a stranger in her husband's home, snubbed by co-wives, forever at the beck and call of her mother-in-law. Not until her sons grew up could she feel really welcome.

Beyond the immediate family—that is, of course, Father's family— there was the clan, the more distant relatives in the male line all sharing the same name, honoring the same founding fathers, and recognizing the same chief. The stick-together "clannishness" of big families is not a strictly African phenomenon. It is to be found the world over. Think of Scotland and its clans. They might not have the importance they once had. Still, everyone named Campbell looks

up to the laird of Argyll Castle, *The* Campbell. Even some Camp-
bells in America might admit to pride of clan. In South Africa groups
of clans soon came to be organized into tribes, and these into the
several great warrior-kingdoms for which the tip of the continent
became famous.

Cutting across kin ties were loyalties of quite another sort—
loyalties which bound all the boys of a certain age together in much
the same way that boy scouts in our world, whatever their family
or state or country, have something in common and share a basic
understanding. This system of grouping boys (and sometimes girls)
in age grades was a custom which had traveled down from cattle
country to the east of the lakes. It was a system which one South
African military genius was able to put to stunning use.

Chaka, King of the Zulu, had learned well the lessons taught by
white men moving into his country. He had seen both British and
Boer soldiers in action. And when he came to power, around 1820,
he organized his nation's age grades into regiments and disciplined
them ruthlessly. Armed with cut-down spears rather like the Roman
short-sword, they were sent out to conquer. And conquer they did.
Surprise as much as superior tactics and weapons operated in their
favor. Traditional warfare involved raids and quick retreats and was
mostly a matter of showy personal combat. Chaka's Zulus waged
total war, war of conquest, war of annihilation. Able-bodied survivors
were spared to become themselves soldiers for Chaka. Captive girls
became Zulu wives and bore future warriors for the invincible regiments.

Chaka's armies turned on their Bantu brethren, doubling back
along the road their ancestors had traveled long ago. Whether this
doubling back was a result of the whites' moving into the area, of the
pressures of population, or simply of one man's restless ambition, we
do not know. But what started in a time of general unrest as a land-
grabbing operation resulted in a gigantic recoil. Whole peoples fled
before the advance of Chaka's regiments. Some became refugees,
some ravaged and despoiled weaker people in their path. Many of
Chaka's own army units, defeated and fearing punishment, went

A.W.O.L. en masse. One group marched all the way to Lake Victoria, turned back, and eventually settled for good around Lake Nyasa. Others moved coastward into what is now Mozambique or into the granite hills of Southern Rhodesia. All of them aped Chaka's aims and Chaka's methods.

And all the time Chaka himself went right on building his empire and driving his people to despair with his cruelty. At his mother's funeral, for example, hundreds of Zulus were sacrificed to accompany her soul. Hundreds more died in a massacre of those Chaka suspected of grieving insufficiently.

Even in ordinary times it was dangerous just being in the royal kraal. Coughing or sneezing while the king ate his solitary meals was forbidden on pain of death. One walked warily or not at all. The king's harem had to be avoided and so did the places where the king's bath water was deposited. For it was powerful medicine. So was the hair from the divine head, the very dirt from the divine person. Perilous tokens for ordinary eyes to see! If one *had* to approach Chaka, one did so in a wriggling crawl, prone on the ground. In a gracious mood, the king might cast a joint of beef one's way. It had then to be worried up off the ground, dog-fashion, lest one defile the king's meat with common, human fingers.

Chaka's tyranny lasted only ten years and ended in assassination, which was arranged by his brother Dingane. That same Dingane succeeded him, and being no better than his predecessor, was himself killed by a man of the Swazi nation. And so it went—brother after brother, and son after son. From battle to battle—with fellow Bantu, with Boer, with the British, until, in a last bloody rebellion in 1906, the fierce Zulu were humbled for good and all, their kingdom broken into the administrative units of colonial rule, their customs weakened, and their king exiled.

Cousins to the Zulu are the Swazi. They come from the same stock, have much the same background and way of life, speak the same dialect, and were also organized into a powerful kingdom. While the Zulu were crushed in battle, however, the Swazi suffered only a "paper defeat" at the hands of the Boers and the British.

Though they ceded away territory and rights, somehow they never lost their identity as a nation. They are still the Swazi of Swaziland, still with their own national songs and dress, still with national pride, still with the king and queen mother who symbolize it all.

Swazi historians can trace beginnings back through twenty-five kings but agree absolutely only on the last eight, starting with Ngwane II, who, in the 1700s, led his people inland from what is now the coast of Mozambique to settle in the land they have held ever since. It is a pleasant land, about the size of Hawaii.

Ngwane's grandson, Sobhuza I, found himself toe to toe with the terrible Chaka. He was brave but not foolhardy. Deciding to put his faith in diplomacy, he sent two of his daughters to grace Chaka's harem. One day, in a towering rage, Chaka killed them. Still Sobhuza held his peace. Zulu regiments came anyway, and Sobhuza led his army to the hills, refusing to face the enemy until the odds improved. This kind of caution, painful and humiliating though it was, paid off handsomely in a strong and consolidated government to be handed on to successors.

The Swazi found themselves truly a nation of parts. There were the people they had annexed, the people who had voluntarily made submission, and after the 1830s—the times of trouble and upheaval in the southland—there were people who fled "to the king's armpit" for protection. All these various groups, while retaining their own languages, customs, and chiefs, nonetheless enjoyed the same rights as the original Swazi. They could speak at the national councils, were entitled to wear the Swazi national dress and markings, and were enrolled with the Swazi in the national age grades. The kings after Sobhuza I tended to copy the Zulu regimental system but were never badly infected with Zulu militarism. Perhaps this is why their kingship survived.

A Swazi king never ruled alone—and he does not to this day. The monarchy is dual. One half is the king—"The Lion," "The Sun," "The Milky Way," "The Bull," "Obstacle to His Enemies." The other half is his mother—"The Lady Elephant," "The Earth," "Mother of the Country." The British anthropologist Dr. Hilda

Kuper, who has spent a good part of her life studying the Swazi (her last visit was in 1961), describes the relationship. The king, she says, is considered hardness personified. The queen is all softness. He is thunder; she is water. She is the powerful rain maker for her people, but he owns the land on which the rain falls. He wears a mantle of oxtails. She wears feathers of the flamingo, the Swazi rain bird. He represents past kings, but she keeps the objects sacred to the royal clan and provides beer for offerings. His is the nation's supreme court; hers is second highest, and in the old days, a man condemned by the king might take refuge with her. The king commands the age regiments, but the leading general and whatever bar-

racks soldiers there are stay at the queen mother's village, which is the capital of the country.

The king and queen mother never share a royal residence. That would be dangerous in the extreme, say the Swazi. Too much royal togetherness breeds quarreling, and royal quarreling "breaks the nation." Better to keep royalty apart. Tradition insists that the king precede the queen mother in death. Actual fact seems to be otherwise. The present king, Sobhuza II, has ruled for very many years, and his mother has long since passed on. A maternal aunt filled the role until her own death. At that point the Swazi chose one of the king's senior wives to function as his "mother" and the nation's queen. People die; the roles remain.

The royal village was (and is) very like a family kraal enormously enlarged and multiplied. Some of the king's wives stayed there and some in other parts of the domain, by their homes and presence upholding the royal image everywhere. To the queen's court flocked the important chiefs, the royal councilors. Often they built "town huts" in a second ring around the royal kraal and established a wife or two there. Both councilors and messengers rushed regularly back and forth between the king's residence and that of the queen, keeping the line of communications and decision ever open.

The royal kraal was the public square of the nation as well as an ordinary cattle pen housing a larger than ordinary herd, the herd whose meat feasted the nation on great holidays. Every year in January the Swazi met (and they meet still) in the royal kraal to help the king bring in the New Year. A good deal more than a greeting was involved. The ceremony that took place—called the *Incwala*—was the most solemn and sacred of the national rites. It was at once a pledge of allegiance, an affirmation of faith, and the glue that bound the people together. In it the king was purified and revitalized for another year, "doctored" with sea water from the Indian Ocean, and protected against all harm. For his health was (and is) the strength of the Swazi nation and its future. During the *Incwala* the king took a bite from the first ripened fruits of the year and blessed the harvest and the planting ahead. He watched as the sacred history of the

Swazi was sung and mimed. And he steadfastly endured as—instead of praise and adoration—his people offered scorn and threats and, in dance, attacked him. They sang:

> "You hate him,
>   Mother, the enemies are the people.
>   You hate him,
>   Mother—the people are wizards.
>   Admit the treason of Mabedla.
>   You hate him,
>   You have wronged,
>   Bend, great neck,
>   Those and those they hate him,
>   They hate the king."

Over and over, the refrain:

> "O King, alas for your fate.
>   O King, they reject thee.
>   O King, they hate thee!"

Here is captured in solemn ceremony an old, old truth: a leader *may* be loved, but he is surely hated. At least, he is hated *part* of the time. He is hated when he has to impose taxes or draft soldiers or punish infractions of the rules. In canny recognition of this fact, African kings have always taken care to associate their unpopular decrees with councils and officials. In a really well-run government, officials automatically took full responsibility for such acts so as not to "spoil the king's name." This was a time-honored Lozi custom. In other kingdoms the people usually blamed a king's brutal whims on his councilors anyway. It was all someone else's fault, wasn't it? One could hardly, after all, hate the king—especially when he was divinity or the next best thing.

The Swazi, however, took pride in blaming the king personally. Since it happened only once a year and in a ritual form at that, the king's feelings were not hurt a bit. If anything, the *Incwala* seemed to make everybody love one another more than ever. Ties between king and people were only the more firmly bound, bound through the expression of feelings that ought, by right, to tear them asunder.

This is not to say that the Swazi king was without advisers who shared the responsibility for his decrees. Indeed, the Swazi still maintain firmly that the king "is king by his people" and "a king is ruled by his councilors." Such are the traditional checks and balances which prevent the despot. Among the Swazi, certain commoner clans claimed the right to provide candidates for all official positions, from prime minister to commander-in-chief to priests. There were judges and men who kept track of the population and men who collected fines and taxes and death duties. There were the regimental cadres who tended the king's and queen's gardens and danced and amused the royal court. And there were, in the old days, young squires in training. All chiefs of clans, leaders, and officials—and any Swazi who was interested—met regularly in the national council. A smaller circle of royal advisers helped to plan things on a day to day basis. A sort of aristocratic steering committee, it was, composed of the great princes and relatives of the king.

The king had good cause to be wary of these relatives. Since he was often an only child, he had no full brothers and sisters to lean on. There were only his half brothers, forever scheming to take his throne away from him. Even his father's half brothers were severe critics. In defense the king gathered about him his blood brothers— men who had mingled their blood with his and so were bound to him forever. So much a part of his life were they that if any one of them died before his master, the king was never told and no mourning was allowed. Royal blood was also exchanged with the king's first two wives, the "takers away of darkness." They were not in any sense "great wives"; they enjoyed no special privilege. But since they shared the royal essence, they were thought able to act as scapegoats, drawing evil away from the king to themselves.

After these two, innumerable wives were taken in an exercise of mass diplomacy. Only by wholesale marriage could the king convince the many Swazi clans of his impartial favor. And he tried very hard to be impartial. Nobody knows how many wives Sobhuza II, the present king, has. Nobody would venture to count his offspring.

A Swazi king ordinarily waited to marry his "great wife" until he was getting on in years and beginning to worry about the succession. He had to choose with special care because the mother of the heir apparent had to be of very high rank. Several noble Swazi clans, offshoots of the royal family, were eligible for the honor of providing a queen mother. "The Bearers of Kings," these clans were called. Sometimes the king asked for the hand of a foreign princess, thereby cementing a new alliance. Even so, the council reserved the right to confirm the king's choice of great wife. And final confirmation did not take place until after the king's death. Always a certain jealousy and uncertainty prevailed in the harem.

The king was old, and his great wife young. And so very often crown princes have come to the throne as small boys without full brothers or sisters. During the years of his growing up, a boy king and his mother were rigorously trained for the future while grandmother (substitute or real) and a paternal half-uncle ran the country. Not until the boy became a man could the full *Incwala* be performed, though a shortened version was used during the years of his minority.

This is how Sobhuza II grew up, a man well trained in the traditions of Swazi life and lore. His education was thoroughly Western, too, and so in time was his grasp of politics. He now heads the major political party of his country and thinks of himself as a constitutional monarch leading a people both black and white. The year 1968 marks the independence from Great Britain of his domain, an old nation in a new role. Can its ancient institutions continue as before? Will the legislative council function in the same way now that it is a modern parliament? Is the *Incwala* on the way to becoming simply a "national dance," meaningless and a little funny, with its sea-water "medicines" brought by automobile instead of runner, with its dancing warriors wearing American undershirts and knee socks under their leopard skins? Or will the distinctive old ways go on, modified perhaps, but filled with meaning?

To his people the king is still the Lion, the Bull, the Sun itself. Clad in his mantle of oxtails, he still dances barefoot in the queen mother's kraal. He dances to renew the Swazi and their land. He dances to hold them together during the difficult times that lie ahead. He dances to join past to future and old to new. And perhaps, in the end, he will succeed.

7. The Kings of Zimbabwe

Riddles and Ruins

Like a child's set of building blocks all in heaps, the low hills and granite outcroppings of Rhodesia stud a flat horizon. It is as if the careless hand of nature had strewn her toys about. And yet, at the top of one such natural heap, other hands were once at work—human hands, patiently binding the great boulders into curving stone walls. Art and nature combined to make of this hill a fortress. Even now the intention is plain, for all the shambles it has become. No wonder the present guardians of the ruin call it "The Acropolis."

A quarter of a mile away and down in a shallow valley is "The Temple"—an oval maze of high stone walls and towers and broken enclosures. Surrounding it is a jumble of smaller structures—one on top of another, all utterly ruined. The inescapable picture is: town clinging to temple (palace?) and the whole dependent on the fortress above for defense or perhaps refuge. This is Zimbabwe—a word translated by some as "houses of stone," by others as "great house." It is not the only one of its kind in Rhodesia. There are perhaps three hundred ruins crowning hills and nestled in valleys around and about, all of stone, all rounded and with walls of the same general design, though none so grand or imposing.

The Temple *is* a wonder to behold. At greatest length, it covers 292 feet; at greatest width, 220 feet. Its walls in some places are thirty feet high and fourteen feet thick. And its immense conical tower (a solid mass of masonry, most specialists now think) is thirty-two feet high. Nobody knows how much was knocked off the top by treasure seekers trying vainly to find a way inside. These measurements, of course, are puny when stacked up against those of monumental buildings in other places, other times. The wonder of Zimbabwe is that it exists at all. Africa is a land of mud houses and mud walls, pounded and sometimes mixed with cattle dung, of pole and mud houses, of pole and thatch houses, and pole and hide and pole and leaf. Stone building is almost unheard of in Africa south of the Sahara. And nowhere else there will you find a ruin of Zimbabwe's magnitude.

It may be argued that nowhere else is the building material so easy to come by. The granite and schist outcroppings break off naturally and cleanly into manageable blocks. But Zimbabwe stonemasons used these materials in ways which are, as far as anybody knows, utterly unique. The walls are dry. No mortar—not even mud —was used to hold the stones together. And nowhere is there to be found a straight line or a right angle. All is curve. Walls (some thin for their height and roughly done, others sturdy and smooth) circle and lean inward, being wider at the bottom than at the top. Even steps seem to flow. Very often the stones are arranged in patterns of chevrons or checks. If you have ever tried (as I have) to build a dry-stone wall, you will instantly appreciate the skill of Zimbabwe's master masons. Simply to balance stone on stone is accomplishment enough. But to add decorative effects as well—there's artistry for you!

One thing more. There is—or at least there was once—gold in these granite hills. Zimbabwe was apparently a center of extensive mining activity which continued for over a thousand years. The news traveled fast and traveled early. There were traders from Arabia already settled on the coast near Zimbabwe in 700 A.D. In time the venturesome Portuguese heard rumors of treasure, and since they already had bases in West Africa, dispatched ships to investigate the situation.

Arriving in the early 1500s, the Portuguese discovered that there was more to the country than just a few Arab settlements on the coast. It was, in fact, a large tribal confederacy, covering what is now Rhodesia and some of Mozambique, and it was headed by a rich and powerful king called the Monomatapa. In the good old-fashioned African manner, the ruler's title gave the country its name. Also in that manner were Monomatapa's style and role.

The Portuguese quickly noted the fact that he was considered a sacred ruler, that he had to be physically perfect and in absolute health, and that he had a mother or mother-substitute of great importance. After their experiences with the Manikongo and sundry other kings of the West African coast, such a state of things must have seemed old hat to the Portuguese. But they may have been a bit surprised at Monomatapa's marriage customs. Of course he maintained a large harem, and of his wives nine bore special titles and filled official roles. But the greatest of these "great wives" was the king's own full sister. Some said that only her child might be the king's heir. Others said any one of the nine was eligible to be king bearer. In any case, these nine, together with the queen mother, were responsible for choosing the new king when the need arose.

All in all, the Portuguese learned a good deal about Monomatapa. They knew the titles of his great wives and the titles of his chief councilors and the names and chiefs of the four subsidiary kingdoms. But they knew very little about Zimbabwe, which was, presumably, Monomatapa's home and capital city. It was, after all, a 170-hour walk from the coast. Being more interested in gold than in architecture, the Portuguese relied on hearsay and wrote that down. And maybe there were other cogent reasons for this. In 1561 a Jesuit priest made the journey and even managed to convert the king, only to be speared the next day for his pains. One Antonio Fernandes did actually see a building project in construction, and he pointedly mentioned the use of stone without cement.

In time Portuguese traders collected in some numbers and grew highhanded in their treatment of Monomatapa's subjects. The king called on Changamira, chieftain of the Rozwi (sometimes spelled *Rotse*), to expel the intruders. It is not clear whether the Rozwi were an offshoot of the royal clan or whether they were a once alien tribe

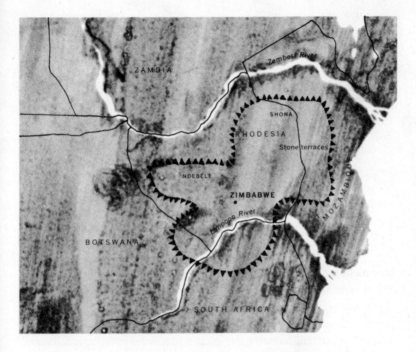

Zimbabwe and Monomatapa
▲▲▲ Boundary of the Empire

that had been incorporated into the empire in much the way that outsiders were accepted by the Swazi. Whatever their antecedents, they were able warriors, the Rozwi. Between 1690 and 1710, the Portuguese posts and even Sofala on the coast were attacked and destroyed. Unable to restrain himself after such a successful campaign, Changamira took Monomatapa's domain for himself.

His title as chief was Mambo, which now became the imperial title as well. All the trappings of the sacred kingship were reinstated —even to ritual death at the end of an appointed period. The Mambo's predecessors had never followed this custom, and some had even objected to taking poison at the onslaught of illness or debility. One nonconformist, upon losing a tooth, flatly told the royal court not to expect a speedy exit on his part. A lost tooth might ruin his smile; it would not ruin the country. The Rozwi chiefs, however, seem to have been conservative in this regard, preferring to return to the old ways. (Or so tradition tells us.)

For a century and more the Mambo Empire flourished. Then, after 1833, three successive hordes—in headlong flight from Chaka's terrible Zulu regiments—overran the empire. The last proud Mambo

refused to flee, and sitting calmly on his throne, awaited the invaders. They skinned him alive—literally. So much for an empire and a way of life.

Two of the marauding bands raged on toward the east and north. The third group settled down to stay. These were the Ndebele, and they knew a good thing when they saw it. The vanquished people— all the various tribes that had collected under the Monomatapa and Mambo empires—were now called Shona—the slaves. And after a while, forgetting their separate tribal pasts, they called themselves Shona, too. Now only these things do they recall: that even their small chieftains had to be physically perfect or die, and that in death the chiefly bodies were always smoke-dried and wrapped tightly in hides. Some Shona still celebrate rites to Mwari, a high god whose priest, they say, used to prophesy on Zimbabwe's tower. And they still build in stone. Crudely sometimes, with mud covering all, but in stone.

From the late 1800s on, Zimbabwe came within the British orbit, and Westerners had free access to the ruin. It quickly became the choicest mystery of a romantic, mystery-loving public. Nobody troubled to ask the Shona living around and about the ruin what they had had to do with it. It was just assumed that no connection was possible. So thoroughly did image affect theory that even Carl Mauch, the German geologist who, in 1871, witnessed one of the last religious ceremonies performed in the "temple," failed to make the connection. He thought the Queen of Sheba had been responsible for the building. Later travelers insisted it had once been the administrative headquarters for King Solomon's mines. The supposed claims of the Phoenicians, the Arabs, the Indians, the Indonesians, and the people of ancient Mesopotamia were also warmly pressed.

In the 1920s, specialists at last questioned the people but neglected the building and its archaeology. The idea that developed from these investigations was that the distinctive features of the Zimbabwe monarchy, especially the king's ritual death, were part of a whole culture pattern that had traveled westward (as we know the yam traveled westward) from Asia. Perhaps early, in a Babylonian package, it was thought; perhaps later, and in Indian wrappings.

In the 1940s, when archaeology and the old traditions were at last brought together—notably by H. A. Wieschhoff, a German archaeologist—there was a quick about-face. Outside influences took a back seat to native invention. Zimbabwe, it was decided, had been conceived in Africa, for Africans, and built with African labor. And what is more, it was not early, but late—medieval, in fact, with the best walls not going up probably until the eighteenth century. And as for the king-must-die theme, Wieschhoff said what a few others had been whispering all along. Maybe this idea had traveled out of Africa eastward instead of the other way around.

Only recently have the archaeologists (armed with carbon-14 tests) and other interested scientific parties reached yet another conclusion. As you might expect, it is somewhere between the extremes of early and late.

According to the new timetable the first immigrants arrived in the area close to the beginning of the Christian Era. Their pottery, which has been unearthed on Zimbabwe hill, is of the kind usually found in association with iron. And sure enough, these people were iron-using and iron-smelting. Their slag has been found if not their iron tools, which would have rusted quickly in Rhodesia's acid soil. They were farming people. The African cereals, millet and sorghum, have been found in their sites, and also the little fertility figurines associated with early farmers everywhere. They apparently met and traded with the Bushmen native to the area. Beads of ostrich egg shell appear in the farmers' camps, and their pottery in Bushman sites among Old-Stone-Age tools. They also married Bushwomen. What skeletons have been found show the double characteristics, Bush and Negroid. What is more, Bush rock drawings changed when the newcomers arrived. Animal and hunting scenes were discontinued, and scenes of elaborate ceremony appeared. The new people are shown, too. Tall people with fat-tailed sheep. Did they have cattle as well? No one is sure.

The new people were the first to have a go at the gold which almost eroded out of the soil while you looked at it. It was only after this surface metal was exhausted that mine shafts were sunk. Sometimes the miners themselves are found on archaeological digs—little skeletons of women. Were they there because of small size or because of their sex? About 700 A.D. the Arabs came, and gold trading commenced.

A few centuries later, still newer people came into the region, probably from somewhere to the northeast. Roger Summers, Curator of the National Museum of Southern Rhodesia, believes these were Bantu-speaking ancestors of most of the present Shona tribes. They brought along a different sort of pottery. (Thank goodness for pottery. Even in fragments, it is sometimes the only thing that lasts!) They brought bronze, too, and much more iron. It was they who built the first walls on Zimbabwe hill, probably in 1100 or thereabouts. Whether their building was the result of influences from the north, whether it was Arab-inspired (though, since it was all dry-wall construction, that is unlikely) we may never know. Certainly there were and had been trade contacts with the Orient, probably via the Arabs, for beautiful ceramic ware from faraway China has been discovered in the various ruins.

Such monumental building required leadership—chiefs with the authority or ritual prestige to command plenty of workers and enough extra grain to feed them. Here, perhaps, is where Monomatapa began. Were his people also the bringers of cattle? Was it for the prospect of good beef that his stone masons labored?

It was perhaps in the fourteenth or fifteenth century that still another people appeared. Not from the east this time but from a westerly direction. They were also builders in dry stone. But their work was more skilled and sophisticated than that of Zimbabwe's first builders. They set their walls in trench slots, they took care to trim their stone blocks and lay them in even rows, and they added decorations—those patterns of checks and chevrons mentioned earlier. Similar dry-wall construction (though only in modest tombs and smaller structures) has turned up in what is now Angola, and along with it, pottery adorned with chevrons and checks. Dr. Summers suggests that these new builders were Bantu-speaking Rozwi and that they were responsible for Zimbabwe's outer wall with its decorated top and for the solid conical tower inside. It must be said that Rozwi tradition even today (and they are now a scattered people) insists they were the original builders. The Lemba—a strange tribe of master smiths—also claim the honor. Perhaps it was a joint venture.

Could the Rozwi be connected with our friends, the Lozi of Barotseland—or, at least, a chip off that block? For the Lozi, you will remember, settled on the upper reaches of the Zambesi. It would have been an easy enough matter to travel downstream and into the empire of Monomatapa. Desmond Clark points out the similarity between the ground plans of Zimbabwe's Temple and of a Lozi king's grass thatched "palace." Both are rounded in form, both have subsidiary walls to shut off various enclosures. Which brings us to another point.

Shona people and their neighbors today use stone walls in combination with mud and thatch. Sometimes the stone is even covered in daub, a fact which prevented many observers from taking note of the widespread use of stone. Sometimes the walls end in huts or lean on huts or surround huts. And this seems to have been the plan at Zimbabwe and at the many other ruins in Rhodesia.

One riddle at least seems to have been solved. Zimbabwe is pure African and so were its kings. But if the builders were first ancestors of certain Bantu Shona, then Bantu Rozwi, who exactly were the first miners?—those hardy souls whose persistent scratching and panning began the accumulation of wealth that was the foundation on which Great Zimbabwe would later grow. Their pottery, dated to 300 A.D., suggests a sort usually associated with Bantu peoples as well as with iron. Yet Bantu could not have been out of the forest and into Rhodesia by that early time. The pottery and the knowledge of iron, too, came with somebody. Who?

Professor Murdock offers as candidates the Chwezi. Remember the Chwezi—those legendary founders of the lake kingdoms, fair of face, long of nose, and masters of every useful art? They were, he believes, neither myth nor ideal, but real people operating in real time—the time when the Christian Era began, the time when the first mining operations were begun. He would go further still. He would give the Chwezi credit not only for the early mines but for the first building at Zimbabwe as well—an event he thinks may be dated at 700 A.D., instead of the more conservative 1100.

The real trouble with his theory is this: no skeletons of Caucasoid people have yet been found in or near Zimbabwe—or indeed anywhere in Rhodesia, the most common type for the early periods being Bushman or Bushman-Negroid mixtures.

There is one more possibility. The knowledge of iron smelting need not necessarily have traveled westward from Meroe and then back east again with Bantu immigrants. Perhaps it moved southward, as well, along the Nile. Bits of typical Iron-Age pottery (though without the customary decorations) have been uncovered in the Sudan. There is, furthermore, the matter of the Jur, a tribe of Sudanese smiths, Nilotic people related to the Luo of Kenya. Some scholars think Jur furnaces and smelters may look very much like the ancient ones at Meroe. How long the Jur have practiced their craft is not known, but their credentials as ironsmiths may well be as good as those of any other group.

As for those Bushman drawings depicting tall, tall people newly arrived in Rhodesia, perhaps anyone would look tall to a Bushman—except perhaps a Pygmy.

Back to the beginning and who came first. Were they Bantu briskly out of the forest and down into Rhodesia betimes? Were they Nilotes driving their cattle before them and acquainted unexpectedly early with the forge? Or were they the fair, the bright, the ever-elusive Chwezi? Not until some lucky find reveals iron, pottery, stone work, and bones of cattle and men all together in the same spot will we know the answer. It is still a riddle. The last riddle of Zimbabwe and perhaps, after all, the best.

8. A King Who Is a Queen

The Royal "She" of the Lovedu

One of these days you are bound to run into *She*, the African adventure yarn by H. Rider Haggard. First published in the 1880s, it still appears regularly in paperback editions. It is still being read. It is also being seen. The first film *She*, made some thirty years ago, now plays the TV late shows, while a glossy new version circulates through the theaters.

In a nutshell, *She* tells the story of an ancient, never-dying Arabian queen, a great magician and absolute ruler of a simple, savage, dark African people. Her domain lies in the midst of a fabulous ruin— a once-great city built by supermen long since extinct. Theirs was the secret of eternal life, and it is her secret, too. Altogether, *She* is almost as fanciful as any other tale about mysterious Africa. But not quite.

Hidden away in a remote South African valley, there was in Haggard's time (and there is still) a real queen. Haggard heard of her often during his service in the British colonial administration. She was beautiful, some said, gracious and fair of face. She was frightful, others claimed, like some ravening beast in human form. According to some rumors, she was a real rain maker. According to others, she brought only drought and plagues of locusts besides. Whatever the conflicting stories, all agreed on one thing: she lived forever. It was this rumor that gave Haggard his heroine.

Another one gave him the setting, the mysterious ruined city where the fictional queen had her domain. The real queen's people, it was said, came long ago from the Monomatapa empire. With a small shift of the imagination one could envision the immortal queen ruling in Great Zimbabwe itself—or something very like it. And that is just the sort of place that Haggard put *She*.

The legends of the real queen's people *do* hark back to such beginnings. That much is true. The word "Zimbabwe" is used among the queen's people, though they do not connect it with the Rhodesian ruins, of which they know nothing. It is true that the queen is considered a mighty magician. It is true, too, that she and her people seem to be unusually fair of face. Perhaps an influx of Arab blood could account for that.

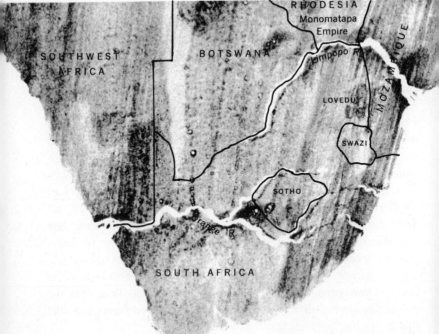

The Lovedu and Neighbors

It is *not* true, of course, that the queen lives forever, though it may appear so to the outside world. Each queen, when she judges herself no longer fit to rule, takes poison and dies. In Haggard's day as in this, her going is kept secret until her successor is chosen and, like herself, named Mujaji. This, plus the fact that Lovedu queens are extraordinarily long-lived, often made it hard for an outsider to know when one reign ended and another began. No wonder Haggard heard only of her immortality.

Take away these grains of truth, however, and the resemblance between fact and fancy—between the real Mujaji and the fabled She—ends. And well it might, for the fact is story enough. Queen of the Lovedu nation (now a native preserve in the Republic of South Africa), Mujaji has always ruled in a man's world and no nonsense about it. The Zulu, the Swazi, all the people around and about were in the old days cattle-keeping warriors, touchy of male honor and male pride. And so were the Lovedu in all respects but one: they were ruled by a woman and had been for several generations of royalty. The last Lovedu king was far in the past and nobody missed him a bit. The Lovedu queen did not rule by default, not through want of a male heir—as have the queens on many a Western throne. No—Lovedu men were ruled by a woman because they would have it that way and no other. (So we are told by J. D. and E. J. Krige, anthropologists of the Republic who lived among the Lovedu during the 1930s.)

Otherwise, the country was run by men. The judges and advocates in court were men. Men arranged the great national ceremonies and were the queen's chief advisers. Women stayed home to mind children and gardens. They did not (especially if they were young women) push themselves forward or presume to set policy. Even Mujaji declined to be bossy. She was, in fact, all but inaccessible, certainly so to foreign male visitors. (The Lovedu have been known to palm off fake Mujajis on European generals and colonial administrators who demanded audience.) She would not even represent her people in regional councils if the other delegates were men.

Because of Mujaji and her exalted position, however, women were given more than ordinary respect in Loveduland. Take, for example, the matter of marriage. Among most South African peoples, a wife does not attain full dignity until she has borne a child, preferably a man-child. Being childless is a matter of aching concern, even shame. A childless wife might be set aside by her husband, overlooked and badly treated. She might be sent back to her people with the demand that her marriage cattle be returned to her husband. He might require instead that her family supply a replacement, a substitute wife, or at the very least, an additional wife to bear children the barren woman is unable to have. Not so among the Lovedu. Marriage cattle were never refunded because of a wife's barrenness, nor was a substitute automatically provided. Etiquette required the husband to bear up cheerfully under his disappointment and be pleasant to his childless wife. The queen emphatically approved this sort of behavior and was warm in her praise of it.

Though women were not free to stand up and have their say during court cases, they did manage to make their wishes known. All during the hearing they muttered comments in loud asides. The judge never banged his gavel and sent them packing as a judge would do in our courts. He loftily pretended to ignore the interruptions, but very often he settled the case as his informal jury of old women had advised him to do with their whisperings. The queen herself refrained from court appearances. She reviewed important cases and had the final say, but she always said it in private.

Loveduland was divided among many clans and tribal groups, some of whom had arrived as immigrants, others as refugees during the

time of troubles in the 1820s. Each was entitled to its own leaders, its own laws, its own district head. Sometimes the queen appointed women to these posts, but most often men. The district heads and great chiefs and councilors made up a formal advisory board. More important to the queen, because its members were in residence at the capital, was the inner council—a sort of kitchen cabinet composed of her close relatives. These acted as "mothers" of the various districts, representing the queen, taking note of matters requiring her personal attention. They intervened in quarrels and strife, bringing the queen's womanly influence to bear. For she seldom commanded and never punished. That was not her role. Before all else, she was the nation's mother.

Royal or not, being a mother was of no mean advantage in Loveduland. Not young mothers, to be sure, but matrons with grown children had all the best of it in terms of honor and support. They had much to say about the disposition of cattle that came to the family when a daughter married. They made all the marriage arrangements for their sons, ruled their daughters-in-law, and took full charge of grandbabies from the moment they were born. This happened because boys and their mothers were always very close. A Lovedu mother was ever ready to defend her son tooth and nail against all other boys and their mothers. And when a boy grew up, his mother was still his best ally. He built near her hut in the family compound. If she left it, he went with her—he and his wives and their children. His wives and his brothers' wives, each in turn, were required to cook in their mother-in-law's kitchen until a new bride brought reprieve. The youngest brother's final wife never got her own hearth.

Mother-in-law and daughter-in-law hit it off a good deal more comfortably if they were also aunt and niece, and that is one reason, perhaps, why the preferred marriage was between a boy and his mother's brother's daughter—his "cross cousin." (Mother's sister's daughter was a "parallel cousin" and off limits as a marriage partner.) The most desirable marriage of all was between the children of a "cattle-linked" brother and sister (her wedding cattle had been used to get him a wife). In all cases, marriage ties bound not only the young people concerned but their families as well in a tight circle of mutual responsibility and assistance—and cattle. It was a circle on which all of Lovedu life was founded.

The Lovedu valued all those qualities which help people to live together pleasantly: willingness to compromise, moderation, geniality, having neither more nor less than anybody else. People did not say "Give *me*" in their prayers. They said "Give me *also*"—me and everybody else. The too-smart child was thought to be bewitched, and the man who chaired a meeting with brisk authority verging on bossiness was considered quite mad. The Lovedu frowned on boastfulness or great displays of emotion. Courage was not rated high in the catalogue of virtues and boys were not ashamed to cry and yell at their initiations when the knife cut and blood flowed. There were no policemen or warriors in Loveduland and had not been since women had begun to rule. "The Queen does not fight," the Lovedu said. And yet, unprotected as they were even in the old days, they always felt quite safe from their predatory neighbors. And they *were* safe, because the queen had armies of another sort, spiritual armies which not even the fiercest generals would care to challenge. She commanded the clouds. And her people—Christian and pagan alike—believe she commands them to this day.

Of all South Africa's rain makers, the greatest was Mujaji. To her court came her neighbors, the great chiefs and kings, humbly begging for rain. They did not threaten or boast but entered her borders quietly, gingerly, bringing many gifts. The powerful Zwide, antagonist of Chaka, was blasted for simply looking his old truculent self while in the general vicinity of Loveduland (or so the story goes, losing nothing in the telling). Chaka himself was wont to apply to Mujaji for rain. He brought her, it is said, a herd of black goats to "loosen her arms."

Whatever her fame abroad, Mujaji's first care was to bring rain for her own people. They depended on her completely and did not concern themselves about private garden magic or employ "doctors" to see to the fertility of their land. But sometimes the rain was slow in coming, and the people worried, asking themselves what they had

done to offend the queen and cause her to withhold the clouds. They gathered before her hut and danced slowly and sadly, begging her to relent. Often they blamed the queen's ancestors for "holding her arms." And they sorrowed with her and offered condolences. For they knew that she had only their good at heart and worked unceasingly for them every day. She worked with her own strength of purpose, her trust, and the secret medicines her forefathers had used long ago when Loveduland was ruled by men.

Mujaji's exalted position was not totally without precedent. Even in cow country—male-dominated and male-centered though it was—women were able once in a great while to play roles other than those of wife, mother, and mother-in-law. In the absence of a male heir, a girl could become a family head and raise up heirs to her dead father just as if she were a son. A really unusual woman could even become a great "doctor." But to do this, she needed courage as well as brains. For this role required her to undergo a dangerous psychic crisis during which spirits were said to contend for her body, a crisis which she might not survive. In both these roles—heiress and doctor—a woman had to play a man's game, dress as a man, and carry a spear.

It was by way of such precedents that the first Mujaji came to rule the Lovedu. Queen and woman she might be in person; her role was that of a king. Like any African king, she maintained a large "harem." Great foreign chiefs or district heads in her own land gladly gave her their daughters to wife. In return she sometimes gave cattle, and sometimes rain. The young women took up residence at her court, honored and retained so long as they were childless. But should they become involved with the young pages and councilors-about-court, and should children result (all of whom would subsequently address the queen as "Father"), the young women would be conferred upon other chiefs and district leaders. And so the queen was bound in a web of duty and loyalty with nearly all her important leaders. To some she was "son-in-law," having taken their daughters to wife. To others she was "father-in-law," having given them women from her "harem." All owed her the honor due to kin as well as to queen. And this, along with her rain-making power, gave her strength.

Some say the nation was founded as a result of a royal family quarrel from which the youngest brother fled in a towering rage. Others say it was begun by a woman. Daughter of the Rozwi chieftain, she was, long before that tribe moved to topple Monomatapa from his throne. The Rozwi princess had made a secret and very unwise marriage to her own brother, so the story goes. And fearing her father's wrath, she prudently stole his rain medicines and fled away with all her people. They settled among the hills of Loveduland, and the princess's son was made their king.

In the disorderly old way, Lovedu princes fought over the succession, killing one another and fragmenting the people. A king did not dare name an heir betimes for fear of his being murdered by jealous brothers. One thought to protect his favorite son by banishment, sending him to live in the bush, humiliating him in public, and only in secret teaching him about the sacred rain medicines and charms. (Following tradition, the Mujaji heiresses suffer exile also and must be taught their duties while abroad.) When this rejected prince at last came into power, he pondered the problem. If a woman were king, he thought, how different things would be. Royal wives would not intrigue for their children but would turn their energies to holding the nation together. And the predatory warrior-kings poised on the borders of Loveduland would be confounded by the presence of a royal woman. Her very weakness would be her strength. It would secure the tribe forever.

Realizing that the heiress must be doubly of the blood royal, he took his own daughter to wife. She was the first Mujaji, founder of a line of rain queens who might marry secretly but must be husbandless in public; whose daughters were eligible for the throne but whose sons must be excluded; whose first illness must be the last; and who were to terminate their reigns with poison, self-administered.

Even with these powerful sanctions there was, on a queen's death, contention for the throne. All who thought they had a legitimate claim gathered at the dead queen's hut, there to enact the ceremony

of the queen's door. Like the legendary stone from which King Arthur drew a sword to prove his right to the throne, the door would not yield save to the chosen one, the one fitted by birth and training for the role. The great councilors saw to that, for they followed the dead queen's wishes to the letter. Behind the door was a commoner of the kingdom, instructed to open only for the royal princess, successor to Mujaji. In the old days he was later killed to keep close the secret.

When the door opened, the princess rushed in, snatched up the shield and spear, insignia of her office, and rushed out the back way, pursued by a train of disappointed and angry hopefuls. The councilors, greatest of whom was her uncle or her own brother, hid her away until she could at last be confirmed in her office. Then were the fires rekindled in Loveduland. Then came rains to cool the earth, made hot and angry by the death of the queen.

When the Kriges visited Mujaji in the 1940s, she was sixty years old—hale, hearty, and every inch a queen, though she was hard put to resist the encroachments of foreign governments and modern times. Even then her daughter was in exile, learning the secret wisdom that must be hers as the next queen, rain maker above all rain makers in southern Africa.

Not so long ago, a severe drought hit the Republic. Farmers were in despair at the loss of crops and life. The prime minister (so the newspapers said) exhorted the people to hold thoughts for rain, to visit their churches and pray for it.

I wonder if anyone consulted Mujaji.

Enough hobnobbing with royalty—with kings and dowager queens and their courts. We have scarcely had a moment for the ordinary folk of these realms, the folk for whom and because of whom royalty comes into being in the first place. The air is less rarefied on this level, true. The concerns of commoners turn less on affairs of state and more on affairs of business, relatives, and daily bread, on getting and keeping the good things of life. In this respect, the ordinary citizen of any African kingdom then and now—for all his involvement in trade and markets, for all his wider knowledge—is more akin to Africa's other people, her humble people, who must work very hard just to keep body and soul together.

Alongside the old states, there are still societies without government and politics, without the formal machinery of courts and rules and taxes (those commonplaces of any state, anywhere), sometimes even without the leadership of chiefs and headmen. Innocent of the notion of tribe—let alone that of state—the worlds of such people are small, bounded by family ties and traditions, by their own bands or clans or villages. Many of them live today much as their ancestors must have lived in Neolithic times, soon after the discovery of farming and the pastoral way of life. Still others—there are not many but they are of great significance to anthropologists—live as did their Old-Stone-Age ancestors, some of them unable to this day to make fire or to fashion metal tools, though they borrow both gladly from their more sophisticated neighbors.

In looking at these simpler, earlier ways of life, perhaps we can catch a glimpse of the roots from which the great African kingdoms grew and flowered.

Part III

IN THE BOSOM
OF THE FAMILY

MBUTI
PYGMIES
Epulu R.
Ituri R. AMBA
L. Victoria

L. Kariba
Okavango
Swamp
Zambesi R.
TONGA
KOROCA
KALAHARI
BUSHMEN
HOTTENTOT
Orange R.

Bushman and Pygmy Areas

9. Of Elephants and Men

The Last of the Great Hunters

Time and inventions may long since have taken most Africans out of the hunting life, but they have not yet taken the hunter out of Africans. Though farmers and herders rarely hunt seriously for food, hunting is still considered the manly thing to do. It is fraught with peril both physical and magical. The hunter never knows what sorts of scary beings he might encounter in the forest or on the plain— ghosts, vampires, visions of death, or visions of glory, not to mention those only too real living killers, the charging buffalo and the skulking leopard. No wonder special hunting gods were once honored in several of the great African kingdoms. The Dahomeans maintained hunting shrines as short a time ago as the 1930s. And among all Africans, personal hunting magic was (and is) intense and complex. Even the hunter's wife at home must observe a strict code of behavior lest by some small infraction of the rules she bring injury to her husband.

With all this reverence for activities long out of date, it is not surprising that Africa's farmers harbor a grudging admiration for Africa's truly big-time hunters, the last to follow a way of life as old as man himself. The admiration is grudging because these mightiest of hunters are also the littlest of men. Kalahari Bushmen are only an inch or two over five feet in height, and Ituri Pygmies are usually four or five inches shorter than that. Though short in stature, both are long on courage. Bushmen pit themselves against those tanks of the animal world, rhinoceroses and hippopotamuses. Their commonest prey, however, are the fleet antelopes of all sizes, which they shoot with poisoned arrows, track for miles, and run to earth. They have even been known to contest a kill with lions, calmly driving the big cats away. The Pygmy's status quarry is the elephant. And this one beast he hunts alone.

Admiration—grudging or not—has not kept tall farmers and herders from pushing the little hunters aside whenever they stood in the way of "progress." And so it is that Africa's hunting people can be found in numbers in only two places: the belt of rain forest across the continental middle and the Kalahari Desert of the southwest.

It was not always so. Not, at least, for the Bushmen. The testimony of the bones declares that ancestral Bushmen inhabited the whole eastern half of Africa during late Paleolithic times. Even today in Tanzania there are remnant bands of hunters speaking a language explosive with the clicks and pops that are uniquely Bushman.

And then there are the pictures. Rock faces and rock caverns from Tanzania to the Cape of Good Hope have been found decorated with the forms of animals and men. Some were painted and some incised; some (particularly those in the south) were gorgeously rendered in many colors, with a sharp eye for nature and a feeling for design. Most often these art works are attributed to the ancestors of modern Bushmen, for many have been found in conjunction with "Bushmanoid" bones. And while living artists have never been surprised at work, the dead body of a Bushman was discovered in the 1860s, still with paint horns tied around the waist.

Heroes of these drawings are often depicted in red or yellow-gold (today's Bushmen prove to be of that same golden shade when their protective "skins" of grease and dust are rubbed away). And they bear certain distinctive physical marks, among them a sway-backed posture and a natural bustle, both characteristic of living Bushmen. Scientists had long thought this exaggerated seat might represent an adaptation to desert life—something like the camel's hump, a storehouse of nourishment for lean days. However, as Dr. Phillip Tobias,

Bushman rock painting in South Africa

the South African anatomist, points out, the bustle and many of the other Bushman features—flat head, baby face, small stature—were acquired long before the retreat into the desert. Other explanations will have to be considered: beauty standards, perhaps, a preference for women who looked one way instead of another; perhaps mineral content in foods (or the lack of it), glandular changes, or just plain mutation.

Besides describing the Bushmen and their old way of life, the paintings in South Africa unfold much of the Bushman's tragedy— by now almost forgotten even by the Bushman himself. Impossible to place in time, unclear about the tribal identities of invading groups, the pictures are nevertheless very specific as to color and as to action. They tell how tall black men came down from the north driving cattle, and how, when the Bushman hunted those cattle (thinking them another, though quieter sort of game), he was punished for his mistake. The paintings tell, too, how tall white men came up from the south, also driving cattle, and riding horses, how they appropriated the Bushman's wells, raided his honey trees, closed in his traps, and killed the Bushman for defending his own. And it was not only black men and white who contested with the Bushman for his hunting grounds. The cattle-keeping Hottentots—larger cousins of the Bushmen—moved in from the west. Little by little the small golden men were pushed back into the hostile desert lands of the Kalahari, certain no one would follow them there.

But they did not go without a struggle, a struggle in which many of their groups were totally destroyed. They fought with their bows and poisoned arrows, shooting with such unerring accuracy that their big enemies—who thought them really no better than wild beasts—paid them the grudging compliment of showing fear. A Zulu chieftain said of the Bushmen, whom he called Abatwa—which means simply, little people:

> "The Abatwa are very much smaller people than all small people; they go under the grass and sleep in anthills; they go in the mist; they live in the up country in the rocks. . . . Their village is where they kill game; they consume the whole of it, and go away. . . . They are dreaded by men . . . for men do not see the man with whom they are going to fight. . . . Their strength is like that of the fleas, which have the mastery of the night. . . . They see them for their part, but they are not seen."

In their long struggle and in the exile that followed, the Bushmen did not lose their language. Far from it. Bushman clicks found their way into many of the Bantu languages of the area, introduced, perhaps, by captive Bushman women. The Kalahari Bushman way of life, moreover, was not without its bleak attractions. Two Negro groups, the Bergdama and Karoca of Southwest Africa, long ago emulated their Bushman neighbors in both speech and culture. And so have many others driven into dry lands during the time of troubles in the south.

The Bushmen of the Kalahari, however, paint no more and have quite forgotten how. Their lives are completely occupied in wresting an uncertain living from their inhospitable land. And even if they had time to spare, there are no suitable "canvases" for their art. But perhaps some remember. Author Laurens van der Post, who led an expedition into the Kalahari in 1957, found two very old people who did remember. He showed them a rendering of a Bushman cave painting depicting some kind of religious ceremony. The couple at first wept bitterly and then performed the ancient dance which the picture was meant to represent.

The Bushman undoubtedly has lost more of his former skills and graces than just the art of painting. And he is a loser still. The desert, which has at least protected his freedom, cannot protect him forever. It may keep out aggressive men on foot but not men in trucks. Farmers and herdsmen—black and white—prize Bushman servants. Docile now and cowed, the little hunters need not even be paid beyond the food to keep themselves alive and a scrap or two of clothing. And so it is that Bushmen in the desert run and hide when they hear from afar the rumbling of truck engines. They know farmers come to entice them away, buy their children from them, or even cart them off by force. Both Colonel van der Post and Elizabeth Marshall Thomas, who, with her family, made many journeys into the Kalahari, attest to this.

It is sad but true that though game is protected in the Kalahari, its human inhabitants are not. The Bushman hunter so injudicious (or innocent) as to kill a giraffe or a gemsbok (a rare kind of antelope) will be tracked down and thrown into jail by policemen from the desert's edge. There the Bushman languishes and dies—confused in the big people's world and lost irrevocably from his own.

His is a world with narrow bounds. Its heart is the Kalahari in what used to be Bechuanaland Protectorate (now independent Botswana). There are also numerous Bushmen in the velds of Southwest Africa, fewer in the southwest corner of Zambia, and fewest of all in the Republic of South Africa. A very tiny remnant, the River Bushmen, live in the Okavango Swamp. "Tame" Bushmen work virtually as slaves on farms and ranches. "Wild" Bushmen, however, follow the old hunting-gathering life, and in this they occasionally are joined by their "tame" fellows, who must now and then refresh their souls by going over the hill to the desert.

Perhaps because Bushmen groups speak different dialects of the Khoisan language, there seems to be a strong sense of differentness—almost a tribal identity—from group to group. Customs differ and so do songs and dances. The groups bear distinctive names descriptive of their home grounds or of common ancestors. At those times of the year when the scattered bands of a group are forced back on permanent water holes, this elementary tribal consciousness is reinforced. Then, as Mrs. Thomas tells us, these bands exchange news, celebrate religious observances, and see to it that young people get to know one another and find spouses. These gatherings do not last long, for there is not enough food for all. Each little band must go its own way, back to its own special territory where the hiding place of every melon, every root is known, and the ways of birds and beasts are mapped and remembered.

The bands are small, each including perhaps an older man and his wife, his unmarried sons and daughters, and his married daughters and their husbands and children. Among the Bushmen it is customary for a man to live with his wife's family and hunt for them at least until three children have been born to him. After this a young married couple may live with whatever relatives they choose or even alone with their children, if that suits their fancy.

A Bushman band knows few formal rules and regulations and has no chiefs, though Mrs. Thomas suggests that large bands may sometimes acknowledge a headman who passes leadership on to his son. In any case, leadership is by courtesy only, for Bushmen cannot order one another about. No one would listen, much less obey. Decisions are usually reached in discussions among the grown men of a band.

The test of manhood among Bushmen is the hunter's test. When a boy bags his first big game, he is considered ready to marry, and boys become men very early. The most suitable marriage for a young man, say the Bushmen, is with a little girl, eight years old or so. It is more a formal engagement than a real marriage, which does not occur until the girl reaches womanhood. Still and all, Bushmen say, helping to raise and nourish one's future wife does insure a happy marriage. Ordinarily a man has but one wife, though really superior providers occasionally take more.

A Bushman band moves ceaselessly on its rounds, breaking camp every few days. There is not much to break. The camp is no more than a collection of grass shelters, or *sherms*, under which are indentations in the ground for more comfortable sleeping. And yet the *sherm* is no less a home for all its simplicity. The ground around it is carefully cleared, the few possessions neatly arranged, and at the tiny fire, man's place and woman's place are clearly marked. If there is no time to make a shelter or no grass for it, a woman will lay out a circle of stick pegs and that will be home, its sanctity respected by all. So home-conscious is the Bushman woman, says Mrs. Thomas, that she will not leave her fireside at night to walk three feet to a neighbor's hearth. People might talk and call her a gadabout.

A woman's possessions are mostly on her body—her apron of skin, her leathern *kaross*, a versatile garment which serves as a skirt, a baby carriage, a market basket, and a warm cape. Kalahari nights are icy during some months of the year, and the *kaross* is all too necessary an item. Her arms are wound with skin bracelets made for her by her hunter-husband, and her neck and hair are hung with bead chains made of ostrich egg shells. How important are these eggs to the Bushman's life! They give him not only food and decoration, but light, portable containers, the only item he still paints. When the rains come, or when he finds ground water, the Bushman stores it in his eggshells, stopping up the holes with grass or dung. Some are carried on the march, slung in big bags of fiber string. Others are buried in the ground, there to keep cool and fresh for the dry times ahead.

Besides her clothes, ornaments, and shell jugs, the Bushman woman prizes her little wooden mortar and pestle for pulverizing nuts, grains, and dried meats. And most important of all is her digging stick. Daily she goes forth with her stick to find the juicy roots and melons which, besides supplying nourishment, are an important source of

liquids. She also looks for nuts and berries, and perhaps small game such as tortoises or lizards. At the end of her search, she may return to the *werf*, the little collection of *sherms*, carrying nearly her own weight in firewood and food, and a baby sitting on top of the load.

Man's work, like woman's in this hard life, is never done. His are the fire sticks, which, when twirled between his expert fingers, can give him fire in a few seconds. He tans the leather for the family wardrobe and cuts the clothes. On his side of the *sherm* are the all-important tools of his trade—his bow and arrows and his poison equipment. The poison he makes mostly from the grub of a certain beetle, though he may, from time to time, add plants or even snake venom to the brew. He mixes the poison with a thickening agent so as to produce a kind of glue, and this he smears, not directly on the arrowhead, but on the shaft just beneath it.

So attuned is the Bushman to the beasts he hunts that he feels their presence even without seeing them, knows their moods, and predicts their movements. The hunter goes early from home, before first light, strengthened by observance of certain strict taboos the night before. He hunts alone, and when he finds game, he nicks it with his little arrow and then returns home. The next day, the other men of his band go with him, and together they track the dying animal. Though herds of other animals have trampled the ground, the hunter knows his quarry's spoor and follows where it leads. Bushmen can travel many miles without tiring. Often—especially when the ground is muddy—they simply run their game down, exhausting the animal long before they themselves are spent.

Triumphantly the meat is carried home, where it is divided according to certain strict rules. Nothing is wasted, neither head nor intestines nor the half-digested contents therein. A large animal will yield, not only meat, which can be dried and preserved, but a good quantity of liquid. This is carefully collected in a hole in the ground, a hole lined with the animal's hide.

Only by wringing every drop of water from his environment does the Bushman survive. Rain falls for just three months of the year, and from one rainy season to the next the weather is first freezing cold then searing hot and dry. So dry that lightning strikes veld fires in the powdery grass. So dry that the Bushman must dig himself into the ground to conserve his own body water by preventing its evaporation in sweat. During these months, his ostrich-egg coolers keep him alive, these and his watery melons and his sip wells. Colonel van der Post describes such wells—dry stretches of sand into which the Bushman thrusts a long, hard, hollow stalk. This he sucks until water comes up from somewhere below the sand and drips down the side of his "straw."

Some say that in really bad times, on long marches, the old and infirm are left behind to die. Others say no, old people are never abandoned. All agree, however, that deformed babies are not allowed to live and neither are those who arrive in a time of harsh drought when the mother already has a baby to feed. The older child's rights must come first. It is not lack of love or humanity which dictates such action. It is the price of life itself, life which is geared to the demands of a brutal environment.

In spite of his rugged existence, however, the Bushman is neither depressed nor dour. His manners are at all times gracious, but being a born mimic, he cannot resist interpreting whomever and whatever he sees in a kind of pantomime play. When a joke (his or someone else's) tickles his fancy, he does not smother a giggle but flops on the ground, howling and shrieking with mirth. He is a musician as well as an actor. His favorite instrument is a little stringed "lyre," from which he coaxes music both sweet and sad. Sometimes he sings to himself in melancholy whispers; sometimes he sings game songs which are loud and boisterous. Often he dances—men and women and children all together. Late into the night they dance when the moon is on the wane, anxious to show their love for her, anxious to bring her back again to light the night. Now and then during the dance men become possessed, fall into the fire, and pick up live coals. In such a trance, a man may heal. From person to person he goes, drawing out from each his sickness, his sadness, his pain, and flinging these evils to the spirits of the dead gathered just beyond the firelight, waiting.

When a Bushman dies, he is buried within his *sherm* and the grass pulled down over the grave. With him go his few possessions. One part of his soul, the people say, remains in the grave, rising as a ghost from time to time to frighten living men. Another part goes to the great, remote god in the sky, there to move among the heavenly animals and the hunting fires men see as stars. To light the soul's way on its journey the family builds a huge fire at graveside. Silently they watch the flames and then move on, leaving their dead—the hunter, the old father, the young wife—behind in the desert. The

desert that, for all its harshness, has been kinder to the Bushman than the big men who live in fairer lands beyond.

Unlike Bushmen, whose ancestors seem to have enjoyed a more prosperous, more complex life than the one their descendants know today, Pygmies seem always to have lived simply, without many of the amenities other folk crave. Most Pygmies are now where they seem to have been for time untellable: in the Congo jungle. And it was theirs alone until Bantu farmers came, and cutting round holes in the forest canopy, let the sun shine through. What happened when farmer and hunter met is unrecorded. Judging by legends popular among several Bantu groups, Pygmies often acted as rescuers and friendly guides. These same friendly guides may have occasionally ended their careers in cooking pots. For the jungle farmers— some of them—are said to have been cannibals.

For the most part, however, the villagers probably regarded Pygmies (as they still do) with a mixture of scorn and superstitious awe. The little hunters were, after all, at home in the forest, the dreaded, menacing forest in which the farmers knew themselves to be intruders. So it was that they made offerings to the Pygmies, the owners of the forest, thinking thus to placate the forest itself.

But they never scrupled to use those owners and to dominate them when they could. When more and more people arrived (or when the original villages multiplied), the farmers took to feuding— one tight little island clearing against another. And in these battles Pygmies came in very handy as scouts and spies. Each village had its own Pygmy contingent, which it paid with farm foods and manufactured articles. We know this was so because such warfare was in progress right up to the time when colonial rule put a stop to it.

Nowadays the old uneasy relationship between Pygmy and villager continues as a sort of trade agreement. It is cast in "family" terms, and Pygmies are the poor relations. Each village family "owns" its family of Pygmies, who bring game and honey from the forest and lend menial assistance in house and field. The village hosts supply food, metal items, and European clothing. They also try hard to pass on their culture to the Pygmies, whom they consider to have none at all, being, in fact, little better than hunted animals in this respect. The villagers will point out that Pygmies have no language of their own, that they cannot make fire, that they have no wedding or funeral ceremonies save for those the villagers themselves provide (and also pay for). And they consider the Pygmies fortunate to have such thoughtful, generous "owners." All this superiority does not quite conceal a note of anxiety. For after all these years and centuries, the villagers still do not feel at home in the forest. They know it belongs to the Pygmies, and in many little ceremonial ways they acknowledge the fact.

The Pygmies know it, too. And far from being the downtrodden slaveys they have always seemed to outsiders to be, they have simply used their considerable talent for mimicry to get for themselves the best of both possible worlds—the world of the village and that of the forest. They may indeed have given up their own language. Nobody knows and nobody can tell, for each Pygmy group is fluent in several languages—in fact, in all the languages and dialects that are spoken by villagers in their particular areas. And all these languages alike are rendered nearly unintelligible to others by uniquely Pygmy accents and intonations. They do celebrate weddings and funerals in village style if they happen to be near a village at the time—but only for the incidental feasting, not because such ceremonies have deep meaning for them. They have their own ways of marking such events. They do insist that their boys undergo a period of hazing and initiation alongside village boys. Such a ceremony does not automatically make a boy manly in Pygmy eyes. But it does according to village standards, and in order to maintain his membership in that world, the Pygmy will put up with the discomfort.

All things considered, he usually has the best of the village-Pygmy relationship. A little self-deprecation ("I am only a poor Pygmy, master!"), a lot of dancing and song (not the same songs he sings in the forest), and now and then a gift of game, and he manages to keep his village "owners" feeling secure and confident. In any case, the forest is always at hand. The Pygmy can retreat at any time, certain he will never be followed and punished by a disgruntled villager who has already been frightened half out of his wits by Pygmy tales of forest spooks and demons.

The plain truth is, the Pygmy does not really need the village except now and then for a change and as a diversion. He lives a full and secure life on the bounty of the forest. There may be Pygmoid groups who have partially adapted to newer ways—the pottery-making Twa of the lakes region, for example. And Pygmies who once inhabited forests along the Guinea coast have all but disappeared. But the Mbuti Pygmies of the great Ituri forest are today much as they must always have been. They have been studied most recently

by Dr. Colin Turnbull of the American Museum of Natural History. He lived with them (those of the Epulu region in particular), hunted with them, and traveled with them for many months, recording their music and their ways. He has also surveyed in one book most of the things other scholars have written about them.

The Mbuti Pygmies favor two styles of hunting. There are the archer bands, whose territories lie in the eastern part of the Ituri forest. They hunt with dogs (who never bark), use bows and poison-tipped arrows, sometimes ambush game, move ever silently on the trail. And there are the net hunters around the Epulu River. Each married man owns a net a hundred feet or so long. Once on likely hunting grounds, these hunters spread their nets in a wide semicircle and wait for their women and children, singing and clapping loudly, to drive game into the nets, where it is promptly speared. Whoever owns the net keeps the kill. When animals are caught between two nets, however, or when the nets are loaned by an absent owner, many niceties of division come into play.

Seven nets are considered the absolute minimum number for a successful hunt, and people feel more secure when they can count on twenty. For this reason, net-hunting bands may run to upward of a hundred people. Their numbers and their loud style of hunting make frequent moves necessary, but this effectively keeps them out of the village orbit. The archers tend to hunt in smaller bands and can stay put for longer periods—at the beck and call of their villagers.

For all their skill, however, they bag less game than the net men, who don't mind saying their archery is pretty poor, poison-tipped arrows or no.

All the Mbuti Pygmies—whatever their hunting style—now and again take out after elephant. It is a matter of proving courage as much as anything else, for the Pygmy who hunts this game most often hunts alone. He silently tracks his prey and then runs between the beast's mighty legs, spearing upward as he goes. Covered then by the undergrowth, he freezes, not even daring to breathe while the bleeding, pain-maddened elephant searches for his tormentor. He continues to wait until the elephant bleeds to death or dies of blood poisoning. Then all the band comes to camp beside the carcass, and they eat and eat until every bit of flesh is gone.

For all the excitement of the hunt, meat is not the only item of the Pygmy diet. The forest dispenses bounty in the form of roots, nuts, mushrooms, berries, and greens. All is at hand for the gathering, for there are no seasons in the forest. Only honey—the most prized of all foods—comes but once a year, the joyful time of the year, the Pygmy Christmas, New Year, and Fourth of July all rolled into a few happy weeks.

The forest gives more besides. Bark for cloth, vine for swings and nets, grubs and herbs for poisons and also for their antidotes, saplings for round huts, and leaves for tiles. Most of all, fire, which the Pygmies say is, like the others, a gift of the forest. And though they do not know how to make it blossom and bloom, they can keep it alive, wrapped in fire-resistant leaves, to blaze anew in each camp. Thus every little cooking flame comes, in unbroken lineal descent, from the first fires the Pygmies ever knew. Were they stolen, as the legends suggest? Gathered from a lightning-struck tree? Never having learned to make fire or to forge metal tools, Pygmies are content to borrow these conveniences and let it go at that. Why bother one's head with hard problems? The forest will provide.

The net hunters of the Epulu with whom Dr. Turnbull stayed longest were gathered in a large band of thirty families or so. Most of the men of these families were related, but there were outsiders, too. The band, the economic group, means more to the Mbuti in the long run than blood ties. A man's main loyalties are here, and everyone helps everyone else, related or not. All grownups are "father" and "mother" to all the group's children. All the old folks are communal "grandparents." Each child is "my child." The only time family relationships become a matter for concern is when weddings are in the offing. The Mbuti Pygmies say they "marry far," that is, out of the home band, out of the family, away from attractive cousins.

Engagements are not long and are usually formalized by an exchange of visits between the families concerned. The young groom-to-be then brings a gift of game or maybe a few arrows to his new in-laws, takes his bride home to live in his band and with his parents, and that is that. His only obligation—and it is a stiff one—is to find among his relatives a girl willing to marry a brother or male cousin of his wife. For no group happily gives up an adult member, and the loss must be made good. Sometimes the groom has to do a good deal of searching among his available kin and no little arm-twisting besides to produce the missing link in the exchange. A man normally marries only once, though there is nothing to prevent his taking additional wives if he thinks he can feed them—and if he has lots of unmarried sisters and cousins to exchange.

Sometimes a Pygmy is taken to wife by a villager, who makes good her loss to the family by giving fine presents. She may come home again any time she chooses to resume her former life. But not her children. They belong to the village, and though they, like their father, may come to the forest to visit, they are not invited to stay. The forest is for the Pygmy and protects its own.

There is no such thing as "one's own business" among the Mbuti, and even if there were, nobody would mind it. Every scolding of a child, every lover's quarrel, every marital spat is the signal for everyone else to chime in. And since there is no chief to settle matters, an argument involving the whole band may go on for days until it is resolved to everyone's satisfaction. On matters involving the hunt or moving camp, or some real crisis, all the grown men of the band normally meet around their own campfire, where they listen with greatest attention to the one or two best hunters and the one or two oldest and wisest men. Inasmuch as the women are not shy about pronouncing opinions, however, even these serious matters get a general airing. At least, says Dr. Turnbull, this is true among the net hunters, whose women are valued for their help in the hunt as well as for their other sundry contributions to life and larder.

All the adults of Mbuti bands belong to one of two associations: the women's group (called *elima* by the net hunters) and the men's group (*molimo*). A girl joins the *elima* when her body becomes womanly. This is a joyful occasion, a time for singing and feasting among all her young girl friends. They gather in a special hut where they are taught women's songs and dances. To the hut come—at the girls' invitation—young men of their choice. A boy must, in honor, accept such an invitation, but he may well do so with misgivings. For getting inside the hut is no easy matter. Older girls and grown-up women stand outside with whips and sticks, and he has to fight his way through. It is, for him, a sort of testing of his manhood.

Success in this venture, however, does not qualify him for membership in the *molimo*. Nor does ability in song and dance, though such talents are prized. For the Mbuti, there is only one test—the hunter's test. When a boy proves himself by bringing down his first big game, he is a man and may join his peers nightly at the *kumamolimo*, the men's fire, the "heart of the *molimo*." It is the heart of life as well.

For it is from this tight little group—from the hunters of the camp —that the special songs emerge, the songs that bind the people to their God and bring life and God into harmony.

The forest itself is God to the Mbuti, the constant enveloping presence, the giver of all good things and all bad things as well. For even the bad, say the Mbuti, must have its purpose and meaning. All is well when the forest sees and knows. But sometimes, they say, the forest sleeps and must be awakened to the needs of His children. And so when sickness strikes, when game is scarce, when the end of a wise old person is to be honored, when a hunter in his prime is killed, then the *molimo* meets nightly to sing to the forest. It is not, as Dr. Turnbull explains, in ritual that the god is invoked. It is not even in special words. All the Mbuti say in their songs is, "The forest is good, the forest is good." It is the sound that matters, the beautiful sound, the sound that has the power to heal and to restore. And to heighten the sound, to intensify it and make it lovelier and more haunting, a special trumpet is brought from a secret hiding place.

It is only a long, hollow tube of wood, sometimes even a length of European metal pipe, into which a man can sing and echo the camp-fire songs on deep, deep into the forest. This trumpet is itself called "the *molimo*" and is sometimes personified as a forest animal associated with death and the rainbow. The Mbuti tell stories about it—how men took it away from women in a tug of war, or how men took it away from animals in the same game. The women and children profess to fear it and hide away in their huts on evenings when it is due to appear from out of the forest. Their withdrawal is in reality more a matter of respect than dread.

The villagers know the *molimo*, too. But their *molimo* represents the thundering voice of the ancestors, and it is well and truly feared. Whatever its beginnings, whether among villagers or in the forest, the Mbuti trumpet is not that kind of voice. It is, instead, a voice of joy and celebration. It sings a waking song and a thanking song and a song to make all the world right again—the God's world, the world that shelters His own people, the children of the forest.

10. The Village Universe

To Each His Own

It is easy to be pro-Pygmy. Who could help loving these little people?—so gay and quick and brave; so clever at turning a difficult situation to their own advantage. It is just as easy *not* to like the Pygmy's village "bosses" with their suspicious nature and air of grand superiority.

But is that fair? We have been looking at the forest farmers from one angle only—the Pygmy's angle. Shift position a little, and a different picture emerges. Take the Amba, for instance—one group of Bantu villagers, neighbors to archer Pygmies. Let us look at them through sympathetic eyes, the eyes of American anthropologist Edward H. Winter, who studied the Amba in the early 1950s.

Amba villages used to be scattered all along the eastern edge of the Ituri Forest where it rises in spurs toward the Ruwenzori Mountains. Like all farming villages from Guinea to the Rift, each was an island clearing surrounded by a sea of trees—a sea in which lurked perils uncountable. Each island was a fortress. Each, in the old days before the Europeans came, was continually at war with all other fortress-islands. Each sheltered and held safe a single family. A small family, perhaps—grown sons with wives and children, all obeying grandfather, who ruled the roost. Perhaps a larger family in which brothers or even cousins and their families had managed to remain together after Grandfather's death. In such a larger village no man ruled, for the Amba did not tolerate any authority except a father's. Minor decisions were reached by village elders, who talked and talked until concensus was achieved. They did their best to smooth over family quarrels and settle disputes. But when strife grew really bitter, the family simply broke up, each little segment moving on to found a new village. Families broke up in any case when they grew too large, when family land had been worn out with much planting and would yield no more. For a long time the broken family segments remembered and preserved their ties. Then with the passage of years and generations, the ties grew dim and dimmer still until the descendants were at last enemies.

With all the evidence of breakup before them, the Amba still believed in big families and big villages. For in numbers there was strength—strength to fight, strength to defend—and each Amba male strove manfully to make the numbers multiply. He married as often as possible, hoping thus to accumulate a respectable corps of wives, all producing food and babies in steady supply. Somehow this ideal, like the ideal of the supervillage, remained a dream. Amba men never took female jealousy into account. They were forever at a loss to explain why a woman simply *would not* be content with her own garden, her own house, her pottery making, and a small but equal share of her husband's attention. Why was it, they wondered, that no matter how diligently a man might pursue matrimony, he nearly always managed to have just one wife at a time instead of many all together?

Of course, the traditional system of sister-exchange (familiar among the Pygmies) was not a help. Any divorce, anywhere, set off a chain reaction of divorces until all the girls were back at the original starting point. No wonder prospective husbands often preferred to give bridewealth for a wife. Her father would be much less apt to welcome her home again if he had to return the goats and hoes he had received for her.

Let us not fault the Amba for their ideals. Family, after all, was everything to them, the source of love and protection and sustenance. In their world, people were divided into two distinct categories. They were relatives—or they were enemies. It was as simple as that and nothing in between—neither friends nor neighbors nor acquaintances. A village on one side of a ridge might wage bloody war with another just over the crest, hardly a mile away. The feuding might go on for years without truce or letup until one group of combatants moved away. If, by some odd chance, neighboring and unrelated villages *did* take a fancy to one another, they immediately had to become what we might call "kissing kin." Down to the last rule and regulation, they behaved as if they were really blood relatives. By the same process, neighboring Pygmy "dependents" also became members of the family.

Away from the home village and its immediate environs, a man could always take refuge with his mother's brothers. If worse came to worse, he could stay in their village permanently, though, of course, with a somewhat lower social standing and less security than he had enjoyed at home in his father's village, where he owned property. Uncles were helpful in lots of ways, however. They were duty-bound to avenge any harm to their nephews, and they were helpful in getting wives, too. As the Amba put it, one married where one fought. One did not marry relatives, after all, not even pretend relatives, so what else was left? Uncles often were able to arrange romantic contacts through their own wives.

Even at greater distances, the really venturesome Amba could manage to be at home abroad. The would-be traveler or collector with a taste for exotic foreign ware struck up trading partnerships with men of other tribes. Far from being business propositions, these were looked on as family arrangements in which hospitality and gifts were exchanged, in which all the usual family obligations were undertaken. And the two men *were* family. Brothers, in fact. Had they not, after all, eaten seeds dipped in one another's blood?

If family was the root of good, it was also the root of evil. As with the Pygmy in his forest universe, so with the Amba in his village universe. Only at home did notions of right and wrong, sin and virtue have meaning. Away from home one did what one did; one killed and forgot. And if one happened oneself to be killed in battle, why that was in the nature of things, a fact of life and honor. It was at home that one loved, one shared, one gave. That was only right. But then, what if one's virtue was rewarded with unaccountable accident? What of sickness, of the wasting away of strong flesh and a slow death in one's own bed? Why did it happen? And at home?

The Amba's answer was simple and direct. He blamed his misfortune on the ill-wishing of his relatives—the people who were supposed to love him and who, in sin and error, hated him instead. Not everyone who hated, of course, had the power to do harm, but those who did—and one never knew who they might be—the Amba called witches.

Such an explanation of misfortune was not unique to the Amba. Nearly everywhere in Africa fear of witches and fear of the ancestors were (and still are) dominant philosophical themes.

Now, Africans are reasonable people, practical people, with a deep conviction that the universe is basically run for and by human beings instead of the other way around. And so it follows that little happens without its human cause—a living human or the ghost of one. It is perfectly reasonable to the African that death may occur by way of a lion, a snake, a germ, or some other agent. What he really wants to know, however, is *why*. Why did the lion attack one man and not the other? Why did the snake bite one day and glide away the next? Why did the germ bring death to *this* man and not to that? The possibility of chance is unthinkable. What he wants to know is what *person* sent the lion, the snake, or the germ, and *why*. Was it an offended ancestor? Was it a sorcerer—an ordinary "doctor," perhaps, turned criminal, willing to make his potions and poisons for hire? Or was it a witch?

Far more feared than the sorcerer, the witch is thought to be a person born with a power of evil so intense, so inherent that she (or he) may not even be aware of its existence. Knowing, she may still be unable to keep it within bounds (or may not want to). Uncontrollably, it rises from the witch's belly when triggered by envy or greed and strikes through a glance of the witch's evil eye.

Sorcery and witchcraft alike are unknown to the Pygmies. They laugh behind their hands at the inquests held at every village funeral to unmask a "murderer." In the great states, too, the fear of witch-craft tends to be diluted in the general hum of activity. Everyone has many interests and much to do. And there are, besides, lots of gods, all supervising the business of fate. And not only gods but all kinds of human specialists as well, medical and magical, all seeking to interpret the celestial will and to manipulate it if possible.

But among people like the Amba—stuck in their tight little islands, facing enemies without, and within, the same monotonous companions day after day with not much else to think about—evil becomes an obsession and a galling burden. It is a cloud of fear which never quite goes away. Never.

Over the years and down through the generations, witch stories were told and retold and embroidered until the witchly doings came to be more real almost than the everyday world, and in some ways a lot more interesting. Witches, the Amba said, were clever at concealing their identity. One could never really be sure without a test, but one could guess. Likely suspects were people who looked different from other folks or even wanted different things, things that nobody else wanted. (A good way, surely, of maintaining the status quo.) Cripples and decrepit old folks were always eyed with suspicion. Because of their afflictions, the Amba reasoned, they were just *bound* to be envious of normal people. The witch, they said, did crazy things (indeed suspects might actually have been crazy, playing the part society had framed for the mentally ill). She behaved by day as no ordinary person would dream of behaving: she was hysterical, quarrelsome, overly ambitious, perhaps. At night she was crazier still. For then, they said, while law-abiding folk slept, the witch went about naked, flying over houses, hanging like a great bat upside down in trees. She could turn herself into a leopard or call on real leopards to serve her. When thirsty she took salt instead of water. When hungry she hankered after human flesh—the real thing or the spiritual essence thereof. And to ease her hunger she might slip into a hut and suck up the vital force of a sleeping innocent, leaving him sick and weakened.

Horridly gay and gregarious, Amba witches were thought to be great party givers. To their fêtes they summoned colleagues from other villages, colleagues with whom they had contracted trading alliances for all the world like the blood brotherhoods undertaken by respectable men. The gifts exchanged at these midnight suppers were dead relatives. The plumper the "entree," the warmer the compliments to the lucky hostess.

Haunted by such nightmares, it is no wonder that the Amba dreaded seeing the sun go down. They feared to be indoors and they feared to be out. And yet when a man was sick, his children gladly braved the night, carting him about from house to house, up hill and down dale, lest wandering witches find him. If he died they suspected fellow villagers of causing his death, of wishing it, and they longed for vengeance. Not a word could they utter. Not an accusation could they make. For the village, the core of life, must not be broken.

In this dilemma it was the dead man's maternal kin who acted. Trooping to the funeral fully armed, they conducted the inquest, decided who was guilty of causing the death, and meted out punishment. In the old days, punishment meant the spear or, at the very least, a recourse to the poison ordeal in which innocence was proved by vomiting.

"How savage!" you are saying with a delicious little shudder. But wait. We have a savage past of our own to live down. It was only 250 years or so ago that witches were hanged in New England and burned to death in Europe. And our methods of proving witchcraft had the poison ordeal beat all hollow when it came to cruelty. In Scotland, for example, a suspected witch was bound hand and foot and thrown into the nearest pond, where she could easily prove her innocence by drowning. With us still are many superstitious hangovers from those bad old days. Secretly we put our faith in rabbit's feet and lucky pennies. Not so secretly we support fortunetelling gimmicks by the score. And medical quacks make from us a very good living with their mumbo jumbo and useless machines—and for a very understandable reason. When we are sick and desperate and beyond legitimate medical help, we will try anything and anyone— even as the Amba do.

"If only we could find a way to exterminate our witches," they told Dr. Winter earnestly, "if only the authorities would let us, we would be safe and happy." If the tight little islands could be joined, if life could be made fuller and richer, perhaps then the Amba would be safe and happy. But nobody has been able to manage that. Not the rulers of Toro, the lake kingdom to the east of Ambaland. Not the British when they governed there. It was hard enough just holding the ferocious Amba in check, much less drawing them together.

Now they are under the nominal control of independent Uganda, and already strange stories are floating down from the Ruwenzori Mountains. Newspaper items here and there tell of "tiny, wizened, wrinkled men, their bodies painted white, their teeth filed to points," who have attacked government outposts. Lo and behold, it is the Amba on the move, consolidated at last under their very own ruler, a former schoolmaster whom the Uganda police call "the mad king." At last the villages have discovered the outside world and are attacking that instead of each other. In great leaps they are moving out of a neolithic world and into the modern one. Says *The New York Times* (March 6, 1966), quoting the Uganda police: "They have got everything, just like the central government. They even have clerks who know how to type."

People of a very different sort were the peaceful Tonga, farmers and occasionally cattle keepers who lived until recently along the middle span of the Zambesi. Some were on the plateau above the river, some on the valley floor—the Gwembe Valley, it is called. Always more sinned against than sinning, the Tonga came to be resigned to lightning raids by warlike people around them and by dreaded slavers from the east coast. Somehow they were never absorbed into one or another of the great kingdoms in the neighborhood. In their simplicity and poverty they must not have seemed worth the effort of conquest.

Whatever the Tonga lacked in material wealth or political development they made up for in tenure. The first Tonga settlers may have arrived in the area as early as the eleventh century A.D. This is what archaeological excavations on the plateau seem to indicate. And

Tonga looks, which hint of ancient marriages with Bushmen, also suggest long-time residence. This is what American anthropologist Elizabeth Colson believes. Her studies along with those of geographer Thayer Scudder give us the most recent picture of Tonga ways, yesterday and today.

More protected in their valley refuge than the plateau people above, the Gwembe Tonga seem to have kept faithfully to an ancient way of life. As kin-centered as the Amba, their world has nevertheless had somewhat wider horizons. Perhaps it was because there was no black, dread forest to hem people in, perhaps because life along a river just naturally spreads up and down its banks. Whatever the reason, the Tonga world was not bounded by the one-family village but had stretched to include the neighborhood, a collection of separate families, each including perhaps thirty or forty people who built their homes next to one another in little clumps. The neighborhood might vary from several hundred to over a thousand souls.

How the Amba would have loved to see that many residents all congregated in one spot. Of course he would have been shocked that some were not really related. And he would have deplored their family arrangements. For while an Amba man took his father's name and considered that he belonged in his father's village, a Tonga man took his mother's name and inherited land from her brothers. When a Tonga woman left her husband, she took the children and went back home to her brother. An Amba divorcee had to leave *her* children behind with their father.

The uncles, cousins, and assorted kin who lived together in the local neighborhood might be a Tonga's closest relatives, but they were not his only relatives. He could find distant kin with the same clan name in every other neighborhood in the valley. It was much as if all the Joneses in America were to consider themselves very, very distantly related. (And actually, if one were to trace all the Jones lines far enough into the past, one would likely find them converging in the same ancestor.) Even so, the individual Jones is not likely to be much interested in counting kin among other Joneses—except for the Joneses in his own home town. And that is how the Tonga

felt, too. The home-town Joneses counted in life. They were *family*.

Tonga neighborhoods had a kind of permanence that forest villages could never have known. Because of river silt, Tonga fields stayed fertile over very long periods of time and could therefore be considered family assets of the most crucial sort. Individual houses might be moved from time to time, but the fields were passed down through the generations.

Because neighborhoods included a number of families, nobody really had to leave home to get married. One simply moved into another house. If girls did "marry out," it was usually no further away than into the neighborhood across the river. Families did not want their girls moving into neighborhoods where there were no close relatives to look out for them. They had a point.

Tonga men thought it proper to marry many wives. And as long as each wife was treated with scrupulous impartiality, the system worked quite well. Tonga women seem to have been less jealous about their husbands' attention than their Amba sisters. But when it came to land, that was something else again. Valley soil varied considerably in fertility, being very good by the river, not so good further back. And if a woman suspected that her husband had given her less productive fields than those of her co-wives, she raised a great fuss. She also resented (and said so loudly) the way the children of her co-wives made free with her stored groundnuts and grain. After all, she would point out, she had to feed herself and her own children from her fields. Occasionally she had to feed her husband (his own grain usually went into beer). And there were various and

sundry relatives she had to help along. She certainly needed every morsel of good soil she could get from her husband. If her husband remained hardhearted, she could always appeal to her own people for the loan of a field, the produce of which would be hers alone. They never turned her down. This was the beauty of staying close to home.

Although the Tonga believed in mother right, they also allowed father-residence. A girl went to her husband's home to live, and boys usually remained with their fathers instead of moving in with their maternal uncles—though that is what they were supposed to do. It would be from Uncle, after all, that property would be inherited. In actual practice, Father had quite a good deal to say about his children's life and upbringing. Maybe more than Mother's brother, when all was said and done. It was Father who had first call on his son's labor, and it was he who received bridewealth for his daughter—though some of it went to Mother and some to Uncle, too. He could, if he chose, lend fields for his son's use and help him save up for a wife.

There was constant bickering among the Tonga about whose rights came first, a father's or an uncle's, and a boy often felt himself trapped between two sets of duties. The strain was eased considerably when everyone involved stayed in the neighborhood. The fields a boy had to work—be they his father's or his uncle's—might be scattered hither and yon, but he could at least manage to keep everyone happy.

There were very definite advantages to staying put quite apart from maintaining the old home ties and working the old home fields. The longer one's family name was attached to a particular locality, the better its chance to become the ceremonial "owner." Each neighborhood had its *katongo*, its premier family, descended from the oldest settler. Now, this family might have representatives in other neighborhoods up and down the river, but the spot where its people had been first colonists—where it was *katongo*—that was the important spot for the whole clan. The living head of such a founding family was called *sikatongo*, and he was responsible for the spiritual well-being of the whole neighborhood. It was he who owned the local shrine. It was he who interceded with the spirits (often thought of as ancestors so old as to be nearly forgotten) to bring rain. It was his duty to get the annual cycle of agricultural activities underway in the right order and with due regard for tradition. And, as representative of the first settler, it was to him that the neighborhood farmers brought "first fruits," earliest samples of the harvest. If he failed in his duties, if his ancestral spirits grew angry with him (as signified, perhaps, by continuing drought or illness—only the diviner knew for sure), he could be replaced in the job by another member of his family. If matters became too serious, the whole *katongo* family might itself be displaced.

In the long run, everything in Tonga life depended on the ancestral spirits, the "shades." Although sorcery was not discounted as a cause of misfortune, people tended to see the hand of the shades in most bad things in life and in all the good ones. The shades were always there, always on hand at every moment, because, like property, they were inherited.

When a man dies, said the Tonga, he leaves behind not only his material wealth, but his role in society, his relationships with and obligations to many other people—parents, brothers, children, nephews. His place must not remain empty, his shade must not be allowed to wander rootless and alone. It must be attached to some living person who will give it a home, remembrance, and continued meaning.

Shades, said the Tonga, should be passed down in exactly the same way that property is willed. Therefore, a man's shade was given first to his brother and after that to his oldest sister's oldest son. A woman's shade was willed to her sister, and after sister, to her own grandchild—the oldest daughter of her oldest daughter. But the shade was not real property, after all. It had once been a person. It was a person *still* and could be expected to have personal preferences as to hosts. It might not like the brother (or sister) to whom it had been given and would react by making the host sick. It might, in fact, want to change accommodations any number of times. There was certainly no mistaking a shade's dissatisfaction! Or so the Tonga thought. To minimize these disturbances, the executors of a shade's estate took care to choose just the right legatee. Compatibility and character were taken into account as well as tradition. Quarrelsome individuals and chronic drunks were automatically barred from the inheritance even though they might be in the direct line of succession.

It was an honor to receive a shade, and it was a responsibility, too. The identification between shade and heir was complete. The heir might have to take up the dead man's work—carving or smithing (the fashioning of imported metals, that is; the Tonga have never smelted). Certainly he had all the shade's kinship obligations to worry about. He took the dead man's place in everything, becoming "father" to his children and (if not too young or too old) "husband" to the dead man's wife.

An heir was amply rewarded for his efforts. Because of his super-natural connections, living folks treated him with great respect and a certain awe. His income also enjoyed a boost. For he collected bridewealth when the shade's daughters got married. He had a right to the labor of the shade's sons. And any time the shade was due a present, the heir received it for him. After all, were shade and man not one and the same? In the long run, inheriting a shade usually turned out to be a lot more profitable than inheriting a few parcels of land and a scrubby cow or two.

Down the line of descent a shade was passed, from relative to relative, until the last person who could possibly have known him in life had died too. At this point, whatever lands had been going the rounds, lent to sons and sons' sons, reverted at long last to the original and inalienable owner, the line of the mother. And the shade's name was then forgotten, merged with all the unknown shades summoned in a mystical "et cetera" whenever the recent dead were feasted and implored to bring rain.

Before the Europeans insisted on organizing the Tonga into artificial "village" units and appointing artificial chiefs to run them, Tonga neighborhoods got along with nearly as little formal government as did the Amba villages. The *sikatongo* was a ritual leader only —unless, of course, he had a strong personality, in which case he could exert a good deal of informal influence. There was, ordinarily, no need for judicial machinery. Everything that was done had reference to the shades and their wishes, so the diviner who interpreted those wishes commanded whatever decision-making power there was. Most disputes turned on matters of kinship—allocation of bridewealth, death duties, land rights, family spats, and elopements. And in these cases the family heads (senior mothers' brothers) threshed things out among themselves. Sometimes an intermediary was chosen to patch things up among families who had reached the no-talking stage.

The Tonga liked to trade in a family atmosphere and entered into "bonds" much like the Amba blood brotherhoods. They formed partnerships with one another, with government officials from the outside, and with itinerant traders who always got much the best of a bargain. In such an arrangement, no haggling or setting of prices was possible. The parties involved just kept reciprocating gifts—as if they were really related—and hoped to wind up somewhere close to even. Like nearly everything in Tonga life, trading bonds were heritable and could be handed down indefinitely until one or both parties to the pact finally gave up in disgust.

Tonga neighborhoods seem never to have been as battle-thirsty as Amba villages. Neighborhoods rarely concerned themselves with the activities of others, near or far, being involved each in its own little world. There were, however, occasional get-togethers. Each neighborhood had its own "drum and bugle corps"—a band of girl singers and boy instrumentalists who performed in other neighborhoods in a spirit of friendly competition. Sometimes sportsmanship was forgotten and the contests wound up free-for-alls rather like those that sometimes terminate our own high-school football games.

This is how things used to be with the Tonga but are no more. For in 1957 the Kariba dam began to rise, and the old valley refuge was gone. A great lake formed over the neighborhoods. By 1962 it was a hundred miles in length and, in some places, thirty miles wide. The valley Tonga, over fifty thousand of them, had to move to new homes. Some resisted, but as their old fields disappeared beneath the water, they gave in and went away, sorrowing. How in their new lands, they wondered, could a family ever again be *katongo?* How could they work in fields unhallowed by memories—memories of Mother planting there and Grandmother before her? How could they start again and build again and find happiness and security as before?

Already they have begun to try. And one day Dr. Colson and Dr. Scudder will go back and tell us how the Tonga have fared and what they have made of their new life.

Nilotic and Herero Cattlemen

11. Kin and Cattle

At Home on the Range

Perhaps you have a pet. Most Americans do. No doubt you feed that pet, coddle it, take it to the vet when it is sick, and bury it in a pet cemetery when it dies. But for all your devotion, you could never love your pet half so much as a man of White Nile country loves his ox. Your pet may be a friend and companion, but it is not your whole way of life. And that is just what cattle represent to Nilotic peoples—a way of life.

A young Nilote is given his animal alter ego early in life, and from this animal's name or its special markings he takes his own name-of-honor, his "ox-name." This is the animal of his heart, almost a second self, guarded, cherished, carefully groomed. He hangs around its neck an iron bell, twists and hammers its horns into decorative designs, and composes songs and poems in its honor. When the ox dies, he dies a little, grieving so profoundly that his friends come from afar to visit and condole. If he dies young, the ox is sacrificed to accompany him in death. Rubbing the animal's back, he communes with the god of his fathers and with the ghostly herds which have dwelt in the company of men since time began.

From the herds come sustenance—the milk and blood which are the prized food for men. Meat is too precious to be on the daily menu and is eaten only when an animal dies or must be sacrificed in religious rites. From the herds, too, come clothing (what there is of it), bedding, containers, and shelter. Cow dung is used to plaster homes and to make fires, the ashes of which furnish hair dressing, tooth powder, and the dry paint for sacred markings on face and body. Cow dung soothes and cools the feet of orators delivering lengthy speeches. Cow urine washes wooden containers, curdles milk, and warms cold hands on chilly mornings. Cow bone provides ritual objects, jewelry, and kitchen implements. Just by *being*, cattle give a man the most important thing of all—honor and meaning for his life.

Nilotic peoples can be found, not only along the White Nile and its tributaries, but around Lake Victoria, all the way down past Mt. Kilimanjaro and into Tanzania. The lion-hunting Masai roam there, vanguard of the Nilote advance. To the west of Lake Victoria, ancient Nilotes, together with farming Bantu, organized the great lake kingdoms described in Chapter 4. To the east of the lake, Nilotes remain as they have been for as long as anyone remembers—simple herdsmen, interested in cattle, family, and war.

Nilotes are very tall and mostly Negroid peoples who speak Nilo-Saharan tongues. They are not the only cattle lovers in East Africa. Throughout Ethiopia and along the Red Sea are other herders—mostly Caucasoid in type and speaking Afro-Asiatic languages. For a long time specialists have believed that cattle and the knowledge of cattle-keeping traveled through these people to the Nilotes. Evidence now suggests that things may have been quite otherwise. If, as now seems likely, a native breed of cattle was domesticated right in the Sahara, then the roles of giver and receiver may be just the reverse of what was supposed. Cattle may have traveled from west to east instead of in the other direction.

However and whenever cattle appeared along the White Nile, men there have certainly developed cattle keeping into a distinctive way of life. It is an elementary life in some respects, complex in others, with wider horizons than those of the village folk we have already met. As any tourist will tell you, travel is broadening, and travel is what most of the Nile people do plenty of. The home grounds of many groups are alternately flooded and cracked with drought. During wet times they live in settled villages. During dry times they must take their herds in search of water and pasture. And these great swings set the

rhythms of life and define its boundaries. Although some few of the Nile tribes have gradually settled into farming ways altogether, most leave the matter of crops to their womenfolk while the men live in symbiotic communion with their herds.

The Nilotic way of life involves as little in the way of governing forms as any we have seen so far. Only in a few of the river societies can anything even approaching a chief or ruler be found. Indeed it is hard to imagine these herders submitting to authority of any kind. Tall, proud, touchy, tender of their honor and ever ready to fight in its defense, they are among the world's staunchest believers in equality. No man is considered better than any other man though he have a thousand cows to prove it. Nobody tells anybody what to do. A bossy man is likely to find himself looking down the sharp end of a spear.

And yet, amid all the apparent disorganization of the cattlemen's world, there is order of sorts. Some tribes recognize semisacred personages—rain makers who also try (without much success) to be peacemakers as well. These have no power of decision, however, can give no orders, make no demands on anybody. And there are, of course (as everywhere else), men who just naturally have influence whether they seek it or not. Whatever they do, others copy. Such a man gains influence not only by virtue of his personal qualities but also through his position as eldest of a band of brothers. If he has kept them all together after the father's death, that is achievement enough, and people will flock to his homestead—his sisters' children, various in-laws, and remnants of other, less harmonious families. His children and his brothers' children grow up and marry, and so the village grows, a "herd" around its original "bull."

This is particularly true of the Nuer, fierce fighting men who live near the swampy Sudd—that vast tangle of vegetation that plugs the White Nile as it loops upriver toward the lakes. British anthropologist E. E. Evans-Pritchard has lived with the Nuer and studied their way of life. It is in the wet-season settlement, he tells us, that Nuer ties of love and loyalty are strongest. A pebble, thrown into still water, casts ever-widening rings of ripples. Like a living pebble, the Nuer village casts round itself the ever-widening circles of kinship—circles which give yet another form to Nuer life. Although easily affronted and quick to spear, Nuer village-mates try to maintain good feelings among themselves. If mishaps occur, livestock is immediately offered in reparation. And there are strict rules about village fights, if fighting there must be. Clubs may be used but *never* spears.

Beyond the village, rules of combat weaken with the weakening bonds of kin. Quarrels between neighboring villages often result in a feud with everybody on both sides fighting, even though their

core family lines may be related—making them third or fourth
cousins, say. If, however, the next larger kinship segment to which
our warring duo belongs—the district—were menaced by another
district, then small hostilities would cease and the combatants would
band together to fight the larger war. And so on, all the way up to
the tribe.

Always there are ways of settling differences peacefully within
the tribe. Compensation in livestock may be offered. Guilty parties
can hide out with a spiritual leader, a Leopard-skin Chief, who will
do his best to mend matters and prevent a feud. But with the tribe

one is close to the uttermost boundary of kin and *at* the boundary of peaceful solutions. Differences between Nuer tribes can be settled only in war. But even here a certain decorum prevails. Nuer women and babies must be spared by other Nuer, and their homes left unburned. Outside Nuerland—the last and weakest circle of relatedness—anything goes. Only kin deserve special consideration; any stranger is a potential enemy.

Besides the ties of kin, many of the Nile peoples have a wider unifying bond. It is the bond of age and shared experience. Boys who are initiated together, hazed, and perhaps even scarred together are expected to be friends throughout life. Now, age grouping can mean a lot in a man's life or very little, depending on the end it is meant to achieve. Among the peoples around the Sudd, age sets have little real importance, because men fight as parts of a village or in their lineage sections or as tribesmen and not in regiments composed of age-mates. Nor are there any other requirements for them to fulfill as a group.

Southward, toward the lakes, however, the system becomes a sort of organizing force, a beginning of political form—but with several different ends in view. Some groups—the Masai is one—use the age sets in a military way, as regiments. Age-mates train together and fight together. And the Masai were in the old days notable warriors.

Among the Karamojong (who live east of Lake Kyoga in upper Uganda) the age-grade system is geared to a different goal. It is used to set apart, not young warriors, but the elders, who are near to God—the Sky God, the Great Spirit who dwells in certain treetops and in the hearts of men—the God whom, under different names, all the Nile's people honor and invoke. The elders, because of their nearness to God, can prophesy and beg for rain. They can bless, and they can curse. And they use this power often in decisions which affect all: the time to send out the cattle to dry-weather camps, the time to release the young men for war. They can convene meetings and settle disputes. Altogether it is a beginning of formal order—more order than people such as the Nuer could imagine or endure.

The Karamojong occupy plateau land. For part of the year they expect rain. It rushes down from hills and along dry river beds in raging flood only to sink into the sand, lost from sight. Women dig wells in the sand, wells which deepen as the dry season progresses. During rainy times, they plant fields of sorghum along the river-silted banks, and the crops must grow and ripen before the drought approaches. But in some years the rain is scanty or falls betimes, and in those years the people know famine. Then they must depend upon their herds to keep them alive. In any case, young children are regularly sent with their fathers to dry-season camps. There they will be sure to get ample milk and blood to keep them healthy.

Life is hard at the cattle camps. The men doze fitfully all night, ready to protect the stock, to repel wild beasts or wilder men, and there is no friendly beer with which to cheer the hours unless wives and sweethearts come for a visit. In the daytime, young boys take the animals to grass or water while the men stand guard or perhaps carve wooden milking bowls and the tiny stools which are badges of manhood as well as furniture. There is no time and no inclination for art, unless it be poetry. And there is precious little interest in trade.

Men move out to cattle camps in groups of relatives and band together or wander as they will. Each unit is free to seek pasturage according to its own lights. Men with large herds parcel them out among sons or close relatives, who wander separately, so that one plague or one raid will not destroy an entire herd. Raids are as much a danger now as ever. The Karamojong and their cousins the Dodoth raid with ardor and are raided in turn by the Turkana, a neighboring tribe much like themselves. In 1956–58, when anthropologists Neville and Rada Dyson-Hudson lived among the Karamojong, men were being speared while on cattle raids. It was happening even as short a time ago as 1961, when Elizabeth Marshall Thomas visited the Dodoth. For cattle are still the most coveted item of existence and doubtless will continue to be so for a long time to come. With many cows a man can acquire many wives and from them get many sons who will support him, if not for love, then because of the herds, which may not be divided until his death. With many cows a man can give presents to friends and thus gain allies and make himself felt in the community as a man of wisdom and substance.

Indeed, he must have many cattle—and numerous sheep and goats and donkeys also—if he wishes to see his sons well married. For, when marriage negotiations are underway, the father of the bride will insist that each of her close relatives be given livestock to forestall pique. The groom's problem is to meet the demands while keeping enough cattle to support his bride. Often he makes the rounds of relatives—his uncles, his mother's people, his sister's husband—picking up from each a contribution to the bridal herd. It is rather like our custom of sending wedding invitations and expecting gifts in return.

Comes the wedding day—or the first of a series of wedding days on each of which some special event occurs—and the groom arrives at the bride's homestead wearing a handsome leopard skin draped over his cowhide cape. Most likely that will be all. Nilotes are devoted nudists and believe that an elaborate coiffeur constructed with clay, ash, and feathers, and perhaps sandals and a necklace or two constitute ample dress for any occasion. The bride wears the beaded apron and half skirt of the unmarried girl. Perhaps her lower lip will have been opened to accommodate a decorative lip plug which fits nicely in the space where her lower incisors ought to be and are not, having been removed long since. If she wants to be rude to someone, she can stick out her tongue, just as we do. But if she first removes the lip plug and puts her tongue through the hole, that, says Mrs. Thomas, is considered the ultimate in last retorts.

After the private cattle negotiations are publicly and elaborately re-enacted, the bride is taken to the groom's homestead and installed in the compound of her eldest co-wife until a separate place can be prepared for her. This will consist of a courtyard built into the homestead proper but fenced off from other courtyards and containing several huts for her and later for her children. In such a courtyard she will store and grind her grain, churn milk which her young sons and older daughters have drawn, brew beer, scold the youngsters, and, if she gets along well with her co-wives, live happily ever after.

At her husband's death, the whole vast complex, more often than not, will break up and scatter as the herds are divided. Her own sons —the sons of one courtyard—will move away to form their own joint family. Unless she wishes to be inherited by one of her husband's brothers, she will go with them. And so begins a new segment of the larger family—the family which is forever.

Along Southwest Africa's dry coast there were once other cattle people. Totally unlike and unconnected with the great Bantu kingdoms of the south which were built in equal parts on farming and on cattle, these were a simpler people. And they were wanderers. Hottentots—bigger cousins of the Bushmen—formed one group. The Herero tribes formed another. Of all the Bantu-speaking peoples anywhere, only the Herero followed the pastoral nomadic way of life. Whether they had once been farmers and had grown weary of their fields, whether they had been driven into the wilderness by the pressure of stronger people behind them, we do not know. Neither do we know exactly whence and from whom they got their cattle.

All that is known for sure is this: when the Dutch first came to Southwest Africa, they found the Herero and Hottentots in possession, both with cattle, and both at war—with each other. The hostilities, in fact, continued until both were overwhelmed by colonizing Europeans. The Hottentots were in time either destroyed by the Boers or absorbed into the ranks of other peoples, a mixture which came to be known as the Cape Coloreds of South Africa.

Germans pre-empted what is now Southwest Africa in the late 1800s. Their settlers took Herero cattle in payment of "debts," and the Herero rose in revolt. By 1904 only remnants of the tribes remained on home grounds. Many fled to what was then Bechuanaland Protectorate (now Botswana) and found refuge among the Tawana, a Bantu-speaking people who lived near Lake Ngami. It was among the Bechuanaland Herero that the American anthropologist Gordon Gibson lived in 1956 and their ways that he recorded.

A reconstruction of the Herero past—made largely on the basis of missionary accounts—was attempted in the 1930s by Dr. H. G. Luttig. He believed that in the old days before the white man came, Herero life was more organized than Dr. Gibson found its Bechuanaland remnants to be. Dr. Luttig speaks of priest-chiefs who were advised by councils, various officials including war-chiefs, and even pages who carried verbal messages from chief to chief. If this was so, then the harsh environment and destructive wars have certainly wrought a change. For the Bechuanaland Herero were, when Dr. Gibson studied them, simply family men whose entire attention was focused on wringing a living from a dry land.

Bechuanaland Herero travel with their cattle on ceaseless rounds. The Kalahari and its fringes are not, after all, the most hospitable of grazing lands. Sometimes the men take their herds out to temporary cattle camps when the grass near home is gone. In especially dry times, the whole family group departs to set up a new homestead elsewhere within the particular area they know best, where the women can gather what wild food there is about. Always the animals move and are corralled as a double herd. There are the ordinary animals to be used for food, clothing, and the necessities of life. And there are the sacred animals whose flesh is eaten only in sacrifices. Like herders everywhere, the Herero glory in their hard life and scorn the tillers of the soil. The herds, both sacred and profane, were life and honor, and the man without cows was relegated, Bushman-like, to a hunting-gathering existence.

"Thick milk," as Luttig calls it (curdled, perhaps?), is the Herero's

staple food. It nourishes both body and soul. Perhaps it is this double power which, the Herero say, makes it doubly dangerous for a person to drink without taking proper precautions. Every homestead has its "taster"—father or priest who sits at the sacred fire and, morning and evening, takes the first sip of the milking, neutralizing its sacredness and making it safe for all.

Herero women do most of the milking and even help now and then with the herds when help is needed. Far from being an outsider in her husband's home, a woman is made welcome and bound to the family in many important ways. She is permitted, even invited, to pray to her husband's ancestors. These are symbolized by a sacred *omuvapu* bush, itself representing (in that all but treeless land) the even more sacred tree of life. It is the wife's job (the great wife's that is) to kindle and keep the sacred fire, the fire which betokens the sun and which, surrounded by a thorn-bush fence, burns ever at the center of the homestead. All in all, the wife is a kind of priestess and honored as such. Naturally, the course of every marriage does not run smoothly, and divorces do occur. In such a case, the husband's ancestors are notified of the event and solemnly advised to remove the departing wife's name from the family rolls.

The female element in things magical and mystical goes beyond mere assistance in daily rites. Luttig tells us that in the old days, the far-off high god, Ndjambi Karunga, was both man and woman just as he was both good and evil, life and death. In honor of the god's dual nature, heirs to homesteads regularly wore women's clothes for their first official ceremonies. And none of these was for men only. Now even in our anything-goes world there are a few institutions—bars and gyms and fraternal orders, for instance—that are off limits to women. And most tribal peoples separate the sexes, at least when serious ceremonial business is afoot. Not so the Herero. Even in the case of a young man's coming-of-age, the most exclusively male of all rites, Herero mothers were invited to be present. Whether this is still true today, Dr. Gibson does not say.

The ritual importance of women may have arisen, at least in part, because of the Herero way of reckoning family (or maybe it was the other way around). A man keeps careful track of his descent on both sides of the family—his mother's ancestors as well as his father's—and both, for reasons which we shall shortly see, have their uses in his daily life. The system is called double-descent, and it is a bit more complicated than simply taking all one's relatives into account on the same terms and in the same way.

Perhaps you have noticed that in Latin American countries, a man often tacks his mother's name onto his own surname. Like this: Pablo Garza y Ortiz. Only his mother's name is, of course, really *her* father's name. Now suppose the maternal surname were, instead, a mother's mother's mother's name all the way back as far as you could remember, and you will begin to see how the Herero system works. Under such a system your name might be, say, John Smith-Jones. The *Smith* would represent your father's father's family, and the *Jones* your mother's mother's family. If you were truly Herero, of course, the *Jones* would have to be replaced by something like *Storm* perhaps, for Herero maternal names describe flowers or personality traits or natural phenomena. So you are Smith-Storm.

Now, let's say your Herero homestead includes, besides your father's quarters (he is Smith), three "houses" something like Karamojong courtyards. In each live a mother and her children. All the children of your house are Smith-Storms. The others are the Smith-Happys and the Smith-Roses. Your mother's sister marries Mr. Smith also, and she and your mother build their houses together. Your aunt's son is then considered your own full brother. He is Smith-Storm, too. Remember?

The Smiths (and there are a lot of them in your particular area) keep track of each other and know whether they are second cousins or kissing kin. The lines, in fact, may be plotted over ten generations back to the founder of the Smith clan. (Of course the Storms do the same for their line.) It is Smith cattle you will inherit since you are a boy, along with the Smith name and all the little conventions of dress and food taboos peculiar to Smiths. Your herd, like all Smith cattle, may be of a special color and bear special markings.

But the people you feel closest to are the Storms, your mother's people. Your mother went to her mother's house for your birth. Quite literally you were born "in the lap of your grandmother." Your coming made your mother for a time sacred in her father's homestead, so sacred that she could even "taste" the milk and make it safe. But it is not your maternal grandfather who loomed largest in your childhood recollections. It was always your mother's brother, a Storm like yourself. Your father has many children to see to, but your uncle is interested in *you*. When you visit his homestead he gives you whatever you ask for. He scolds your father for beating you overmuch and may even take you away to live with him. If you were born a cripple or in some way defective, he will certainly adopt you as his own. In the old days he would have willed you part of his sacred cattle. Even today he will try to leave you what he can after the demands of his sons have been met. Certainly he will want to give you his daughter (your cousin) as a wife. And if his love is really great he will overlook the matter of bridewealth.

Service you owe to your father, to his brothers, and to your clan. The marks of your identification as a Herero (lower front teeth removed, notch filed between the upper two) are given in your father's homestead. It is in the homestead that you pray and learn. The homestead is for you the center of Smith territory, the land of all Smiths. But Storms are everywhere in Hereroland. How lucky for you. Herdsman that you are, you may often find yourself pretty far from home. Suppose some night you stop at a lonely homestead and ask for shelter. The owner may be named Smith—a very distant clansman of yours—but that alone will not incline him to hospitality. If he is a Smith-Storm, however, or even if there is a Storm "house" within, you will be assured of a welcome, a good dinner, and friendly faces. For "house" relatives—no matter how distant—are "heart" relatives as well. They can be so precisely because—unlike "homestead" relatives—they have no cattle to bequeath, no honors to give, no marks to identify the wearer, no religious rites to offer. They have only love to give to one another, and that is gift enough.

Meanwhile, suppose that back at the homestead Father is gathered to his ancestors. The eldest Smith-Rose is designated as homestead heir. But you and your brothers dislike the Smith-Roses. So do the boys of Smith-Happy. Besides, it is the middle of the dry season, and there is not pasturage enough for a common herd. So you all decide to take your mothers and your cattle and go your separate ways.

Smith-Rose argues and protests, but in the end he lets you go, sending with you a bit of cow dung from the sacred family fire that you may use it to kindle the first fire in your own homestead. He must bless your going in this way lest the ancestors blast you for your presumption and bring sickness on the lineage. And quite beyond these practical considerations, he must let you go willingly because he wants you to come back for family prayers. For he is now the homestead priest, and by letting you go peacefully, he has transformed what was once simply an extended family into a congregation, a religious congregation which will meet at the founding family's sacred fire and remember the family that has gone beyond as well as the living one that remains.

Besides the family men of forest and plain, there were African peoples who managed life and pursued happiness in other ways. Their territories were not so large as those of the great kingdoms, their rules of order a good deal less intricate and involved. But at least they were not bound to a tight little family world. Their interests were wide enough to include all sorts of activities and all sorts of individuals, individuals who were not necessarily relatives. They had developed a well-defined tribal consciousness and true tribal leaders. In terms of organization, they were the in-betweens. And like in-betweens everywhere, there were lots of them.

Part IV

THE IN-BETWEENS

12. Age Grades and Graduations
Like Father, Like Son

We live, you and I, in a competitive world. We get ahead in it sometimes by luck but mostly by using our wits. For us there is no real social security. We are as good as our last big deal, the grade on a final examination. All our lives we struggle to get on top and, once arrived, to stay there. No wonder it is hard for us to understand societies in which position is rigidly determined by birth. More incomprehensible still is the world in which ability counts for little, in which honor is measured in terms of age, in which a man can be utterly sure, not only of social position, but social promotion, too—all in good time and the fullness of years. There are people who order their societies on this principle. And the Kikuyu of Kenya are one of them, or were in the old days before the white men came.

The system of age grouping is one way of getting large numbers of people, perhaps widely scattered people, organized. It was (and still is) a popular pattern in East Africa. For simple herdsmen like the various Nilotic tribes we have met, age grouping represents the faint beginning of government beyond pure family rule. Among the great Bantu states of the southeast (Zulu and Swazi, for example), it was only one feature—and mostly a military feature—of an already complex government. Among the Kikuyu, the age-grouping system *was* the government, the whole government. Its leaders were chosen not by birth, not by election, not even by divine appointment. They arrived at their posts by accumulating birthdays. And as government

Kikuyu and Nyakyusa

was by "committee"—there were no formal chiefs in the Kikuyu system—every man could hope to stand at least once in the limelight and,
with his fellow "committee" members, to direct tribal policy.

The entire tribe was divided into halves, rather like the American
two-party system. Each half had its full complement of elders, judges,
and parliamentarians, all up and down the chain of command. But
while the officials of one half acted, officials of the other side could
only listen, and when invited, consult.

Every forty years the halves switched roles. Men of action gave up
their power and resigned themselves to a back seat in the affairs of the
tribe. Some Kikuyu were unlucky in their birthdays and spent their
entire lives in the consultative role, more's the pity.

If the age system was a kind of government, it was also a kind
of school—a school in which one learned one's duties. And for the
Kikuyu it provided continuing education. There was no final gradua-
tion from the system. One just went on to a higher degree.

"School" began for the Kikuyu boy or girl when he or she was
initiated. That was sometime around age thirteen for girls. In the old
days boys were eligible for initiation at eighteen. It was at this point
and this point alone that the student could flunk. To refuse through
fear to submit to ritual cutting and scarring was to be an early drop-
out. Almost no one declined, for the uninitiated was condemned to
perpetual childhood. Forbidden to the fearful one were all the things
that mattered most in life: marriage, children, homestead, battle.
Initiation was matriculation in the age-grade system and pain the
qualifying test. No exceptions allowed.

After initiation, progress was roughly similar to our own progress
through school. At least, this was so for boys. Girls had no connection with war or government, so the age-grade system was mostly
a way of sorting out possible husband material.

In our world, the moment you enter first grade you and all the
other first graders in town become "The Class of _____" (whatever the date will be twelve years later when you are due to be
graduated). If yours happens to be a particularly lively group, your
teachers might call you (privately) "The Rowdy Class" or maybe

just "THAT class!" The name has a way of sticking all through school. Kikuyu groups were named, too, but after the outstanding event of their initiation year. "Drought," a class might be called, "Victory over Masai," or "Cattle Died," or even "White Men Came." Recalled in sequence, the names constituted a sort of living record of tribal history. Among some peoples in East Africa, class names were repeated in every other generation, so that a group of old men and one of young boys might have the same class name at the same time. If confusion resulted, there is no record of it.

As in our schools, Kikuyu classes moved from grade level to grade level, in each learning different and more difficult duties. There were not twelve grades in the Kikuyu "school" but five. And though new age groups were initiated every year, there were not yearly promotions. These usually occurred every six to eight years. Matriculation made a youth into a junior warrior. He and his initiation class fought as one regiment—a beginner regiment as he entered the grade, a senior one when he left the army after twelve years or so of fighting. Each regiment had its own elected leaders. The warrior regiments also acted as a kind of police force under the direction of the elders.

Sometime during a young man's warrior career he was required to marry, found a homestead, and father a child, and not until he had achieved these things could he move with his class up to the next grade—the grade of apprentice elders. There he sat at the old men's feet and listened and learned to judge, to deliberate, and to arrive at decisions.

In time he advanced to full elder—consulting or active according to whether it was his tribal half's turn to be "in" or "out." When his own child reached the age of initiation, he was graduated into the

Council of Peace—the grade of senior elders whose members were eligible to take part in district or all-tribal councils and guide the greater destiny. These councils each elected "spokesmen" who were not, in any sense, chiefs but more like committee chairmen in our scheme of things.

When a man's senior wife no longer bore children, he entered the final grade—the religious council. Now his duties were priestly ones. He acted for his family or sub-clan in offering up prayers and sacrifices to Ngai, the great god whose dwelling was atop Mt. Kenya and in the groves sacred to Kikuyu everywhere.

All these things happened at nearly the same time to his age-mates. And so it was that all through life they were together—the men of his class, his fellows, the boys with whom he had been initiated so long ago, who had stood together in the icy rivers singing to keep fast their courage and awaiting the knife. Close as brothers, close as kin they were, these men of his class, bearing the same identity, one and all. Thus his wife called his age-mates, like himself, "my husband," and considered herself jointly married. Children of the men of a class were children of all and were alike "my child." And to those children, all their father's age-mates were "Father." Never was a man alone in life, bereft and friendless. What if he never became an extraordinary man (which was considered not quite seemly anyhow)? He could never be entirely ordinary, either. For all men knew honor and enjoyed prestige—no man more than another—in due course and at the proper time.

The Kenya Highlands, say the Kikuyu, have been home ever since the god Ngai put his people there. (Or, as other northeast coast legends have it, since friendly Bushmen led them there out of the wilderness.) From this homeland the Kikuyu expanded southward and, so the story goes, found ugly little people who lived in holes in the ground. Now, pit dwellings of prehistoric folk have been uncovered in the area, and it may well be that Kikuyu pioneers did encounter a remnant few still living there. Later still and still expanding, the Kikuyu wished to enter forest land owned by the Wandorobo, a living hunting people who may be Bushman in origin. Portions of Wandorobo land were acquired by a system of purchase utterly unique to Africans of that time. It has been described by Dr. L. S. B. Leakey, who grew up among the Kikuyu, speaks their language, and was initiated into their age-grade system. According to him, the terms of the sale required a Wandorobo family and a Kikuyu family to adopt one another . Thus the ancestral spirits of neither group would be disturbed by the new land arrangements.

Once established in their new fields, the Kikuyu learned the way and the myth of cattle from their neighbors, the fierce Masai. But cattle never became all in all to the Kikuyu, as they were to the Masai. Wealth, yes; food, yes; a matter of sentiment, no. Cattle did not figure in Kikuyu religious rites; goats and sheep were the ancient animals of sacrifice. Milk products were not prized. Even milk itself was hardly ever tasted by adults.

It was not cattle but land that meant most to the Kikuyu—the land in which his father's bones were buried and his father's father's all the way back to the first man of the tribe ever to stand facing Mt. Kenya. It was the land—the mother of the tribe—by which he swore his most binding oaths. It was the land and the fruits thereof that gave life meaning and continuity. Men did not scorn the work of the land and spent as much time at it as did their wives. In the old days certain crops were raised entirely by men (bananas, tobacco), while others belonged to the women.

Jomo Kenyatta, first prime minister of independent Kenya, was in his youth a student of anthropology and wrote then a fine account of the Kikuyu, his own people. He spoke eloquently of their attachment to the land, explaining that each field was family-owned and inherited and that it could be lent to tenants but never lost to its original owners or their descendants. What rare sales there were took the form of marriage ceremonies with the desired field as bride. He went on to explain how, in time, the land was lost to European settlers, who thought they were buying it from Kikuyu owners, who, in their turn, meant only to lend the land's use; and how those owners suddenly found themselves only tenants on fields which, by the newcomers' law, belonged to them no more. In addition, there were in

the early 1900s several outbreaks of sickness and years of drought which caused a drastic population reduction. The incoming Europeans thought the unused fields mere bushland, theirs for the taking. Without papers and documents, Kikuyu families could not substantiate their claims and so lost their lands. It was the loss of land—and with it honor and self-respect—that eventually drove the Kikuyu to killing and despair.

In the old days, says Mr. Kenyatta, the Kikuyu were prosperous farmers but not, by any means, ordinary peasants, mere soil tillers, narrow-minded and uninformed. Their world was wide and full of many things. There were home crafts to be practiced. Women made pots and baskets in their spare time. Men carved in wood and kept bees for the fun of it and for the honey-beer to come. There were professional people such as herbalists who diagnosed ailments and applied cures. There were markets in which women could sell the surplus of their fields. Here the work of the ironsmith clans could be bought and the leather goods of the tanner clans. (Occupation tended to hinge on family training as it still does in most parts of the world.)

Often men did not wait for buyers to come to them but took their goods and their livestock afield. It was great fun to trade with some neighboring tribes. But businessmen had to go where business called and so even the fierce Masai were not overlooked. Of course, one knew one was on enemy land, and one took the proper precautions. A careful man cultivated trading partnerships among the enemy, arranged for safe conducts, and traveled in convoys.

Kikuyu ways and Kikuyu life began, say the legends, with Gikuyu, the first man. To him great Ngai gave land—the land around Mt. Kenya—and a wife into the bargain. From their marriage nine daughters were born but no sons. Again Ngai was generous and provided nine grooms for the nine girls, and they all lived happily at father's homestead—for a while. Then the girls began to grow bossier and also bigger until they were veritable giantesses. Alarmed, the little men conspired and bided their time against the day when their wives should all be busy with new babies. And when that time finally came, then also came the revolution! That is why, say the Kikuyu, father right has been practiced ever since in the Kenya highlands. Even so, the nine Kikuyu clans—much scattered—were named for the nine hapless giant-wives.

Women did not entirely lose their importance, however. They were, like their brothers, initiated and age-graded. They assisted in religious ceremonies, particularly those having to do with crops and planting. They also shared the glory when their husbands were elevated to the next higher grade. But, of course, they also shared their husbands. Like nearly all African people, the Kikuyu believed polygyny. And if you disregard the romantic love aspect (so important to us, so negligible in the African scheme), the system does have definite advantages. No woman with co-wives about ever lacked for a baby-sitter. No one woman was burdened with too many children, borne one after another. There were no spinsters and no widows, either, and no woman was ever without masculine support and protection. But then, no women was ever the sole object of her husband's affections. Mr. Kenyatta insists this was a matter of no importance. Children, he says, were taught early to share their love, and the habit stuck in matrimony. Wives are described as urging their husbands to take additional brides and even lending a hand in the wooing. The word "jealousy" is seldom mentioned by Mr. Kenyatta. It was, apparently, an attitude as frowned upon as personal ambition. For after all, individuality was rated last in the Kikuyu catalogue of virtues—if virtue it was. One's connections, not one's self, were what counted (one was addressed as "so-and-so's mother" or "son of so-and-so"), and solidarity was the watchword always.

And yet, in spite of all the ideals, there *were* jealous women and ambitious men, eccentric men, men stubbornly determined to be individuals even if they had to turn bad to do it. The Kikuyu believed that one might recognize the potential rebel by his self-seeking ways and by the company he did *not* keep. Unlike his gregarious peers, he liked to be alone and to live alone. But in time, they said, on some black night, a night without a moon, such a man would go to join others like himself and together they would form a council of evil very much like the daytime Council of Peace. They were said to meet, these eccentric men, in secret places, wild places far away from everyday human haunts. They wore no clothes and painted their faces black with white dots around the eyes so as not to be recognized by one another. And they traveled by zigzag routes so as not to be followed. And no wonder. They were the wizards, the sorcerers of the Kikuyu. Their life work was the manufacture of deadly poisons or of even deadlier spells which brought misery to the good people, the ordinary people at whose pleasant conformity the wizards took so much offense.

Of all possible crimes wizardry was thought to be the worst. The suspected wizard was spied on, followed, and hunted down. Haled before a judge and council, he was made to take frightful oaths or to taste his own "medicines." And if the spectators were still not convinced of his innocence, he was condemned to death. His family had first to disown him, his age group to cast him out, and then— beyond all belonging and all redemption—he met his death, and society closed ranks behind him. There were no revolutionaries among the Kikuyu!

13. Peers and Neighbors
Men Who Play Together, Stay Together

The Nyakyusa of Tanzania believe in segregation. Not the segregation of castes or classes or sexes or races. It is the generations which they feel should be kept apart. A man does not ordinarily eat with his father or grandfather, does not spend time in their company, and never passes so much as a night in their homes. Father and grandfather are not companions, mentors, and certainly not pals. A man learns instead from his playmates and lives with them, too. Such, at least, was the way of things with the Nyakyusa in 1934–38 when the British anthropologists Godfrey and Monica Wilson lived among them.

Each Nyakyusa settlement then was really three villages in one. There was a village for the family men, the men who ran things; a village for their fathers, who managed religious affairs; and a village for their sons, who were learning to be men. It was the ultimate in age grading, and it was practiced only by the Nyakyusa and their near neighbors. Living as they did (and still do) at the head of Lake Nyasa, hemmed in and protected by mountains and by the spears of their own formidable warriors, the Nyakyusa were able to keep to their ways during times when other tribes were harried by slave raiders, armies from the south, and the attentions of colonists from abroad. Even trading contacts were limited. The Nyakyusa were not market fans or traders, and beyond traditional ties with neighbors who brought metal and salt to exchange, there were no commercial travelers to bring in newfangled ideas. Even today what few stores there are belong to Indian or Swahili businessmen. And though in process of change (men now go away to work, and Christian missions have won many converts), the old ways were still recognizable when Dr. Monica Wilson paid a return visit in 1955.

The Bantu-speaking Nyakyusa used to divide their interests and activities almost equally between farming and herding. But not at the same ages. The daily business of cattle tending was delegated to boys. And since wives did the barnyard cleaning, a man had all the joy of his stock and none of the care. A boy began taking his father's cattle to pasture when he turned six. He did not go out alone but in a small troop of boys his own age and a little older. Out in the pasture land, they occupied a world of their own—cooking their own food, playing games, wrestling and fighting to see which was strongest, the acknowledged leader of all, the one whose orders would be obeyed.

At about eleven a boy began to think about leaving home. If he delayed too long his friends would tease him and call him a Mama's boy, or the Nyakyusa equivalent thereof. Even his parents might hint broadly that it was time to go. For it was considered highly improper for boys to intrude on their elders' privacy. So off the youngster went with his friends to start a new village—a collection of rude, unmudded bamboo huts surrounded by new-planted banana trees. This was not just for the fruit, though bananas were a favorite food. The Nyakyusa have always adored trees of any sort—rare trees, exotic trees—and to this day are forever planting and tending them.

Actually, the boys' huts were built right next door to the home village, so the break was not, all things considered, even so definite as a boy's departure for boarding school in our world. Besides, the Nyakyusa boy came home to his mother's hut for meals. But not alone. He brought his friends along and, like a swarm of locusts, they descended on one mother's larder after another. This pleased the older men. Every night a father wanted to know how many young guests had been fed. If there had been a house full, the proud response usually went something like this: "Ah, my son! He's a regular chief, that's what he is!" But the unpopular boy, the boy who

was a solitary eater might very well get a hiding to incline him toward winning friends and influencing people.

Soon after the move into boys' town, cattle tending was passed on to younger brothers. The older boys then began to help their fathers with the hoeing. Mothers and daughters did the planting and harvesting. All the farm work was nicely divided according to sex.

When boys reached age eighteen or so they closed their village to further members. New eleven-year-olds had to take up residence in boys' groups elsewhere. Unless brothers and half brothers were close in age, they seldom landed in the same village, to be pals through life,

though of course they always shared various family obligations and relationships. "You can't choose your relatives," our old saying goes, "but you *can* choose your friends." The Nyakyusa not only chose their friends, they lived with them.

Girls married early among the Nyakyusa—soon after the arrival of puberty. But not boys. A boy needed cattle in order to marry. Stock had to be given to the bride's father, who then put them aside for her brother, the brother who would use her wedding cattle as a down payment on his own bride. Accumulating bridal cattle took such a long time that a man and his first wife were ten years apart in age and sometimes more. With each additional wife the age gap grew wider still. A very young widow might, on her elderly husband's death, be inherited by a whole succession of her husband's brothers and then by his sons before she found herself married to someone close to her own age and life expectancy. Stinginess with cattle was not the only reason why young Nyakyusa men married late. Fathers enjoyed seeing their bachelor sons strut about and insisted on their having plenty of time to "sow their wild oats" (as we would call it) before settling down.

So it was that the first wife in a youth village did not ordinarily appear until its oldest residents were over twenty-five. Her coming was the signal for everyone to stay home for dinner and sample her cooking. Suddenly she found herself married, not just to one man, but to all his friends as well—at least in terms of cooking and cleaning and fetching wood and water. To all she had to give the proper greeting—a profound bow, sinking low on the ground and turning her gaze respectfully aside. Harried and overworked from dawn to dusk, worn out with obeisances, she could only console herself with the thought that the others would *have* to get their own wives some day. And they did. Forever after, then, she was honored above all the women in the village, for she had been first and had worked the hardest. Honoring, however, did not include invitations to dinner parties or gab fests. Convivial conversation was for men. Nor could she leave off the usual obeisances. But at least she no longer had to carry loads of firewood home. The other women did it for her.

As wives trickled in, the young men's houses were moved further apart, more trees were planted in between, and bits of land were put into cultivation. The large fields, however, were still under the control of the main village—the village of the fathers—and a young man hoed there for his father and for his father-in-law, too, if he came from the father's village. Land was always owned by the village as a whole and was allocated by the village headman to village residents and to newcomers alike.

Not unnaturally, as their families grew the young men chafed under their restrictions and their obligations. They wanted their own fields, parceled out by their own headman, and they wanted their own homesteads, too. How beautiful, how dignified those homesteads would be with their clean-swept yards, their elegant huts—made round or rectangular to suit individual taste—and over all the arching trees. And so, in time, the older men had to make way for their sons, moving their own houses out of the way, thus returning the settlement to its original narrow dimensions. They handed over the fields (though not the trees that they had planted and certainly *not* the cattle). And they handed over political power, too. This happened in an impressive ceremony called the "coming out" which marked the abdication of an old chief and the installation of his sons in office.

The Nyakyusa lived under the rule of chiefs. And there were lots of them—something over a hundred, all told, when the Wilsons were there. In the old days some were allied and some fought with one another, cattle raiding and killing men, but there was never one chief paramount over all. The chiefs and chiefdoms continued to multiply because each chief's domain was divided at the "coming out" between his two eldest sons. And each of these married two great wives whose eldest sons would again divide the chiefdoms at *their* "coming out." You would think that the endless process of division and subdivision would reduce the Nyakyusa chiefdoms to mere plots of land. But no, each chiefdom simply expanded into surrounding pastures and maintained a respectable size. Of course, this could not have happened if the land had been unavailable or occupied by other well-entrenched people. The law of diminishing returns, however, has overlooked the Nyakyusa. They started out in a largely vacant area (it is still full of wild game), and since the soil was (and is) extremely fertile and well-watered, they have not even yet begun to feel pinched as to space.

They came to their present country, the people say, long ago and found only a few Pygmy hunters in residence. Their ancestors were without the knowledge of fire, perhaps even without crops—though this is a point of some question. Then came the "heroes," very fair of skin, bringing the gifts of fire, of cattle, of crops, and of iron. These newcomers possessed in their own bodies the power of rain and fertility, the power to make all gifts of their bringing grow and multiply. And because of it they came to dominate the earlier Nyakyusa settlers. But their power was possessed at a price, and a high one. They were not allowed to live past their prime or to suffer illness lest the land itself diminish in fertility. The growing parts of their bodies, indeed, their very breath signified growth and power and life for the Nyakyusa people. And so it was that the headmen chosen to end a chief's life removed his hair and nails and smothered him to keep the last magic breath from leaving his lungs.

Forever after the heroes came—and Dr. Monica Wilson judges this to have been between 1560 and 1650 A.D.—men of their blood were chosen to represent them in the three sacred places of Nyakyusa and neighboring Ngonde. These men were called kings but had no actual power—especially in Nyakyusaland. Their function was simply to be divine. They existed to promote and preserve all the good things of life—the rain, the crops, health, growth, happiness—and they purchased their divinity with their very lives.

The chiefs of Nyakyusaland had political roles to play. But since they, too, were thought to be descended from the immigrant heroes, they shared something of the priest-kings' divinity. They also shared the prospect of ritual death. At least, this was the custom in the old days. For as long as any Nyakyusa can now remember, chiefs have lived to a ripe old age.

Tradition holds that the heroes came down from the north and east, and Dr. Wilson is inclined to agree. Whether the age-grade system filtered down as well nobody knows. What does seem clear is that a chiefly order was imposed on an older one—one stubbornly democratic in nature—and that the two have since been in almost equal balance. Nyakyusa chiefs were certainly no tyrants—not, in any case, when the Wilsons visited. Doubtless the heroes had brought many gifts to Nyakyusaland and had the power of fertility. But the people there before them possessed power, too. It was, say the legends, the power of darkness, the power of witchcraft. And so chiefs have always listened to commoners—"the men of earth"—fed them beef, shared power with them, married their daughters.

Old chiefs were always as loathe to give up their rule as the fathers of villages were loathe to give up their fields. But abdication could not be postponed forever, and each old chief had finally to make way for his sons.

Young chiefs-to-be were locked up for months in a darkened house where they were instructed in their duties. With them were the young commoners who would be village headmen, the future judges and leaders of the people. It was from this hut that they were called to "come out," all together, into a new life of responsibility and power. On this same day throughout the chiefdom, fathers belonging to the old chief's age group gave over village rights to their sons.

Each of the two young chiefs selected two villages as his capitals and in each installed a great wife. The headmen of these capital villages acted as his advisers throughout his reign. And so close was the collaboration between chief and headmen that the people called it a "marriage."

When a chief died, his senior headmen became leading priests at his burial grove, the grove that had been planted at his "coming out." To this grove came in pilgrimage all the men of his generation, the men who had "come out" with him. To the grove came his two chiefly sons, and in time, four chiefly grandsons as well, all to be led in worship by the headmen-priests. Each priest was followed in office by his own eldest son and his son's son after him until the day when the old chief had been at last quite forgotten.

It was not only the chiefs who lived in constant partnership with their commoner subjects. The sacred "kings" in their shrines were also attended by commoners, priests who felt perfectly free to chide and scold when the "king's" ceremonial behavior was not up to snuff. And special rain priests—often junior brothers of chiefly families—were themselves supervised by commoners. It was a fine balance, all around, of respect and fear. The commoners respected and

feared the chiefly powers of fertility; the chiefs feared the headmen
and the powers of witchcraft. And all feared the "breath of men."

In our terms, this could be translated as the fear of public criticism,
of disapproval. Criticism was thought to cause sickness, and therefore
criticism could kill. The chief who fell ill was told it was because he
had postponed his sons' "coming out." And when, soon after, he
died, his death was attributed to a general withdrawal of love. His
subjects had preferred his sons to himself and with their "breath"
had wished him away. To the Nyakyusa, popularity was power and
safety as well. Even today it is so.

When men of a village fail to live up to village values, they are
liable to "the breath of men." The man who stays much alone, who
fails to share, who boasts and brags, who keeps an untidy homestead,
who is silent at gatherings invites censure and ill fortune. The cardi-
nal sinner is, of course, the man who eats alone—or, worse still, with
his wife. Unforgivable!

But such a one, falling ill, does not see his plight as punishment for
his sins but as the result of pure witchcraft. It all depends on the
point of view. Has he, he wonders, been too diligent in his farm
work and outstripped his fellows? Has he had too many good things
to eat recently, particularly meat and milk? For these are things
which are said to stir a witch to jealousy, releasing his power to harm
whether he consciously wills it or no.

Most Africans consider the power of witchcraft to be inherited—
the way blue eyes are inherited, or curly hair, or the tendency to run
to fat. But notions about the way it is inherited and the way it is
used differ from one group of people to another. The forest Amba,
as we saw in Chapter 10, accuse their relatives of being witches.
Among the Nyakyusa it is not relatives who fear and resent one
another. It is among friends, those supposedly loving and unselfish
companions, that resentment smolders unexpressed. It smolders because there are rich men in an age village and poor men, too. And
nowhere do these differences show more plainly than at a meal,
traditionally shared with friends. It is at the shared meal that jeal-
ously arises, and that its evil, like the common cold, is most easily

caught and spread. No wonder feasting friends harbor fear and accuse one another of ill-wishing.

An accused man is not necessarily condemned, however, or driven to seek refuge in another village. And if he speedily confesses, he is welcome as ever to remain. Indeed, he is considered a distinct asset. For the confessed witch is a good witch, one who will now be able to "see" the secret evil all around and protect the village.

Witchcraft and criticism are not all the Nyakyusa fear. Living together as closely as they do, stressing love and loyalty as strongly as they must, it is themselves they fear as well and the corrosive effect of their own anger. For anger is twice-cursed; it curses the angry man and it curses his victim. It brings guilt along with sickness and misfortune. And so anger, say the Nyakyusa, must be rooted out, confessed, and in confession, destroyed, else harm will come to all.

The Nyakyusa New Year is the time of throwing out rubbish, the time when fires are extinguished and the old ashes—the ashes by which too many ancestral shades have lingered, in which perhaps too many witches have cooked forbidden food—are scattered. Now must the people acknowledge their anger and any resentments which they may harbor secretly against a friend. Now do they dance and fight mock battles, letting out the bad feelings inside, the angry feelings, so that they may be dispelled. Now do they kindle new fires on the swept hearths. It is a time of purification and beginning again, rather like the old Roman season of rubbish burning and purification which they called Februo and which is still our February.

For the Nyakyusa it is a very necessary rite—necessary because they live lives of closeness and dependence on one another, because, even in a time of change, they still value above all things the virtues of togetherness, of comradeship and harmony. Though their acquaintance with the great world and its ways may be slight, they know well and interpret well the secret places of the human heart.

14. Uniforms and Fancy Dress
The Happy Joiners

Perhaps nowhere outside the continental United States will you find so many enthusiastic clubmen as among the peoples of West Africa. Some societies support only one big fraternity and one big sorority, and the membership is neatly divided by sex. Others like secret associations whose members wear masks and play dirty tricks and (like gleeful little boys) just generally think of themselves as being up to no good. Still others go in for church sodalities and civic groups, patriotic groups, and groups of dance enthusiasts or amateur musicians. The Bamileke peoples of the Central Cameroons—up in the highlands between savannah and forest—support organizations of all these types and some others besides. For they are the happy joiners who believe in a club for everyone and everyone in his club.

The Bamileke, and all the peoples of the Cameroons Highlands, are particularly interesting for yet another reason. They have by no means the sort of impressive unity that the big kingdoms once had, not the size, and not quite the cosmopolitan outlook. (And bear in mind that I am comparing, not in terms of vast technological and urban societies, East or West, but in terms of Africa alone.) But when it comes to liveliness of interest, variety of taste, and just plain complexity of social form, the Bamileke rival any of the people we have met. Each of their little chiefdoms, though fast being absorbed into new, independent Cameroon, still provides a peephole show of all the things once to be found in the great old kingdoms. They offer a summary and a digest, and, with them, we come full circle—back to where we began.

It was probably from the Cameroons Highlands that Bantu-speaking peoples, newly equipped with yams and iron, ventured into the Congo forest. The peoples who live in the area today, however, should not be thought of as descendants of laggard Bantu who waved the pioneers on and themselves stayed comfortably at home. Since that time—whenever it was—the Cameroons tribal stream has been muddied and mixed, and although Bantu languages are spoken in the area, nearly everyone there now claims to have come from somewhere else.

The Bamileke say they arrived in their present land long ago—sometime in the seventeenth century, that might have been—and that they came from lands just to the north. Who knows where before that. The religious wars of the ever zealous Fulani—northern converts to Islam—later pushed many people hither and thither, and the Bamileke were one of them. In whatever shape they may have

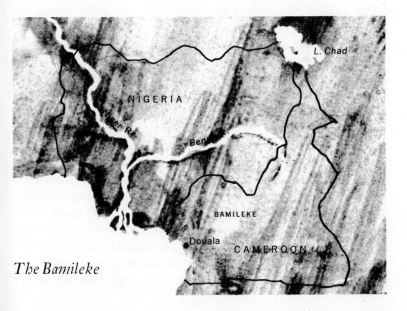

The Bamileke

entered—in family groups, as stragglers, as armies—they are now cut up into ninety or so little chiefdoms. Less land was available to them than to the Nyakyusa, and they were always surrounded by peoples as strong or stronger than themselves. Warfare was constant before the Europeans came—with neighboring peoples such as the Bamun, and among the Bamileke chiefs themselves. Some chiefdoms capitulated, others allied themselves with stronger powers, some were born as subdivisions of larger states. And so it is that now the chiefdoms vary in size—some having as many as twenty thousand people, some as few as five hundred.

The Bamileke are not an urban folk, according to Miss Margaret Littlewood, who, in 1954, surveyed the ethnographic writings about the Bamileke. There are seldom even good-sized villages—except for the chief's capital, which is, after all, only an extra-large residence housing the people of the court. Common folk live each individual family in its own compound and on its own land—that is to say, land assigned by the chief. Families tend to be small—not the gaggle of uncles, cousins, and what not around which villages collect in other parts of Africa. And yet, there is no such thing as isolation or loneliness, either. People of Bamileke chiefdoms are forever congregating for one reason or another. In these tiny states, distance is seldom a problem. Markets convene every four days. Clubs hold meetings every week. And since a man normally belongs to several, that adds up to a lot of social activity.

Nearly every club has its own clubhouse and its own drums. These are pounded to call the meetings together, and every member knows which drum is calling whom. Regular attendance is compulsory, and members who are persistently tardy or absent without a good excuse might wake up one morning to find their crops trampled and their goats gone. Even without the prospect of punishment, however, people would attend, because they enjoy it. Club going is one of the best ways around to make a name for oneself. Each club is organized in ranks—rather like the "degrees" of the Masonic Order—so that a man's prestige increases according to his length of membership and his attainments in the club. His rise is marked quite literally by an

elevation in seating arrangements. He graduates from the ground to a variety of ever taller, ever more elaborately carved stools on which he sits with ever greater girth and dignity as the years go by.

Best of all, every two years each club stages a big dance for the local chief. Nonmembers watch and admire as the clubmen show off their fancy uniforms, their masks and sacred carvings, and their headdresses. It is, all in all, rather like an American Shriner's convention with the whole chiefdom turned topsy-turvy for the festivities.

All the men in each chiefdom usually belong to one large fraternal order. Boys join as apprentices at age twelve. At eighteen they become second degree-ers and join in club work. Like the Chambers of Commerce in American cities, Bamileke men's clubs involve themselves in civic improvement projects. They also collect taxes for the chief. Perhaps there is a connection between the two functions. Perhaps not. Third degree members are flatteringly called "our bravest" and "our strongest." In the old days they may have been the war leaders. Nowadays they make a name for themselves as dancers. Enormously talented and long-winded, they not only sing about dancing all night, they do it—regularly.

Some chiefdoms have two societies for ladies, one managed by the chief's mother and the other by his number-one wife. Both groups are devoted to general good works and cooperation in the fields—especially when the fields in question belong to the royal queens. They also stage the equivalent of luncheon parties during

which current business is discussed and plenty of palm wine put away. The queen wife's club enrolls about fifty members, mostly her co-wives and the wives of notables. The queen mother's club is larger and more democratic. All diligent farmers are invited to join, whatever their social position. Belonging to the queen mother's club may be an honor, but lots of women groan when they receive their invitations. This honor, like all honors, is not without its strings. Members have to spend so much time in the queen mother's gardens that they wind up neglecting their own. And so it is that, honor or no, prospective members sometimes visit the queen and ask to be excused.

Besides the large associations, there are burial societies whose members are sworn to attend one another's funerals and mourn long and loud. There are musical groups and priestly groups whose members concern themselves with ceremony. There are the various guild associations for the offspring of chiefs and for the servitors of chiefs. These function more or less as historical societies, keeping in their care various of the national treasures and national archives—the drums, the chief's ancestral skulls, the royal wardrobe and insignia.

You will not find all these groups in every Bamileke chiefdom, and new ones crop up all the time. When European money came to be a potent force, some chiefs organized their own clubs, special clubs designed to keep the new commodity flowing into the royal treasury. In some ways the chiefly clubs might be compared to the American President's Club. Both have proved to be dandy fund-raisers. Wealthy, influential men—there as here—are invited to join; they are also invited to pay a stiff entrance fee. What they get for their money is the chance to sit around with the chief, swapping opinions on national affairs and drinking palm wine like old buddies. On these occasions they wear special veiled headgear, and nobody has to bow and scrape to the chief. To complete the whole heady show of equality, everyone drinks out of the same wine dish—chief included. Being the crony of a leader is pretty fancy stuff in any world. As for the chief, what he loses in majesty, he makes up in profit.

The warrior groups have used this system to their own advantage for quite a long time, inviting older, wealthy men (who could not possibly fight) to play soldier for a fee. They met regularly (veiled again) to give their opinions on military matters—a sort of *ex officio* defense council.

Some Bamileke clubs are frankly political and busy themselves with the machinery of government. One warrior group functions as an informal police force—under the chief's orders, of course. Another, consisting of representatives of the "founding families"— rather like the Daughters of the American Revolution in this respect —acts as the chief's advisory council. It helps to decide matters of policy and chooses a chiefly successor should the chief fail to nominate an heir. If the royal choice happens to be clearly unsuitable— a young man given to the bottle, say, or known to have thievish habits—the council can simply set aside the king's choice and elect another successor.

All in all, the chief is not really so much a tribal leader as a vest-pocket king. So it seemed to Mr. F. Clement C. Egerton, a British

writer and traveler, who lived in the court of the ruler of Bangangte, a middle-sized chiefdom in the southeast part of Bamilekeland. Actually, he lived in the king's own house. This was for some months during 1938. Mr. Egerton tells us that once, long before his visit, the king's power had been absolute. Life and death, banishment, slavery, and eviction were all his to decree. True, clubs did exercise some restraining influence. So did the queen mother, for she was nearly as powerful as her royal son. Always she lived in her own compound away from the king's village. Her home was a sanctuary as were those of the king's brothers. If a culprit could get close enough to lick a royal hand, any royal hand but the king's, all the safer for him.

Throughout Bamilekeland the queen mother still has the right of membership in any male club whose meetings she chooses to attend. Only she of all the women in the chiefdom is so honored. The king's sisters in the old days were petted and pampered and kept at home. Sometimes dynastic marriages were arranged for them. Sometimes they were simply left to their own devices. During Mr. Egerton's visit in Bangangte, the royal sisters had become a royal scandal, tooting off to Douala, the Cameroon big city on the coast, whenever they pleased and doing what they pleased while there. Everyone in the chiefdom gossiped about them. And even the king, who ordinarily doted on his sisters, was embarrassed to tears.

Besides being the supreme judge, the king of Bangangte was also the chief priest, a living connection with the ancestors, a person right next door to divinity if not already there. He was approached on bended knee and always addressed as "Leopard." Subjects never spoke to him without first cupping their hands over their mouths so as not to contaminate the royal air with their common breath.

The king was supposed to control the elements, and so when thunder storms or even epidemics struck, the people did a lot of muttering about the king and how he had done it out of spite. The poor innocent king of Bangangte had to dash out into the market place and perform the tortoise test. In the old days, it was the only way he could prove his good intentions. This is what happened: royal henchmen went in search of a suitable turtle, split it, and cut its heart into tiny pieces. Before the assembled citizens, the king's brothers and other courtiers volunteered each to eat a bit of turtle heart declaring the while, "If the king has been responsible, may disaster strike me and mine." Then everybody went home and waited. If, within a reasonable period, none of the guarantors had been lightning-blasted or snake-bitten or some such, then the people were willing to agree that the king had not, after all, been responsible for the original disaster.

Bamileke kings are still thought to be responsible for fertile soil and good farming as well as the collective weal. Land, after all, belongs to them. The newly-married youth ready to set up house-keeping must apply to his king for a grant of land. And though he prefers to settle close to his own family, he takes what fields he is given and thanks the king nicely.

In the royal compound are a king's talismans of office, sometimes tended by guilds which function as a sort of department of antiquities, sometimes by royal wives. These heirlooms are never sold or given away. Most important of all are the ancestral skulls. Family skulls are treasured by all Bamileke—invoked and given offerings and honored in the huts of their inheritors. Skulls of men go to their eldest male descendants; skulls of women to the eldest woman in a line. Chiefly skulls are particularly precious, for in them are thought to rest the ancestral spirits who, far more than the vague, faraway creator god, bring good things to the chiefdom.

Besides the skulls there are, in the royal treasury, other items of value. Drums and gongs, "medicines" and ornaments, thrones and stools on which a chief sits to give judgment. All these "crown jewels" require many huts for safekeeping. Many huts, too, are needed for the king's family. The king of Bangangte had, in 1938, over seventy-two wives. Their housing alone—in a special compound with enclosed court and dancing pavilion—required an establishment of truly impressive size.

At the Bangangte capital village were also the huts of five chosen great lords who comprised the secretariat. And there were various other officials—stewards, subchiefs of "quarters," court recorders (men noted for their powers of memory)—who required housing. In other, more prosperous days, long before Egerton's visit, this basic list of courtiers would have been augmented with heralds, messengers, special "doctors" to attend the king's wives in childbirth, priests, servants, and slaves.

In other days courtiers were expected to maintain bachelor quarters while in attendance on the king. Youthful heralds and messengers could not marry in any case until the king provided wives for them. Older councilors either commuted to home compounds or took periodic furloughs. Unauthorized males did not often live in the court of the king of Bangangte. Even the royal sons were seldom to be seen. They were usually sent elsewhere for rearing and for safety's sake as well. Besides, the king was usually nervous lest they become too popular and hatch revolt. Sometimes the king sent his boys to a royal neighbor for upbringing, sometimes to his own mother's brother. This special uncle, always a favorite, was nearly always treated to whatever difficult responsibilities the king wanted to delegate.

Tiny though the chiefdoms are, a Bamileke ruler's goings and comings are still attended by pomp and ceremony. At special club meetings and dances he appears in garments handed down from his ancestors and hallowed with age and divinity. Sometimes he wears leopard skins. These animals are sacred to royalty. The hunter who bags one must take it at once to the capital. Pythons belong to the king, too. And it is whispered that the king can assume the living shape of these fearsome creatures—leopards and pythons—and in their coats of skin wander at will through the bush.

Other men, too, are believed to possess the power of transformation. But they do not use it as the king does—for fun, as an escape from the burdens of rule. They use their power for evil. Who these animal-men are nobody knows or wants to tell, though of course they suspect this one or that one and quake with fear.

In the Bamileke world of clubs even evil is organized, and the animal-men are just as much joiners as the civic-minded clubmen they mean to harm. A man inherits from his father the right to

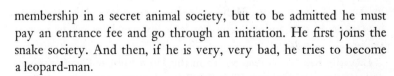

membership in a secret animal society, but to be admitted he must pay an entrance fee and go through an initiation. He first joins the snake society. And then, if he is very, very bad, he tries to become a leopard-man.

The young hopeful is not admitted to this club just because he wants to join or can afford the fee. He must first *prove* his talent for evil, and he does this by murder. Not any murder, if you please. No passing stranger and not necessarily a hated enemy. The victim must be the applicant's wife, his first wife preferably, or else his eldest daughter. Once the deed is done, he can continue unhindered on his wicked way, turning into a leopard whenever he wants, and ambushing unwary strays in the forest. To help him in his career there soon appears (or so it is believed) a real, live leopard who is his familiar (like the witch's black cat) and who carries out his commands.

Imagination, you will say. Real leopards, yes. Were-leopards, leopard-men, no. It is true, of course, that there were until recently (and perhaps there still are) plenty of real leopards in Cameroon. And there have been many deaths—not only in Cameroon, but throughout West Africa and into the Congo—caused by long claws and sharp teeth. But not all those fatal claws and teeth have belonged to the cat family. Now and again colonial police have captured the murderers: men dressed in leopard skins, armed with talons made of iron and carrying wooden tools with which they could imitate the footprints of leopards.

Why such secret societies were ever formed nobody really knows. Some say they came into being long ago when women were bossier and more important than nowadays. Joining a secret society was one way for a man to even the score. Others say the secret clubs were nationalistic in character, meant to protect the social order and punish those who tried to change it or do it harm. Still others see the secret societies as opposition to the king. Perhaps it is safest to think of them—as the Cameroons people themselves often do—as havens for criminals, for the antisocial individual, or (we might add) for madmen. No clucks of disapproval, please. Societies for evil are not, after all, entirely unknown elsewhere in the world. In Sicily and in America there is the Mafia, as evil as any society the Bamileke have ever devised and as secret—at least, its members *try* to keep it secret.

Like the Kikuyu, however, we in the West hunt out our criminals and madmen if we can. The Bamileke, left to their own devices, put their faith (characteristically) in yet another club—and another animal club at that. It is a club for good, and its members are chimpanzee-men. Now real chimpanzees are long gone in Bamileke country, but there are plenty of baboons around, and they serve as substitutes for the real thing, giving the chimpanzee-men "mascots" and animal brothers-in-arms. The chimpanzee-men pit their primate strength against the leopard-men's feline strength, not in actual combat, but in moral duels. The chimpanzee-men, and they alone, can uncover the evil ones, exposing them to the public view and public scorn. With exposure comes defeat, a withdrawal of evil power, a loss of magic, the hidden, animal magic of the dark forests. Not alone do the Bamileke face terror. They fight fire with fire. And club with club.

Bamilekeland changes now with every passing day, growing ever more surely absorbed into independent Cameroon. There are national soldiers and national police to protect the people from leopard-men, and modern knowledge challenges the benevolent power of the chimpanzee-men. Bamileke chiefs now meet with their colleagues in regional councils, councils which are very like small Houses of Lords and just about as impotent. But when voting time rolls around, then the chiefs are courted and flattered by all the new politicians of the capital. For as the chiefs go, so goes an election. Among his own people, the chief, the vest-pocket king, is still considered more than a little bit divine. And he means to stay.

Most Africans learned about the outside world in Arabic. The Arabs came early to Africa. They saw, and they remained. They also adapted. And after the seventh century, when they espoused Islam, they did even better in their new land. For Islam was attractive to many Africans. It was neither complicated nor especially demanding. It did not interfere overly with local customs. The African family with its many wives would have been thoroughly approved by the Prophet. Arabs were greedy, often cruel, but they were never snobbish. No wonder that Islam spread rapidly all across North Africa and down to the jungle's edge, and with it Arab ways and Arab ideals. The old patterns shifted and changed. How much they changed and how permanently is something else again.

Part V

THE ARABS IN AFRICA

East Africa and the Ocean Trade

15. Arabs in East Africa
Sultans, Spices, and Slaves

It is romantic to think of Africa as a forgotten land, a land un-traveled and very largely unknown. Romantic, perhaps, but not quite correct. Not, certainly, for the long eastern coast. As far back as the archaeological records go and for nearly as long as men have had boats, the African east coast has been known to traders, and known well.

The Red Sea has never presented much of an obstacle to travel. Bab al Mandab, the strait between Africa and Arabia, is little more than twenty-five miles across, a mere hop and skip for any vessel, however leaky. Even the Indian Ocean, for all its width and wild-ness, carried its share of commercial traffic. It was the peculiar nature of the winds in this part of the world that emboldened travelers to set sail. Because of these winds (called, appropriately enough, the trade winds), an Indian merchant could take ship any time between De-cember and February, certain of being wafted westward in plenty of time to sell his goods and catch the return winds home again in April.

The peoples of Africa's east coast bear witness in their faces and customs and tongues to all the many traveling salesmen who came to do a little business and settled down to stay. Before the Christian Era began, Malaysians came in great outriggers bringing root crops and bananas, then moved down the coast to Madagascar, where they made a permanent home. Persians came and Indian traders, whose descendants (or modern compatriots) are there still, dominating small business ventures all up and down the coast. And always there have been the Arabs, easing their triangular-sailed dhows into every port of call.

It is as the land of Punt that East Africa first appears in the annals of trade. Egyptians had long prized the perfumed myrrh trees that grew in "god's land," as Queen Hatshepsut called Punt (she never got there in person, it must be said). During her reign—1486–1468 B.C.—an expedition was sent to collect myrrh trees along with numerous other wonders, and the voyagers returned to write about the sights they had seen. One in particular impressed an artist, who recaptured in stone the enormously fat queen of Punt, hostess to the Egyptian expedition. Just where Punt is no one knows for sure. Somewhere along the coast of what is now Somalia, most people think.

Across the sea from Somalia lay Arabia Felix—Arabia the Happy—so called because its coast line had rather more water and fertile soil than the arid rest of the peninsula. Prosperous states were in existence there probably before 1000 B.C. An inscription made by Sargon II the Assyrian in 715 B.C., which details the tribute paid him by an Arabian queen, mentions gold and spices. It also mentions slaves. These must have come from the coast of Africa, where busy Arabian merchants were by then already settled. Some had even moved into the highlands of Ethiopia, where their inscriptions (dated to these times) have been discovered. Descendants of these early immigrants, along with Cushite natives, were later to found the Kingdom of Axum, which in 350 A.D. destroyed Meroe on the Nile. Meroe—last gasp of ancient Egypt. Soon after that Axum turned Christian and embarked on a modest expansion back into Arabia, whence its people had originally come. Prosperity was not to outlast the short-lived conquests in Arabia. After 600 A.D. or so, Christian Axum was imprisoned in its mountain fastnesses, surrounded by a sea of Islamic converts. There, long cut off from the Christian world, it maintained its character, its ancient language, its religion, and its land, which we know today as modern Ethiopia.

As for the coastal region, seven hundred years were to elapse between those first tantalizing references to Arab-African trade and later appearances in the records. In 80 A.D. or thereabouts a Greek shipmaster from Berenike on the Red Sea wrote a book for his fellow sailors. A sort of combination sailing manual and travelogue, it was, describing ports and people, the perils of navigation, and the trade goods to be found around the shores of the Indian Ocean. Africa he called "The Continent of Azania." He cited trading town after trading town, all the way down the coast line to what is now Dar-es-Salaam in Tanzania. Each, he said, was inhabited by "tall men," and each was ruled by its own chief. Were these tall men black or white; relatives of the many mixed people of the Horn or Nilotes from the interior? He did not say. He mentioned only that their language was spoken by the Arabian merchants resident in the ports. What that language was we cannot learn from him.

He did say, however, that most of the coastal towns were under the overlordship of Ausan, once a state in southern Arabia. The Ausanian merchants exported ivory and rhinoceros horn and slaves, the area near Ras Hafun (a promontory on the tip of the Horn) being especially noted for "slaves of the better sort."

There is simply no telling how long this traffic in human misery had been turning profits for enterprising traders. From the time of Egypt's pyramid building, at the very least, though records are not explicit until later times. Slaving continued to be profitable right into the twentieth century. For all Africa's gold, her ivory, her exotic animals, her jewels, it was her people who became Africa's principal export. In the last two or three centuries alone perhaps fifty million of them have been torn from their homes to live out their lives on other shores. Surely double that number died in transit. And double again the number killed in trying to defend their villages from attacking raiders. Enough, all told, to depopulate whole regions. Enough to retard natural development and stifle native invention. But who in the business thought much about that? Slaves, after all, were not supposed to have ordinary human feelings. A Chinese merchant of the thirteenth century, writing about slaves from Madagascar, reflected this sort of wishful thinking. Black men far from home, he observed, did not grieve for their kinfolk, were perfectly content in their new surroundings.

The fact is that slavery has always been—until comparatively recent times—an accepted institution throughout the world. Slavery upheld the economies of Greece and Rome as well as that of the American antebellum south. It was practiced among Africans themselves. And when the outside world arrived with its insistent demands for slaves, many an African chief or king was glad enough to sell his own subjects. The necessity of seeing people as people and not as things has only recently begun to be recognized among human beings everywhere. And about time, too.

Arab dhows carried slaves from Africa's east coast across the Red Sea and the Indian Ocean to places as far away as Persia. Even China was not overlooked. Arab merchants, it is true, never developed the sort of mass processing and mass transportation boasted by other slave-trading nations—Portugal, Spain, Holland, England, and the United States, among others—whose ships plied Africa's west coast for the most part. But Arabs were in the trade longest, long before Europeans discovered Africa's human "commodity," and long after.

Sometime in the early centuries of the Christian Era, Bantu peoples from the forest began to appear along the coastal fringes, and by the seventh century Arabs everywhere had accepted Islam. These two events produced in East Africa a hybrid people speaking a hybrid language, a people Moslem in religion and African in character. The people were called Swahili, a word whose root comes from the Arabic *sahil*, or "coast." So they were simply people of the coast: some purely African, some nearly Arab, and all the mixtures in between; freed Arab slaves, tribal groups, and townsmen who had lost their tribal identities and become wise in the ways of commerce. Their language is called Swahili, too. A Bantu language with a strong Arabic infusion, it has become the trade language for most of East Africa.

Scholars and travelers of the Moslem world were already touring

Africa by the tenth century A.D. In 930 or so one Al Mas'udi was writing about the coast of Zinj—"land of the blacks." He spoke of the city of Sofala, already rich in gold from the inland mines of Monomatapa. Sofala, he said, was ruled by an elected king paramount over all the other trading cities of the coast and powerful enough to field 300,000 men in battle. And yet he ruled with justice or he ruled not at all, said Al Mas'udi, for unjust kings were killed. The native language, he said, was spoken with great elegance by professional orators and also by quite ordinary folk. And though the people had not yet been converted to Islam, the ruling family were properly Moslem, having come originally from the north part of the coastline. There was a good deal of intermarriage among Swahili royal houses. Some writers have called the coastal collection of trading cities—each with its local royalty—an empire, the Empire of Zinj.

Chinese writings of Al Mas'udi's time and earlier mention the island of Zanzibar and its trade in ivory and gold; Madagascar and its trade in slaves. Other records take note of Mombasa, Kilwa, Mogadishu, and the island of Pemba. In the 1300s the irrepressible Ibn Battuta wrote of the beauty of Kilwa and of its sophisticated people, mostly black, he said, scarred with tribal markings. In some of the coastal cities Swahili literature was already being produced—chronicles and poetry of a high order—most of which has been lost. Later records made by the incoming Portuguese expressed amazement at the splendor of the "Moorish" cities, the majesty of the Moorish kings, and the beauty of the Moorish women—gorgeously dressed in silks and jewels, their skins tawny or black. ("Moorish" was, roughly, the Portuguese equivalent of "Swahili.") Mention was also made of the variety of languages spoken along the coast, of the richness of the trade—the ships, the merchants, the exotic and beautiful wares sent eastward over the sea—and the slaves.

The city people of the coast seem to have been in almost constant conflict with the tribes of the interior and made slaves of whatever captives they could take or exact in tribute. Now and then the inlanders took their revenge, massing in hordes and overrunning the cities of the coast.

More recent writings tell us about Swahili people somewhat past their prime. W. H. Ingrams, a British observer, lived on Zanzibar from 1919 to 1927 and recorded the history of the island and its people. For a long time, he tells us, the Hadimu—the conglomerate Swahili "tribe" of Zanzibar—had been ruled by native dynasties. These somehow managed to survive the occupations of foreigner overlords who arrived and departed with the regularity of clockwork. There were the Persians, the memory of their visit preserved in the Hadimu royal clan name, Shiraz, an echo of the Persian word for prince. The Malays came, too, their memory not a pleasant one. There were many Arabs and Indians, sundry Greeks, and goodness knows who else besides. A regular potpourri, it would seem, judging by the cultural relics that remain.

In 1503 the Portuguese sailed into Zanzibar harbor. They had first appeared along the Zinj coast six years earlier. They were in search of the gold, the slaves, the precious things they had heard of half a world away, and they did not intend to leave one harbor unvisited, one stone unturned. Quickly they subjugated Zanzibar and the neighboring islands of Pemba and Tumbatu. A century and a half they stayed, only to be ousted and replaced by the Arabs of Oman. The final sea battle was fought just off Zanzibar, and the Omanis then moved in to enjoy the fruits of victory.

They did not then occupy neighboring Pemba but many years later received a hospitable invitation to do so. The Swahili Pemba wanted to depose an unpopular local dynasty and applied to the Oman sultan for help. He was only too glad to oblige. The wily Pemba chiefs, however, insisted on drawing up a treaty in which the sultan had to agree to certain conditions of faith and good treatment of his future subjects. All parties then "exchanged blood" in the old-fashioned African way to make the pact truly binding. The Oman-Pemba treaty served its purpose, apparently, for the people of Pemba were not deprived of their lands or enslaved. Neither were the treatyless Hadimu of Zanzibar. Their name means "servant" or "serf," but indications are that they remained as they had always been, free men. Perhaps no longer in the upper levels of society, but free to keep to their ancient customs, free to revere (though no longer to obey) their ancient line of kings.

Al Mas'udi said all the Swahili people of Zinj called their kings *waklimi*, which many authorities think a misreading of *wafalme*, the Bantu name for kings, the singular being *mfalme*. This is close to what the Hadimu first called their own rulers. Later the title was changed to *mweny mkuu*, "the great owner." Even this recalls other royal titles to be heard in the continent's interior, far from Zinj: *mwana matapa* (Monomatapa) of Zimbabwe, *mwata yamvo* of the Lunda people, *umwani* of the Burundi. Like all African kings, the Hadimu ruler was something special, even sacred to his people, who came into his presence on their knees. Like them all, he received taxes and tribute and was assisted by a complicated officialdom. He had his own treasured heirlooms, and by his side were powerful royal women, who could and sometimes did rule. History mentions for the year 1653 one Mwana Mwema, a queen of Zanzibar with a traditional name, and later, one Fatima. Each married an Arab and converted to Islam, but neither was Arabian in outlook. Islamic rule forbids women to leave their houses unnecessarily, much less rule a world of men. Not so for the royal house of Zanzibar.

After Sultan Said came to settle in Zanzibar as overlord, the native rulers were obliged to make way, to busy themselves with minor local problems and leave the ruling to Said. Even so, the old royalty became something of a thorn in Said's flesh. Once, so the story goes, Said quarreled with the local ruler and banished him from the island. Not a drop of rain fell until, in desperation, Said brought the "owner" back again. The last Mweny Mkuu died in his palace in 1865 and a successor was never appointed, though, says Ingrams, the Hadimu still do reverence to his heirs.

There were, in Ingrams's time, several native towns and many villages in addition to the sultan's residence, which was the capital. Some Hadimu townsmen were artisans, traders, porters at the docks, sailors, smiths. Most others were small farmers or worked for wealthy Arab planters and were thus at some remove from city ways. All, however, faithfully sent their children to school to learn the Koran. Very often the teacher himself did not understand Arabic and so the lessons were recited by sound and rote and without real comprehension. Allah of the Koran was honored and prayed to, but in keeping with the typically African concept, he was thought to be far away, remote from human concerns. Much nearer were the spirits of rain and thunder, the spirits of the dead, the spirits of nature and of spite, the spirits which possessed a man and made him ill or raving. These were called djinns in deference to the Arabic point of view. To combat the spirits were "doctors" whose formulae of exorcism sound something like Alice's " 'twas brillig and the slithy toves . . ." except with a very Arabic ring. One, to quote Ingrams, went like this:

> O Sultan Koran, come to us. O Sultan, Sultan, pat me. Where are you, Sultan? You are one of the prophets of Solomon, son of David, the prophet, together with your following of djinns, born from the hottest water. . . .

Magic was just as popular in Zanzibar as it was (and is) on the coast or in the interior, and sorcerers, the purveyors of magic, were feared as much. On Zanzibar, however, they were organized in guilds with quite up-to-date methods and techniques. They operated the same kind of protection racket once popular among hoodlums and toughs in the United States. Ingrams, who attended in disguise certain forbidden rites, wrote that when a rich man fell ill, the sorcerers demanded money to insure his recovery. If he refused, they gathered outside his house, dancing and singing and drumming down his death upon him. In an agony of fear, he usually paid up promptly.

It was in 1840 that Seyyid Said, sultan of Oman and absentee overlord of Zanzibar, decided to move his capital. Worn out by palace intrigue, by predatory neighbors, by the power politics of the West, he longed for a peaceful haven. Zanzibar seemed to be just tailormade to suit his needs. It was, moreover, lush and green, a veritable paradise to eyes long accustomed to the arid wastes and incessant glare of Oman. Said brought with him an understanding of intrigue and a considerable talent for business. In Zanzibar he became a

despot—though a benevolent one—and in despotic fashion he commanded the landowners, large and small, to concentrate on a new crop.

All the world at that time relished the taste and the fragrance of cloves. But cloves would not grow just anywhere, and their places of habitation were all too few to suit the market demand. Sultan Said discovered that cloves would grow on Zanzibar. And grow they did, to the exclusion of almost everything else. Even today Zanzibar is the chief supplier of this perfumed commodity. And all the time Sultan Said took his cut and grew rich in the spice trade.

The slave trade made him richer still. And being nothing if not a superb organizer, he so arranged matters as to insure an uninterrupted supply of raw material. Until Said's day, slavers had depended on the natives of the interior to bring their own people to market. They had depended on them to do the dirty work of attacking villages and grabbing captives. With Arab guns warrior people like the Bemba were able to move ever farther afield, raiding their neighbors ceaselessly. The whole of the interior, in fact, was in almost constant turmoil due to the demands of the coastal slavers. This system of supply was too undependable to suit Said. Much better, he thought, to eliminate the middle man. And so he encouraged merchants to organize their own expeditions into the interior. In this he was ably assisted by the notorious Swahili slaver, Tippu Tib.

Arab and Swahili and Indian trading posts soon appeared in the lake region, where they were found by English explorers intent on discovering the source of the Nile. As the supply dwindled, slave caravans traveled farther still. Sometimes slaves came all the way from the west, having traveled from one depot to another and through a succession of slave drivers to arrive at last (if they survived the journey) in the great market of Zanzibar.

Here they were bought and packed, layer by layer, in the cramped holds of slave ships from practically everywhere. England was the first of the great Western nations to become conscience-stricken, ban the trade, and bring pressure to bear on African rulers to do the same. With the loss of colonial possessions in the New World, other nations followed suit. Finally the trade in human cargoes was outlawed everywhere.

But though the slave trade was abolished, slavery was not. Not everywhere. London's Anti-Slavery Society says it can still be found in many parts of Africa. Travelers bring back similar reports. And now and again there are newspaper accounts of slave labor's flourishing in some out of the way place. It must be remembered that slavery in many parts of Africa was hallowed by local custom. It was also sanctioned by the Koran. Slavery in Arabia continued to be legal

until 1962. Hard to come by and expensive to keep, slaves had long since become status symbols for the wealthy there—much as large cars and fur coats are to the American. As an institution, slavery, old-fashioned slavery, is on the way to extinction. But as long as people anywhere can use others—can force their labor, limit their freedom, command their skill—then we are not done with it yet. To mankind's shame and sorrow.

16. Arabs in North Africa
Jihad

The Arabs came early to East Africa, and in the beginning, at least, they came in peace. They arrived in North Africa at a later date. And they came with the sword—the Sword of Islam.

Riding the crest of a successful sweep through Arabia, a Moslem army took Egypt in 640 A.D. and by 681 had rolled over the North African coastal strip all the way to the Atlantic. They found in their path the farms and cities of a mixed folk who reflected in their faces and customs and languages the imprint of countless foreign settlers: Greek, Carthaginian, Roman, Byzantine, the Germanic Vandal. In the hills, untouched by the waves of immigrants that had spread across the coastal plains, were native farmers whose ancestors had doubtless been responsible for some of the ancient rock paintings and engravings still to be seen in the Atlas Mountains or on Saharan cliff faces. Egyptians had long known these people west of the Nile, spoke a similar language, had adopted many of their ways. Egyptian Pharaohs had married their princesses, Egyptian armies had fought their warriors, and Egyptian traders had brought them goods for time out of mind. In Egypt the westerners were called the People of Put. The Romans called them Libyans. The Arabs, newly come to the land, called them the Berbers—a corruption of the Greek term for barbarian, a person who says "bar-bar-bar," all innocent of proper speech. Proper speech was, to the self-centered Greeks, their own language, of course.

Ancient Kingdoms of West Africa

In the desert, behind the coastal hills, the Arabs found people of another sort. They were camel herdsmen, for the most part, and warriors, always on the move, always a threat to the unwary traveler. Some of these nomads spoke a Berber tongue, and (contrary to Arab custom) believed in veiling a warrior's face to his eyes while permitting women to go about with faces brazenly uncovered for all to see. These veiled men were the Tuareg, Caucasoid in race. Other nomads, like the Teda, were Negroid—fiercer, some thought, than even the Tuareg and speaking a quite different language. Both sorts of nomads had long controlled the major caravan routes of the Sahara, carrying goods themselves or demanding toll payment from others. Stones along the old oasis paths from Egypt have long since been polished smooth by the feet of traders and their patient donkeys and oxen. After the introduction of camels during Roman times (around 45 B.C.), the nomads had ranged ever more widely and to more fearsome effect. Horses had been known and prized since ancient times —possibly before they had been introduced into Egypt—but these beautiful animals were hard to keep in the desert. The open terrain below the desert—Beled es-Sudan, "Land of the Black," as the Arabs called it—was a more congenial home for horses.

The nomad groups were based on oasis farms where their Negro serfs raised grain and dates for their use. It is likely that these serfs had been where they were (and are still) ever since the great drying-up had trapped them in their little islands of fertility—relics of a time when the Sahara had been all green and giving and had lured farmers up from the south. The nomads were dependent on towns, too—oasis towns or those on the desert's edge—where their merchant cousins sold the merchandise they carried. It was salt and luxuries that the nomads took to the south, and from the south they brought back slaves and ivory and gold.

This precious merchandise, so the Arabs heard, originated in cities just below the desert's edge—rich cities in rich kingdoms where gold was so common as to be used like iron in the ordinary business of life. And it came, so the stories ran, from an inexhaustible source— from bush mines whose workers traded their metal for salt, never showing themselves, but hiding shyly in the woods while the transaction took place. Such stories had been rife since Carthaginian times.

The Arabs longed to get at both the rich cities and the rich source. And about 735, on the strength of the stories, they sent a raiding party into the desert. Miraculously the raiders won their way to legendary Ghana and to its capital city. But the young bandits never found the source of the gold. In spite of fire and sword, resolutely applied, no one was willing to divulge the secret. (It is a secret still.) The Arab warriors had not counted on that. They had to struggle home, the few that survived, not quite empty-handed, but feeling dazed and cheated all the same. And the people of Ghana, when Ibn Haukel visited them some years later, were as prosperous as ever and, quite without rancor, allowed Moslem traders to build the mercantile city of Koumbi nearby. El Bekri, a Moslem traveler, visited it sometime during the eleventh century and recorded his impressions.

Something else the invading Arabs had not counted on in North Africa was the fierce opposition of its people. Three times the Berbers —townsmen and nomads alike—combined to throw the invaders out, back to their base in Egypt. Undiscouraged, the Arabs always returned, picking up converts to Islam here and there among the Berbers and getting these into uniform until they had a big enough army to invade Spain, where they had better luck at pacification than they had had on the opposite shore. North Africa was not, in fact, thoroughly Islamized until the eleventh century, when hordes of Bedouin Arabs invaded, and moving out into the desert, challenged the Tuareg on their home grounds.

Arabs in Africa grew less and less interested in spreading the faith and more and more interested in grazing grounds or profit. Such lukewarm evangelism attracted only lukewarm converts. Everywhere could be seen an Islamic veneer while life beneath the surface remained true to its old ways. It took a native saint to rouse the Tuareg and even he managed more by the sword than by any real upsurge of religious enthusiasm.

His name was Ibn Yacin and he was from the caravan town of Sijilmassa. So irritated was he by the religious ignorance and indif-

ference around him that he went from tribe to tribe pleading, exhorting, teaching, reproving, setting examples and citing the Koran, and finally—with an army at his back—demanding. After this came followers. He called them Marabouts, which meant simply holy men. To the rest of the world they would be known as the Almoravids. This army of revival split in two. One half moved victoriously into Moslem Spain, and the other turned against old Ghana. This was pure pleasure for the Tuareg, who had raided and harried the cities along the desert's fringe for as long as anybody could remember. They were released to pillage and plunder as they would and given a blessing to boot, for Ghana's people held stubbornly to the old gods. And in 1062 Ghana's capital city fell to rise no more.

The Almoravid empire, north and south, did not long survive the conquest. After the death of Abu Bekr, the commanding general in the south, the tribes withdrew one by one, back into the desert and back to older, more congenial ways of life.

The Tuareg today are much as they have always been. Pastoral

nomads tend to be a conservative lot, inordinately proud of themselves and their style of life, loathe to change. And the Tuareg are
no exception. They have been raiders, traders, herdsmen, and land-
lords as far back as the written records go. And they have only recently been persuaded (by French money and French arms) to give
up the raiding part. So reports Lloyd Cabot Briggs, an American
anthropologist who spent several years during the late 1940s, early
1950s with the Tuareg tribes of the Ahaggar mountains and with
other peoples of the Sahara.

Though the Tuareg are now inhabitants of the deep desert, they
may not always have been so. Henri Lhote suggests that they may be
descendants of the Garamantes, powerful charioteers, raiders, and
traders once based in the Fezzan, now part of modern Libya. The
ancient Greek historian Herodotus knew of the Garamantes, of their
cattle, which had to graze backward lest the curving horns stick in
the ground, of their chariots, in which they hunted cave-dwelling
"Ethiopians," (in those days, the term for any dark-skinned African). The Romans knew the Garamantes, too, for they gave trouble
aplenty until quelled at last by Roman legions on forced march into
the desert. Did the Garamantes retreat, after this turn of events, to
more remote strongholds? E. W. Bovill, the historian of the Sahara,
suggests there may be no connection with the Garamantes. Some
Tuareg tribes, he thinks, may already have been well established by
100 A.D. in home ranges near their present ones. The Tuareg themselves claim to be descended from Tin Hinan, a noble lady of
Morocco who crossed the desert on a white camel sometime in the
fourth century A.D. They still point out her tomb, a little stone building in the desert mountains of Ahaggar, now part of modern Algeria.

At least one thing about the Tuareg is clear. The addition of
turban and face cloth to Tuareg dress is a recent innovation, as in-
novations go. It is not mentioned in the old historical records until
the time of the Arab invasion. Tuareg men today say the face cover-
ings are "proper" and "comfortable." And they are worn at all
times, night or day. Even food is deftly maneuvered so as to keep
the mouth always under wraps. Some writers have called the practice

a very sensible precaution in view of the scorching sun and sand. Others insist it is a matter of high style, pure and simple. Perhaps one might read a clue into the fact that a Tuareg gentleman always adjusts his veiling with special care when in the presence of his social superiors. It is considered unthinkably shocking ever to reveal one's mouth (and thus one's expressions, one's feelings?) to anyone —above all to one's betters. The veil gives a man lots of "cool"— psychologically if not actually.

And he needs it. For the Tuareg are very, very rank-conscious. Each tribe is divided into a number of clans, one or more aristocratic, the others vassal. It is the aristocrat's duty to scout out grazing grounds (and, in the old days, fat caravans) and to protect his dependents. It is the vassal's duty to mind the precious camel herds, to do battle on order, and to contribute to the support of the aristocracy. If exactions become too severe, however, a whole vassal clan might simply decamp, transferring its allegiance to a tribe whose aristocrats will be more moderate in their demands.

From the leading clan in each tribe the chief is chosen. Family heads in this clan choose him, and family heads in the other clans confirm his election. The most blue-blooded clan of all the tribes of a Tuareg confederation is privileged to provide the paramount chief —the *amenokal*, the "owner of the land." (There are three Tuareg confederations: the tribes of the Tassili-n-Ajjer, those of the Adrar-n-Ifoghas, and those of the Ahaggar.) The *amenokal*, too, must be confirmed in office, and he can be removed for bad behavior. His insignia of office is a special drum, *tobal*, just as it is the insignia of any self-respecting chief of any tribe in Africa.

The office of *amenokal* normally passes from a man to his eldest sister's eldest son, for the Tuareg inherit clan affiliation and rank through their mothers. And although a man lives with and inherits property from his father's people, he can improve his own social standing and insure high rank for his children only through a fortunate marriage. For this reason, perhaps, Tuareg women occupy quite exalted positions in the scheme of things. Though they have no voice in political affairs, they are by no means mere chattels as are their

Arab sisters. The Tuareg marry only one spouse, and they marry late—twenty-five or so for women, thirty for men—and a man has to work hard at the wooing. A woman expects and gets a long courtship embroidered with poetry and song, sighs and tears, brave deeds and gallant attentions. One is reminded of the "courtly love" of the European Middle Ages and wonders whether this charming custom began in Europe and traveled south or whether, after all, it was a Berber invention.

When a girl finally marries, she settles down to a life of aristocratic ease, if she is the daughter of a wealthy, high-ranking family. She retains full rights to her own property, and there are servants to take care of it and do the household chores as well. She is free to devote herself to arts and letters. It is she who transmits tribal lore and the unique Tuareg written script to her children. Perhaps she plays the Tuareg one-stringed violin and will become in time a famous lady musician, sought out for parties and other social occasions.

However the Tuareg came by their system of family arrangement —inheriting rank and titles through one's mother and property from one's father—it is certainly different from the custom of any other herding people anywhere. Very different from the Arab code, which honors the male principle in all things and consigns women to the lower social levels. Indeed many pious Moslems think it doubtful that women have souls.

The Tuareg are like other herding colleagues in one matter, however. They share a common disdain for the farming life or for manual labor of any sort—excepting the work with animals, which, after all, is more joy than work. Tuareg depend on their tenant farmers, serfs really, to produce the grain they eat (most often mixed with goat cheese and water in a thin gruel). Hereditary slaves labor in Tuareg salt mines and do the really dirty work around camp. Slavery is now supposed to be a thing of the past. Technically, slaves are free to leave their Tuareg masters. Most remain. Unaware of the law or unable to imagine any other sort of life, they continue to be servants who work for their keep and nothing more. The Tuareg often establish their "slaves" and tenants in large towns. Famous old Timbuctoo in modern Mali still has its quarter for Tuareg dependents, called Bela by the townsfolk. Not so long ago the Tuareg came as highwaymen to plunder and extort. Now they visit the outskirts of Timbuctoo to unload their caravans and collect farm goods and tribute from their people. But they disdain to enter the town. Indeed they cannot even speak the language of the townsfolk and rely on Bela spokesmen, who are bilingual, to do the necessary translating.

Timbuctoo began its rise to fame as a trading center not long after Ghana fell to the Almoravids. The vast trading empire and the shy, silent people who produced the gold were both in time inherited by Mali, the kingdom of the Mandingo people, by then enthusiastically converted to Islam. In 1324, Mansa Musa, the Mali king, made a pilgrimage to Mecca. So prodigal was his largesse, so dazzling his displays of gold and exotica from the Sudan, that the Moslem world began to think of Black Africa as Mansa Musa's realm entire.

Ibn Battuta visited the kingdom during the reign of Mansa Musa's successor and was greatly impressed by the safety and security that prevailed. Why, a man could go anywhere, he said, without fear of

brigands or thieves. He praised the quality of Mali justice ("The Negroes . . . have a greater abhorrence of injustice than any other people.") and the honesty of Mali officials, who scorned to exploit a stranger's ignorance. If a traveler died in the country, his wealth was held in trust until his kinsmen could claim it. The general nakedness, however, shocked Ibn Battuta's sensibilities. Other customs he found simply amusing. The habit of "dusting" in the king's presence was one such. Another was the appearance of poets costumed and masked as birds who reminded the king of his ancestors' meritorious deeds and exhorted him to be, like them, good and merciful. Ibn Battuta was told that this was an exceedingly old custom, but he found it outside the realm of his own experience and difficult to understand.

Mali territory had spread along with Mali's fame. Both Ghana and Tekrur had been annexed, and the Songhai kingdom—including its two chief river cities, Gao and Timbuctoo—had become a tributary. A century later the tributary swelled into the main stream, and Mali shrank to a brook. The Songhai king then made his own pilgrimage to Mecca, not, perhaps, with the sort of grandiose display Mansa Musa had put on, but in fine style none the less. King Askia of Songhai considered himself as devout a Moslem as the next man, and so he mounted a small holy war against the stubbornly pagan Mossi kingdom to the south and a larger *un*holy war against the Hausa city-states to the east, as Moslem as the people of his own realm. He also chastised the raiding Tuareg, keeping them well at bay and his country's roads and villages secure. But he did not trouble either to raid or to convert the simple, silent miners at the source of gold. Only they knew just where that source was, and heaven forbid that they should cut off the supply. As things were, the kingdom had gold in plenty, so much that the people hardly knew what to do with it and gladly squandered fortunes on slaves and horses, fine textiles from Europe, and, especially, salt.

It was during the Songhai ascendancy that Timbuctoo came into her own as a center of learning as well as trade. A fine Islamic university grew up there. Books came in the caravans from Barbary, and scholars of the Koran gathered to learn and expound holy writ and grow holy themselves in the process. For the Marabout is not one trained especially for the priestly profession. He is the scholar whose saintliness may be measured in exact proportion to his knowledge of the Law.

In 1590 this heady success came to an end. The Sudan was again invaded from across the desert by armies of the north. And again it was for the gold. The Moroccan ruler, or *shereef*, sent a picked troop—well trained and hard-bitten—out to take over Gao and Timbuctoo. And much to everyone's surprise, it did. Of course, the Moroccans had firearms, and the Songhai troops did not. Even so, the march over the desert was no breeze. Neither was the subsequent battle, few as the Moroccans were against thousands.

For all their success in arms, however, the raiders found little gold. Most of the Songhai people had fled with their movables. The source of the gold was never found, either, though an empire was wrecked in the search. The Moroccans stayed in Timbuctoo, defying their ruler in his faraway palace and running things to suit themselves. Most married local women, and their descendants—part Moroccan, part Songhai, and called *Arma*—are today Timbuctoo's ruling class, along with the merchant Arabs. The remaining inhabitants, says Horace Miner, an anthropologist who lived in Timbuctoo in the 1950s, have their own parts of the city. There is a quarter for Arma serfs, another for Arab slaves, still another for Tuareg slaves, the Bela. And all the residents of Timbuctoo—today as in medieval times —are as enthusiastically mercantile as ever—out to turn a dollar, honest or not. Let the buyer (or the country bumpkin) beware.

In spite of the bustle and hurry, however, Timbuctoo is today only a shrunken shadow of her former self. After the Moroccan conquest, most of the trade caravans moved eastward to the Hausa mud-walled towns. Kano was a leading Hausa city then. It is still a leading city in modern Nigeria.

Each of the Hausa towns had its own king and its own interests, and little thought was given to consolidating an empire or even a confederacy. In each there was a concentration of industrious farmers and peerless craftsmen. Indeed, the Hausa people claim their forebears were a tribe of smiths, which is a novel beginning indeed. Smiths elsewhere in the Sahara are very nearly outcasts—tolerated for their skill, feared for their magic powers, and loathed for their lack of social standing. Something of a necessary evil, you might say. The Hausa claim very ancient Tuareg ancestry as well, and since their language—now the trade language of West Africa—belongs to the Afro-Asiatic family, as does that of the Berbers, this may indeed be so.

The Hausa had been converts to Islam since the fourteenth century, and having borrowed the Arabic alphabet, had written down the remembered records of their past. These were the famous Kano Chronicles, which were later to be largely destroyed or lost during the last of the great Jihads, or Moslem crusades.

For this story a bit of backtracking is necessary—west in space and several centuries in time, back to when gold-rich Ghana flourished. It was not alone in fame. Along the Senegal River lay the Kingdom of Tekrur, whose people were as enthusiastic about trade as the Ghanaians. The people of Tekrur were, it would seem, herdsmen as well as traders. At least (the records are vague and thin) this was true for some. It was perhaps these people who came in time to be known variously as Fulani, Fulbe, Peul. As fanatical converts to Islam, they were to be among the final soldiers of Allah.

They have long been a people of mystery. Pale and proud, keepers of cattle in a dry, harsh land, they have excited scholarly imaginations since the first Western explorers made their acquaintance (sometimes at great personal peril). Both Gypsies and Saharan Jews have been suggested as possible ancestors. Professor Murdock believes the Fulani are descended from pastoral cattle-keeping Berbers who, pushed from behind by invading Arabs, settled among the people of Tekrur, intermarried with them, and persuaded some to the herding life. Dr. Lhote believes the Fulani to be the last remnants of the "Bovidians"—the cattle herders of the once-fertile Sahara whose beautiful paintings (we saw some in Chapter 1) grace the cliff walls

from Tassili to Tibesti. And there is much about the living Fulani—their faces, their dress, their coiffeur, their huts—which does recall the rock paintings. For a long while linguists insisted the Fulani language was utterly unique, or perhaps Berber in origin. It now turns out to be a bona fide member of the Congo-Kordofanian family, most closely resembling the languages spoken by other tribes living today near the Senegal River.

Whatever their origin, the Fulani began early to move. They spread from the Senegal all the way to Lake Chad—half a continent away. (Remember that the Sahara itself is larger than the continental United States.) The herding Fulani kept to themselves—like all nomads, haughty to a degree, descent-proud, occupation-proud, and loathe to change. They moved around settled areas. Farmers were happy to have them make camp nearby and even paid the nomads to tether their herds on harvested fields where the accumulated manure served to fertilize the soil.

The herding Fulani, for all their uppity ways, were neither businessmen nor political enthusiasts. They left such affairs in the hands of their kinsmen, men of the leading Fulani clans, who had become city slickers and devoted Moslems. After years of intermarriage with town belles along the line of march, they had come to be darker of hue than their brethren of the bush.

By the thirteenth century the Fulani—both town and bush varieties—had arrived in the Hausa states. Some moved still further on. Others stayed and, joined by more and more relatives, eventually became an important force in Hausaland. The town Fulani found their hosts regrettably lacking in religious zeal. Islam had been picked up by the Hausa only to be dropped like an old shoe, and this had happened a number of times since the original conversion. In addition, they unveiled their women, took to drumming whenever it suited them, and drank intoxicating liquors, all forbidden by the Koran. At last, in the early 1800s, a Fulani evangelist of the town, Usuman don Fodio by name, arose and called for a revival. The local Hausa ruler had the bad sense to impose persecutions, and like Mohammed before him, Usuman took flight. A multitude of the faithful flocked to his side, and he made of them an army. In the way of all zealots, he was passionately determined to make men good by force if not by persuasion.

The Hausa cities went down one by one. And still the Fulani rolled on into the pagan country around them. But Usuman's fanatical troops were barred from the east by the kingdoms of Bornu and Kanem, trading states like all the other kingdoms along the desert's edge. These remained steadfast until Turkish armies from the Nile, since the sixteenth century in control of Egypt, moved against them.

One Fulani army spawned another. The Fulani of Massina rose like their brothers in jihad and pressed what had once been Songhai cities and Songhai land. Timbuctoo was held in virtual siege, and the Tuareg and Arab chieftains bowed to yet another master.

The town Fulani of the Hausa states set up their capitals at Sokoto and Gwandu and, as emirs, took over the administration of city and countryside. The native Hausa simply carried on with crafts and farming and trade and the problems of city government. They were accustomed by now to foreign overlords.

The cattle Fulani remained as aloof as ever—considering themselves vastly superior to the land-bound Hausa among whom they moved and, secretly, superior even to the ruling Fulani of the towns. Whatever their personal attitude toward their urban cousins, this connection gave the cattle Fulani much importance in the eyes of local farmers, who appealed to them for protection. With added status and prosperity came the opportunity to acquire slaves who would free them from the despicable business of raising grain. With prosperity, too, came leisure. They began to study the Koran and take on scholarly airs.

Except for the fact that slaves are once again out, the cattle Fulani are—a hundred years and more later—unchanged still. Or so reports the British anthropologist C. Edward Hopen, who lived with cattle Fulani around Gwandu, Nigeria, from 1952 to 1955.

Cattle are still all to the Fulani: the means of marrying, of setting up a family, of achieving wealth and importance and even popularity. All conversation turns on cattle and the things that will harm the cattle: bad behavior (running around in town, for example), dry weather, scanty forage, taxes. For the cattle's well-being, nights are spent sleeping on the wet ground, always guarding, always worrying about the precious herds. "If the cattle die," say the Fulani, "we die." And a haunting look of fear—fear of change, fear of the unknown—fills their eyes.

Fulani live and travel in small family units—a man, his wife or wives (seldom more than two), his sons and unmarried daughters. The boys are economic assets. Long days at a time they are out in the bush alone with the cattle. Father sees to the fields—now an onerous necessity—or now and again relieves the boys on watch. But he keeps them unmarried as long as he can, for then they will take what cattle he gives and leave him. This is a cause of much conflict among herding families, but since family groups nearly always fall apart in this way, the father's efforts are understandable. Ahead of him is a bleak future. He will have to work and herd alone until his strength fails. Then must he go, a beggar, to his sons to be cared for grudgingly until his death.

The Fulani are staunch believers in masculine supremacy, but though men own the cattle, their women own the milk and can take it to market and sell it whenever they please. Men resent the women's frequent trips to town but can do little about it, for the money is needed at home. It will provide, at least, the fripperies women long for. The husband asks only that his wife return early enough to give him porridge without bugs. A return at dusk when the insects are out means a ruined meal and an irate husband.

Men and women talk little to one another. So little, in fact, that they very nearly speak different languages. Literally. The feminine dialect is distinct from the masculine one in which men grumble to each other about the women, their laziness, and their dreadful carryings-on. All of this is mostly hearsay, for it is considered unmanly among Fulani to be much in female company. Even when husband and wife are alone they studiously ignore one another—unless, of course, they are certain no one will notice and comment.

The preferred marriage partner for Fulani has always been a cousin—preferably a child of one of Father's brothers, but Mother's niece is all right, too. Perhaps childhood familiarity helps to ease the strain of conversational avoidance.

The husband is considered a guest in his wife's hut—a rough sort of dome, sometimes only a windbreak when traveling in the dry season. However simple, it is always very formally arranged. Huts face west with their entrances overlooking the cattle corral. On the right hand as one enters is the man's side of the house, his sleeping mat ready whenever he cares to occupy it. To the left is the woman's domain, which she occupies with her children. To the rear is a shelf on which are neatly arranged the simple collection of metal and wooden pots that represent a woman's whole trousseau, her housekeeping establishment. The groom's wedding gift buys them, but they are presented by the girl's mother only after the first baby has been born. Until then the young wife has had to cook with her mother-in-law. She goes to her mother's home for the birth. After a long stay there, she returns to her husband—a real married lady with her pots and pans and her baby to prove it. And as a family at last, the young couple take their herd and move away, on their own.

There have been no more jihads in the Sudan—not by the town Fulani, who were themselves already in decline before ever the British reached them in 1900, not by any other people. But Islam is still spreading. Perhaps this is because Islam arrived, not as an importation of alien white men, but as local property, taught and sometimes even imposed by black men. And there is more. Islam offers much and demands little in return. Under the new banner, old ways can go on without a break. Polygyny, for example, is a tenet of Islam as it is a custom among most of Africa's people. Reverence for ancestors and the belief in witchcraft continue in only slightly different guises. Burial customs and marriage customs and even systems of inheritance may move in their usual channels. For Islam is largely an unorganized faith, spurred by profound reverence for the Law and pride of origin. There are no hierarchies of priests to root out sin and transform local ways.

In pride of origin there is, however, a potent lure which African converts have not resisted. Rank and holiness, in Islamic society, are determined by descent. The closer one can come to the Prophet in one's genealogy, the greater one's position in the world. Failing the Prophet, one shoots for a regional saint. Failing a saint, there is always a local hero. Failing a hero, there are, for Africans, the Arabs to fall back on. Or, as a last resort, the Tuareg. And this is why, says Professor Greenberg, the family trees of so many Sudanic ruling houses start out with foreign founders and sometimes with Mecca as a country of origin. Westerners have taken this sort of ancestor-shopping with perfect seriousness, dutifully jotting down every princely foreign name they were given. And in the long run, the devout status-seeking served only to obscure the reconstruction of history, to lessen in Western minds the very real accomplishments of the high African states. Many scholars have liked to credit Arab influence or even Arab manipulation for the efficient administration of these states, for their complex courts, for their sophistication in trade, taxes, census, and worship—all certainly to be favorably compared with the achievements of any European monarchy of the

Middle Ages and even into the Renaissance. If not Arab-inspired, so the thinking has run, why then, these states must certainly have had a model at some time, from somewhere. Egypt, perhaps? Tuareg, perhaps? Tuareg, at least! Very few scholars have even considered the possibility of talents and achievements home-grown and home-developed. Talents for law, for organization, for politics.

And yet, the evidence points ever more certainly in that direction. Even among humble villagers this talent can be observed. And the kingdoms of the Sudan were in existence, some of them, long before the Arabs came. Perhaps before the Tuareg were more than an occasional irritation. There can be seen in these kingdoms a particular pattern. A pattern roughly cut long, long ago, perhaps when hunters, herders, and farmers from the north met and mingled with hunters, herders, and farmers from the south. A pattern cut from the life ways of many races, many cultures. An African pattern, brought to its highest expression in Egypt, but surely to be seen all across and up and down the face of the continent.

The pattern was not changed in its essential form by the coming of Islam. Only a hundred years ago did the pattern waver, for then the explorers from the West began to penetrate the interior. After them came the missionaries. And after the missionaries came the colonizers. And after the colonizers, the insistent demands of the twentieth century.

But that is a story for another book.

Epilogue

A Fable of Yesterday for Today

Books may come and books may go, but the storyteller is forever. He is as much a favorite among Africans who read as among those who do not. For he is newspaper, poet, critic, and seer all rolled into one. And though he slyly casts his tales with animal heroes, everybody knows exactly what and who he means.

"A story, a story!" the people cry whenever he walks abroad. "Let it go from you, let it come to us." And if he decides to oblige, the tale he tells might begin just so:

Once there was a land that was something like your land and something like my land but not altogether the same. Parts of it were green and steamy, and others were dry and hard, as poor as the others were rich.

In this land lived animals of all sizes and shapes and sorts. They lived together, each among his own kind, some in the rich places and some in the poor. The lions and the leopards and the rabbits each had a king and obeyed the laws he made for them. The leopards were afraid of their king because he would just as soon bite his own subjects as the animals that didn't belong to him at all. The lion king was feared by everyone in the land because he liked to lead his soldiers out to kill and conquer all around. But the king of the rabbits liked peace and order and fair treatment for his subjects. He preferred talking to fighting, and his people did, too. They got along nicely with the shy, simple wildebeests, who startled and fled at the slightest noise and whose main object in life was to keep out of harm's way. The rabbits also lived at peace with the turtles and baboons, who knew very well how to take care of themselves and were neither shy nor vainglorious but somewhere in between. They even put up with the greedy hyenas, who were cringing and savage by turns, out to get what they wanted and never mind how.

All the people of the land lived as they could and as they must. Some were kind and wise, as you have seen. Others were foolish and cruel, just the way folks are anywhere else in the great world. But none of the animals of this particular land knew very much about that, because they had never been away from home to find out. Neither did the inhabitants of other places know very much about them, because there were high mountains all around that barred the way in and the way out.

And then one day some elephants from the outside world got over the mountain, and after them came others and still others until they were in all the green places and all the dry places. They were everywhere. And nothing was ever quite the same again. The elephants were not only big and strong, but they also knew a lot of things the animals below the mountains had never heard of. They had mighty weapons besides.

The elephants looked at the creatures around them and said, "You are behind the times." And that was true enough.

"You are sick and poor," they added. And that was certainly true.

"You are uneducated." And the animals had to agree, for they were not educated. At least, they were not educated in the learning of the elephants.

"You are savage and have no government," the elephants said finally as the crushing verdict. Now this particular charge was not exactly true. For though some of the animals of the land did not have government—at least, not government of the sort the elephants were used to—there were others who did. But the elephants had weak eyesight—as all the world knows—and very often could not tell the difference.

So they set about putting things in order as they conceived order to be. They divided the land into what they called "countries." In these countries they lumped the creatures of big kingdoms and the shy creatures of the herds and the angry scavengers all together. And everyone had to obey the same laws whether they understood them or not. Sometimes mortal enemies were made to live side by side. But of course they could no longer fight because the elephants did not let them.

In time the elephants found the new responsibilities to be more than they had bargained for. What they gained in wealth never quite made up for what they had to spend to keep things going. Sometimes they managed to change matters to suit themselves, to educate the animals to modern ways. Sometimes they did not. But altogether it cost so much that when the animals began to grumble and push at them, and when the rest of the world put on long, disapproving faces, the elephants were glad to go.

After they left, the "countries" all gave themselves new names, but they tried to run things the way the elephants had done. Sometimes the elephants' way continued to work, and sometimes it did not. The lions and leopards soon remembered how much they had hated one another in the old days, and they fell to fighting again. Animals who had gone abroad to elephant country scorned the humble folks back at home and used their ignorance for personal gain. One after another, ambitious and sometimes greedy leaders rose in the various states and tried to be king. And one after another was hauled down again, and not so gently, either.

All the time the elephants sat on the surrounding mountain tops and groaned. "Just look," they complained, shaking their great heads, "just look how the animals are wrecking our good work, our effort, our care. What was ever the use of all the wealth and time we spent down there. They will never manage, never!"

And then one day, hearing the mournful conversation floating down the mountainside, a rabbit hopped up to the highest hill he could find and called up loudly, "Stop groaning, you elephants! We are doing the best we can down here. While you ruled us we forgot most of our old ways. And yet we never entirely learned to be like you, for we were never allowed to do that. What we are looking for now is something between our old ways and your new ones—something we can make truly our own.

"Even then you won't like us all, you know. We are not one creature, but many. We come in all sizes and shapes and dispositions. Some of us are kind and wise; some of us are cruel and foolish. Some of us will make a mark in the great world. Some of us will fail. And you must just make up your minds to that. After all, isn't that exactly the way of things among yourselves?"

"This," says the storyteller, "is my tale which I have told. If it be sweet, make it your own. If it is not sweet, give some away and let the rest come back to me."

BIBLIOGRAPHY

Bibliography

Titles marked with an asterisk are nontechnical in nature and will be of interest to the general reader.

GENERAL

Anderson, Edgar. *Plants, Men, and Life*. Little, 1952.

Bohannon, Paul. *Africa and Africans*. Natural History Press, 1964.

Fage, J. D., and Oliver, Roland. *A Short History of Africa*. Penguin Books, 1962.

Fortes, M., and Evans-Pritchard, E. E., eds. *African Political Systems*. International African Institute. Oxford, 1940.

Gluckman, Max. *Custom and Conflict in Africa*. Free Press, 1955.

——————. *Order and Rebellion in Tribal Africa*. Free Press, 1963.

Murdock, George Peter. *Africa: Its People and Their Culture History*. McGraw, 1959.

Ottenberg, Simon and Phoebe, eds. *Cultures and Societies of Africa*. Random House, 1960.

CHAPTER I

Alimen, Henriette. *The Prehistory of Africa*, trans. by A. H. Broderick. Hutchinson, 1957.

Clark, J. Desmond. *The Prehistory of Southern Africa*. Penguin Books, 1959.

——————. "Africa South of the Sahara," in Braidwood and Willey, eds., *Courses Toward Urban Life* (Viking Fund Publications in Anthropology, Aldine, 1962).

Cole, Sonia. *The Prehistory of East Africa*. Macmillan, 1963.

Coon, Carleton. *The Living Races of Man*. Knopf, 1965.

Dyer, Gurney W. *"Guelta of the Bleak Sahara," *Natural History Magazine*, November, 1965.

Garcia, L. P., and Perelló, E. R., eds. *Prehistoric Art of the Western Mediterranean and the Sahara*. Viking Fund Publications in Anthropology. Aldine, 1964.

Greenberg, Joseph H. *Studies in African Linguistic Classification*. Compass Publishing (Branford, Conn.), 1955.

——————————. "Africa as a Linguistic Area," in Bascom and Herskovits, eds., *Continuity and Change in African Cultures* (University of Chicago Press, 1959).

——————————. "The Languages of Africa," *International Journal of American Linguistics*, Vol. 29, No. 1 (January, 1963).

Howell, F. Clark, and Bourliere, Francois, eds. *African Ecology and Human Evolution*. Viking Fund Publications in Anthropology. Aldine, 1963.

Leakey, L. S. B., Tobias, P. V., and Napier, J. "A New Species of the Genus *Homo* from Olduvai Gorge," *Nature*, Vol. 202 (April, 1964).

Lhote, Henri. *The Search for the Tassili Frescoes*. Dutton, 1959.

——————. *"The Fertile Sahara," in Edward Bacon, ed., *Vanished Civilizations* (McGraw, 1963).

Stamp, L. Dudley. *Africa, A Study in Tropical Development*. Wiley, 1961.

CHAPTER 2

Arkell, A. J. *A History of the Sudan*. Oxford University Press, 1961.

——————. "The Iron Age in the Sudan," *Current Anthropology*, October, 1966.

Arkell, A. J., and Ucko, Peter J. "A Review of Predynastic Development in the Nile Valley," *Current Anthropology*, April, 1965.

Blanc, A. C. "Sur le Facteur Fondamental des Mouvements des Cultures Pre- et Protohistoriques en Afrique du Nord: La Fuite du Desert," in Garcia and Perelló, eds., *Prehistoric Art of the Western Mediterranean and the Sahara* (Viking Fund Publications in Anthropology, Aldine, 1964).

Breasted, James Henry. *A History of Egypt*. Scribner, 1905.

Donadoni, Sergio. "Remarks about Egyptian Connections of the Sahara

Rock Shelter Art," in *Prehistoric Art of the Western Mediterranean and the Sahara.*

Fairservis, Walter A., Jr., *The Ancient Kingdoms of the Nile.* Crowell, 1962.

Frankfort, Henri. *Kingship and the Gods.* University of Chicago Press, 1948.

Guggenheim, Hans. *"Smiths of the Sudan," *Natural History Magazine,* May, 1961.

Mori, F. "Some Aspects of the Rock Art of the Acacus (Fezzan Sahara) and Data Concerning It," in *Prehistoric Art of the Western Mediterranean and the Sahara.*

Wilson, John A. *The Culture of Ancient Egypt.* University of Chicago Press, 1963.

CHAPTER 3

Burton, Sir Richard F. *A Mission to Gelele, King of Dahomey.* Tylston & Edwards, 1893.

Clark, J. Desmond. "Africa South of the Sahara," in Braidwood and Willey, eds., *Courses Toward Urban Life* (Viking Fund Publications in Anthropology, Aldine, 1962).

Cordwell, Justine M. "African Art," in Bascom and Herskovits, eds., *Continuity and Change in African Cultures* (University of Chicago Press, 1959).

Davidson, Basil. *The African Past.* Atlantic, Little, Brown, 1964.

Forde, Daryll. "The Cultural Map of West Africa: Successive Adaptations to Tropical Forests and Grass Lands," in *Cultures and Societies of Africa* (Random House, 1960).

Fagg, Bernard. "The Nok Culture in Prehistory," *Journal of the Historical Society of Nigeria,* Vol. 1 (1959), pp. 288–93.

Greenberg, Joseph H. "The Negro Kingdoms of the Sudan," *Transactions of the New York Academy of Sciences,* Series 2, 11 (1949), pp. 126–35.

Herskovits, Melville J. *Dahomey: An Ancient West African Kingdom.* J. J. Augustin, 1938.

——————————. *The Myth of the Negro Past.* Beacon Press, 1958.

Mercier, P. "The Fon of Dahomey," in Daryll Forde, ed., *African Worlds* (International African Institute, Oxford, 1954).

Murdock, George Peter. *Africa: Its People and Their Culture History.* McGraw, 1959.

Parrinder, E. G. *The Story of Ketu*. Ibadan University Press (Nigeria), 1956.

Reference Note

The quotation on p. 62 is from Herskovits, *Dahomey, An Ancient West African Kingdom*, Vol. I, p. 68.

CHAPTER 4

Albert, Ethel M. "Women of Burundi: A Study of Social Values," in D. Paulme, ed., *Women of Tropical Africa* (University of California Press, 1963).

Beattie, John. *Bunyoro: An African Kingdom*. Holt, 1960.

Burton, Sir Richard F. *The Lake Regions of Central Africa*. Horizon Press, 1961.

Mair, Lucy. *Primitive Government*. Penguin Books, 1962.

Maquet, Jacques J. "The Kingdom of Ruanda," in Daryll Forde, ed., *African Worlds* (International African Institute, Oxford, 1954).

――――――――. *The Premise of Inequality in Ruanda*. International African Institute. Oxford, 1961.

Morris, H. R. *The Heroic Recitations of the Bahima of Ankole*. Oxford, 1964.

Oberg, K. "The Kingdom of Ankole in Uganda," in *African Political Systems* (International African Institute, Oxford, 1940).

Roscoe, John. *The Banyankole*. Cambridge University Press, 1923.

Stenning, J. D. "The Nyankole," in A. I. Richards, ed., *East African Chiefs* (Frederick A. Praeger, 1959).

Taylor, Brian K. "Nyankole," in *The Western Lacustrine Bantu*, Ethnographic Survey of Africa, Part XIII, East Central Africa. International African Institute (London), 1962.

CHAPTER 5

Gluckman, Max. "Kinship and Marriage Among the Lozi of Northern Rhodesia and the Zulu of Natal," in Radcliffe-Brown and Forde, eds., *African Systems of Kinship and Marriage* (International African Institute, Oxford, 1950).

――――――――. "The Lozi of Barotseland," in Colson and Gluckman, eds., *Seven Tribes of British Central Africa* (Oxford, 1951).

――――――――. "The Reasonable Man in Barotse Law," in *Order and*

Rebellion in Tribal Africa (Free Press, 1963).

_____. "Succession and Civil War Among the Bemba," *Order and Rebellion in Tribal Africa.*

Greenberg, Joseph H. *Studies in African Linguistic Classification.* Compass Publishing (Branford, Conn.), 1955.

Richards, Audry I. *Hunger and Work in a Savage Tribe.* Routledge, 1932.

_____. "Mother Right Among the Central Bantu," in Evans-Pritchard, Firth, Malinowski, *et al.*, eds., *Essays Presented to C. G. Seligman* (Kegan Paul, French, Trubner, 1934).

_____. "The Bemba of Northeast Rhodesia," in *African Political Systems* (International African Institute, Oxford, 1940).

_____. "Some Types of Family Structure Among the Central Bantu," in *African Systems of Kinship and Marriage.*

_____. "The Bemba of Northeast Rhodesia," in *Seven Tribes of British Central Africa.*

_____. "The Bemba, Their Country and Their Diet," in *Cultures and Societies of Africa* (Random House, 1960).

Torday, E. "The Influence of the Kingdom of Kongo in Central Africa," *Africa*, Vol. 1 (1928).

Reference Notes

The quotation on p. 93 is from Richards, "Mother Right Among the Central Bantu," p. 279.

The quotation on p. 102 is from Gluckman, *Order and Rebellion in Tribal Africa*, p. 188.

CHAPTER 6

Barker, Dudley. *Swaziland.* Her Majesty's Stationery Office (London), 1965.

Gluckman, Max. "The Kingdom of the Zulu," in *African Political Systems* (International African Institute, Oxford, 1940).

_____. "Kinship and Marriage Among the Lozi of Northern Rhodesia and the Zulu of Natal," in Radcliffe-Brown and Forde, eds., *African Systems of Kinship and Marriage* (International African Institute, Oxford, 1950).

_____. "Rituals of Rebellion in Southeast Africa," *Order and Rebellion in Tribal Africa* (Free Press, 1963).

Krige, Eileen Jensen. *The Social System of the Zulus*. Shuter & Shooter (Petermaritzburg), 1936.

Kuper, Hilda. *An African Aristocracy: Rank Among the Swazi*. International African Institute. Oxford, 1947.

_____. *The Swazi, A South African Kingdom*. Holt, Rinehart & Winston, 1963.

Reference Note

The quotation on p. 112 is from Kuper, *An African Aristocracy: Rank Among the Swazi*, pp. 204–5.

CHAPTER 7

Clark, J. Desmond. *The Prehistory of Southern Africa*. Penguin Books, 1959.

Cole, Sonia. *The Prehistory of East Africa*. Macmillan, 1963.

Guggenheim, Hans. *"Smiths of the Sudan," *Natural History Magazine*, May, 1961.

Haleman, J. F. "Some Shona Tribes of South Rhodesia," in Gluckman and Colson, eds., *Seven Tribes of British Central Africa* (Oxford, 1951).

Murdock, George Peter. *Africa: Its People and Their Culture History*. McGraw, 1959.

Rayner, William. *The Tribe and Its Successors*. Frederick A. Praeger, 1962.

Summers, Roger. "The Southern Rhodesian Iron Age," *Journal of African History*, Vol. II, No. 1 (1961).

_____. *"The Riddle of Zimbabwe," in Edward Bacon, ed., *Vanished Civilizations* (McGraw, 1963).

_____. "The Iron Age of Southern Rhodesia," *Current Anthropology*, October, 1966.

Theal, George McCall. *Records of Southeast Africa* (printed for the government of Cape Colony). Vols. I, II, VI (1898).

Wieschhoff, H. A. "The Zimbabwe-Monomatapa Culture in Southeast Africa," *General Series in Anthropology #8*. George Banta Publishing Company (Menasha, Wis.), 1941.

CHAPTER 8

Krige, E. J., and Krige, J. D. *The Realm of a Rain-Queen*. Oxford, 1943.

_____. "The Lovedu of the Transvaal," in Daryll

Forde, ed., *African Worlds* (International African Institute, Oxford, 1954).

CHAPTER 9

Pygmies

Turnbull, Colin M. "Initiation Among the Bambuti Pygmies of the Central Ituri," in *Cultures and Societies of Africa* (Random House, 1960).
——————. *"Children of the Forest," *Natural History Magazine*, August-September and October, 1960.
——————. *The Forest People*. Simon & Schuster, 1961.
——————. *"The Lesson of the Pygmies," *Scientific American*, January, 1963.
——————. "The Mbuti Pygmies: An Ethnographic Survey," *Anthropological Papers of the American Museum of Natural History*, Vol. 50, Part III (1965).

Bushmen

Clark, J. Desmond. *The Prehistory of Southern Africa*. Penguin Books, 1959.
Fourie, L. "The Bushman of Southwest Africa," in *Cultures and Societies of Africa*.
Schapera, I. *The Khoisan Peoples of South Africa*. Routledge & Kegan Paul, Ltd., 1930.
Thomas, Elizabeth Marshall. *The Harmless People*. Knopf, 1959.
——————. "Bushmen of the Kalahari," *National Geographic*, June, 1963.
Tobias, Phillip V. "On the Survival of the Bushman," *Africa*, Vol. 26 (1956).
——————. *"Physique of a Desert Folk," *Natural History Magazine*, February, 1961.
Van der Post, Laurens. *The Lost World of the Kalahari*. William Morrow & Company, 1961.

Reference Note

The quotation on p. 146, cited by Herskovits in *The Human Factor in Changing Africa* (Knopf, 1962), is from an article by the Rev. Canon Calloway which appeared in 1868 in the *Memoirs of the Folk Lore Society*.

CHAPTER 10

Amba

Taylor, Brian K. "Amba," in *The Western Lacustrine Bantu*, Ethnographic Survey of Africa, Part XIII, East Central Africa. International African Institute (London), 1962.

Winter, Edward H. "The Aboriginal Political Structure of Bwamba," in Middleton and Tait, eds., *Tribes Without Rulers* (Routledge & Kegan Paul, Ltd., 1958).

—————. *Beyond the Mountains of the Moon.* University of Illinois Press, 1959.

—————. "The Enemy Within: Amba Witchcraft and Sociological Theory," in Winter and Middleton, eds., *Witchcraft and Sorcery in East Africa* (Frederick A. Praeger, 1964).

Witchcraft and Sorcery

Gluckman, Max. *"The Logic in Witchcraft," *Custom and Conflict in Africa* (Free Press, 1955).

Nadel, S. F. "Witchcraft in Four African Societies: An Essay in Comparison," in *Cultures and Societies of Africa* (Random House, 1960).

Turner, Victor W. "Sorcery: Taxonomy versus Dynamics," *Africa*, Vol. 34 (1964).

Wilson, Monica. "Witch Beliefs and Social Structure," *American Journal of Sociology*, Vol. 56 (1951), pp. 307–13.

Winter, Edward H., and Middleton, John. Introduction to *Witchcraft and Sorcery in East Africa* (Frederick A. Praeger, 1964).

Tonga

Colson, Elizabeth. "The Plateau Tonga of Northern Rhodesia," in Colson and Gluckman, eds., *Seven Tribes of British Central Africa* (Oxford, 1951).

—————. *Social Organization of the Gwemke Tonga.* Manchester University Press, 1960

Fagan, Brian. "The Iron Age of Zambia," *Current Anthropology*, October, 1966. Includes a letter from Elizabeth Colson relating to antiquity of Tonga.

Scudder, Thayer. *"Environment and a Culture," *Natural History Magazine*, April and May, 1960.

CHAPTER 11

Nilotes

Butt, Audry. *The Nilotes of the Anglo-Egyptian Sudan and Uganda.* Ethnographic Survey of Africa. International African Institute (London), 1952.

Dyson-Hudson, Rada. **"Men, Women, and Work in a Pastoral Society," Natural History Magazine,* December, 1960.

_____. *"Marriage Economy: The Karamojong," *Natural History Magazine,* May, 1962.

Evans-Pritchard, E. E. *The Nuer.* Oxford, 1940.

_____. "The Nuer of the Southern Sudan," in *African Political Systems* (International African Institute, Oxford, 1940).

_____. A selection from "Nuer Religion," in Charles Leslie, ed., *The Anthropology of Folk Religion* (Random House, 1960).

Greenberg, Joseph H. *Studies in African Linguistic Classification.* Compass Publishing (Branford, Conn.), 1955.

Mair, Lucy. *Primitive Government.* Penguin Books, 1962.

Thomas, Elizabeth Marshall. **The Warrior Herdsmen.* Knopf, 1965.

Herero

Gibson, Gordon D. "Double Descent and Its Correlates Among the Herero of Ngamiland," *American Anthropologist,* Vol. 58 (1956), pp. 109–39.

Luttig, H. G. *The Religious System and Social Organization of the Herero.* Kemink En Zoon N.V. (Over Den Dom, Utrecht).

CHAPTER 12

Gluckman, Max. "The Magic of Despair," in *Order and Rebellion in Tribal Africa* (Free Press, 1963).

Kenyatta, Jomo. **Facing Mount Kenya.* Secker and Warburg, Ltd., 1938.

Leakey, L. S. B. *Mau Mau and the Kikuyu.* Methuen, 1955.

Prins, A. H. J. *East African Age-Class Systems.* J. B. Wolters-Groninger (Djakarta), 1953.

CHAPTER 13

Wilson, Godfrey. "The Nyakyusa of Southwest Tanganyika," in Colson and Gluckman, eds., *Seven Tribes of British Central Africa* (Oxford, 1951).

————————. "An African Morality," in *Cultures and Societies of Africa* (Random, 1960).

Wilson, Monica. "Nyakyusa Kinship," in Radcliffe-Brown and Forde, eds., *African Systems of Kinship and Marriage* (International African Institute, Oxford, 1950).

————————. **Good Company*. International African Institute (London), 1951.

————————. *Communal Rituals of the Nyakyusa*. International African Institute (London), 1959.

CHAPTER 14

Delaroziere, R. "Les Institutions Politiques et Sociales des Populations Dites Bamileke," *Etudes Camerounaises*, Vol. 11, Nos. 25–26 (March–June, 1949).

Egerton, F. Clement C. **African Majesty: A Record of Refuge at the Court of the King of Bangangte in the French Cameroons*. Scribner, 1939.

Lindskog, Birger. "African Leopard Men," *Studia Ethnographica*, Upsaliensia VII (1954).

Littlewood, Margaret. "Bamum and Bamileke," in *Peoples of the Central Cameroons*. Ethnographic Survey of Africa. International African Institute (London), 1954.

Ritzenthaler, Pat. **The Fon of Bafut*. Crowell, 1966.

CHAPTER 15

Cole, Sonia. *The Prehistory of East Africa*. Macmillan, 1963.

Coupland, R. *East Africa and Its Invaders from the Earliest Times to the Death of Seyyid Said in 1856*. Oxford, 1961.

Davidson, Basil. **The African Past*. Atlantic, Little, Brown, 1964.

Hitti, Phillip K. *History of the Arabs*. Macmillan & Co., Ltd., 1956.

Ingrams, W. H. *Zanzibar: Its History and Its People*. H. F. & G. Wetherby, 1931.

Moscati, Sabatino. *Ancient Semitic Civilizations*. Putnam, 1957.

Prins, A. H. J. *Coastal Tribes of the Northeastern Bantu*. Ethnographic Survey of Africa. International African Institute (London), 1952.

Schoff, Wilfred H., translator. *The Periplus of the Erythraean Sea*. Longmans, 1912.

CHAPTER 16

Baulin, Jacques. *The Arab Role in Africa*. Penguin Books, 1962.

Bovill, E. W. *The Golden Trade of the Moors*. Oxford, 1958.

Briggs, Lloyd Cabot. *Tribes of the Sahara*. Harvard University Press, 1960.

Davidson, Basil. *The African Past*. Atlantic, Little, Brown, 1964.

Greenberg, Joseph H. "The Negro Kingdoms of the Sudan," *Transactions of the New York Academy of Sciences*, Series 2, 11, (1949), pp. 126–35.

_____. "Some Aspects of Negro-Mohammedan Culture-Contact Among the Hausa," in *Cultures and Societies of Africa* (Random House, 1960).

Hopen, C. Edward. *The Pastoral Fulbe Family in Gwandu*. International African Institute. Oxford, 1958.

Ibn Battuta. *Travels in Asia and Africa*, trans. by H. A. R. Gibb. Routledge and Kegan Paul, Ltd., 1929.

Lhote, Henri. *"The Fertile Sahara," in Edward Bacon, ed., *Vanished Civilizations* (McGraw, 1963).

Miner, Horace. *The Primitive City of Timbuctoo*. Princeton University Press, 1953.

Murdock, George Peter. *Africa: Its People and Their Culture History*. McGraw, 1959.

INDEX

Index